MW00478218

A STORM OF MIST AND THUNDER

ALSO BY MARION BLACKWOOD

Marion Blackwood has written lots of books across multiple series, and new books are constantly added to her catalogue. To see the most recently updated list of books, please visit: www.marionblackwood.com

CONTENT WARNINGS

The Oncoming Storm series contains quite a lot of violence and morally questionable actions. If you have specific triggers, you can find the full list of content warnings at: www.marionblackwood.com/content-warnings

A STORM OF MIST AND THUNDER

THE ONCOMING STORM: BOOK FIVE

MARION BLACKWOOD

Copyright © 2020 by Marion Blackwood

All rights reserved. No part of this book may be reproduced in any form or by any electronic or mechanical means, including information storage and retrieval systems, without permission in writing from the publisher, except by reviewers, who may quote brief passages in a review. For more information, contact info@marionblackwood.com

First edition

ISBN 978-91-986387-2-1 (hardcover)
ISBN 978-91-986387-1-4 (paperback)
ISBN 978-91-986387-0-7 (ebook)

Editing by Julia Gibbs
Book cover design by ebooklaunch.com

This is a work of fiction. Names, characters, places, and incidents either are the product of the author's imagination or are used fictitiously. Any resemblance to actual persons, living or dead, events, or locales is entirely coincidental.

www.marionblackwood.com

For all the wildfires pretending to be candles

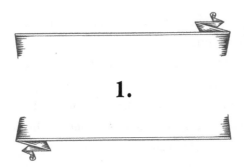

1.

Gray mountains towered before us. They were so tall I had to crane my neck, and even then I couldn't see them fully. Thick white mist swirled around the jagged peaks, hiding the top of the mountain from view. I drew my cloak tighter around my shoulders as a brisk fall wind snatched at my clothes.

"I still can't believe mountains this big actually exist," I said while gazing up at the wall of stone before me.

"I still can't believe the Queen ordered me to come with you," Elaran muttered.

Trotting up next to us, Haela threw her black ponytail behind her shoulder and fired off a wide smile. "Hey, where's your sense of adventure?"

Crossing his arms while on horseback proved inconvenient, so the grumpy elf had to settle for an extra deep scowl. "Last time I went on an adventure with her, she got us captured by the star elves and I had my death faked."

"Like I said." The female half of the twins spread her hands. "An adventure."

Her brother shook his head. "Elaran is right. We need to be careful." Haemir shot his sister a pointed look. "We're here on a diplomatic mission, remember?"

"Yeah, yeah, whatever." She flashed him a teasing grin before urging her horse on.

Keya let out a soft giggle next to me while Elaran and Faelar just watched exasperatedly as the energetic twin galloped across the plains. After a shrug, Haemir clicked his tongue and followed. Yellowing grass flattened under our horses' hooves as the rest of us hurried to catch up as well.

The wide grasslands eventually gave way to rugged foothills full of moss-covered boulders. A brook trickled down through the stones. After stopping to refill our waterskins and let our horses drink, we started out again.

"Are you sure this is the right place?" Elaran demanded.

Turning slightly in the saddle, I frowned at him. "You're the tracker, you tell me."

"You're the one with the map."

"Yeah, which I gave to you. And you led us here."

"Then we're in the right place," Haemir cut off before Elaran could retort. He squinted at the ground ahead. "But we should probably get off and walk our horses from here. The stones are getting worse and it gets pretty steep up there."

Swinging a leg over her back, I slid down from my trusted horse. After Zaina had sailed us back to Pernula, I'd returned to Travelers' Rest to retrieve Silver. Livia had been sad to see her go but she'd taken great care of her while I'd been stuck in the City of Glass.

"Alright, let's get going then!" Haela called and marched up the slope with her horse in tow.

Pebbles clattered down the hill as the six of us and our respective horses navigated the rocky surfaces. The overcast sky combined with the mass of stone around us painted the whole area in dusky gray hues. I steadied myself against a boulder while climbing over a particularly tricky passage before following the others down the slope on the other side. At least the wind had died down.

"Elaran," Faelar suddenly said, a sharp note in his voice.

"I see it," the auburn-haired archer replied.

"What are you..." I began before following his gaze. "Oh."

Scattered across the hillsides all around us were figures dressed in gray. Their garments were a mix of darker and lighter shades, making them incredibly difficult to spot against the stone, and even the bows they'd drawn on us were of that same color. I stared at them. Mountain elves. *Oh*, indeed.

"Storm, any time now would be good," Haemir said.

My mind snapped out of its dysfunctional state. Shaking my head, I cleared my throat and raised my voice. "Thunder is calling."

For a moment, nothing happened. The mountain elves continued watching us like silent statues while keeping sharp arrows pointed at us. Doubt crept into my chest like the cold legs of a spider. Had I got it wrong? Or had this just been a very elaborate trap? Then, a man's voice spoke up.

"And the wind answers." An elf with long dark brown hair pulled back in a ponytail took a step towards us and motioned for the others to lower their weapons. "You know the passphrase."

"Yes," I said.

"Why so many of you?" The leader of the mountain elves moved down the hillside with nimble steps. His long face seemed to constantly be stuck in a serious expression. "And why so many wood elves?"

"We're here on another mission," Elaran said. "Queen Faye of Tkeideru sent us. She wishes to form bonds of friendship between our people."

The serious-faced elf stopped a short distance from our group. Now that he was closer, I could make out the color of his eyes. I stared at him. They were ice blue. The same color as a clear winter sky seen through a sheet of ice. It was a quite striking color.

His pale blue eyes narrowed. "There is no Tkeideru."

My five elven friends all drew back in a gesture of synchronized shock. I flicked uncertain looks between them and the strange mountain elf. What had he meant by that? Of course Tkeideru was real.

"I do not understand," Keya said, voicing the thoughts on everyone's minds. "What are you saying?"

His stern gaze moved from one to the other before he raised his dark eyebrows with a puzzled look on his face. "Your words are sincere. Interesting." Running a hand over his jaw, he considered. "Welcome then, wood elves of Tkeideru, to our home." He jerked his head towards the other side of the gorge, making all the other mountain elves start in that direction. "I'm Ydras."

"Nice to meet you, Ydras," Keya said and proceeded to introduce herself as well as the rest of us.

When she was finished, Ydras leveled those striking eyes on me. "You knew the passphrase, so I'm guessing you're the one."

I nodded. "Yeah."

He tapped a finger against his huge gray bow for a few seconds before nodding back. "You'd better follow me, then. The Storm Casters await you."

My heart skipped a beat. Maesia had told me the truth back in Starhaven when she gave me that map. The other Storm Casters actually lived here. I could barely believe it. After everything it had taken to get their location, I was finally about to meet them. My people. Nervous excitement sparkled through me as Ydras led us further into the mountain range. I was finally about to learn what it meant to be a Storm Caster.

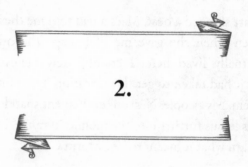

2.

Dense woodlands spread out across the slopes of the valley before ending in a wide clearing at the bottom. Casting a glance over my shoulder, I looked from the barren rocky landscape behind us to the forested one in front. This mountain was incredible. It was as if each valley was a world of its own, and they were all connected by winding paths across the rocks. Ydras waved us forwards. I let my gaze drift over his sure-footed moves before following. We would never have found this place without him.

"It's beautiful," Haemir said.

Yellow, orange, and red leaves painted the woods in an iridescent fall coat. Birds chirped in the trees while a pair of squirrels scurried past on a thick trunk. I swept my gaze across the sea of colors. Haemir was right. It really was beautiful. Silver snorted her agreement as I led her down the gentle hill.

Before long, the sounds of a settlement drifted through the vegetation. My heart rate sped up. After all the obstacles to get here, all that remained were a few good-natured trees and then I would meet them. My people. I wondered what they were like.

We broke through the edge of the forest.

"Wow," I breathed.

The vast clearing was dotted with log cabins made of dark wood on one side and large swaths of grass that looked to be training areas of different kinds. People moved about on the damp ground. I stared at them while trying to keep my heart from leaping out of my chest in nervous excitement.

Two blond wood elves were practicing their archery skills a few strides away while a mixed group of elves and humans sparred further in. White hair and violet eyes flashed past in front of me as a star elf jogged by on his way to a cabin. The most astonishing sight of all, though, was the battle raging between a dark-haired wood elf and a short stocky human.

Black clouds swirled around the elf as she raised her arms. The human snapped a hand to the side. Even from this distance, I could feel the vibrations in the air as he hurled a gust of wind at his competitor. Trees shook in terror as the wood elf swept her arm to the side, redirecting the blast. My mouth dropped open.

"Wow," I repeated.

"Ydras!" a tall human called after detaching himself from the sparring group in the middle. He ran his fingers through his dark brown hair as he jogged over. "It's good to see you. What brings you here?" Golden-brown eyes moved between members of our strange group. "And with this many wood elves?"

"The wood elves are here for us, Marcus," the leader of the mountain elves said before nodding at me. "But this one is for you."

Inside, I bristled at the choice of words. I wasn't *for* anyone. But I figured starting a fight within two minutes of arriving would be a bad first impression so I held my tongue while Marcus shifted his gaze to me.

My dark green eyes met his across the grass as we sized each other up. He looked to be around my age but he was built like a fort. Tall and broad-shouldered with the athletic body type of someone who spent a lot of their time wielding weapons. More specifically, the heavy longsword at his hip. But the expression on his face was one of kindness and excitement. It canceled out the air of aggression his muscles and strong jaw otherwise would've given off.

"You're a Storm Caster?" Marcus asked once he had finished his own assessment of my appearance.

"Yeah."

A wide smile spread across his lips. "Welcome! It's been a while since we had a new recruit."

Dry leaves rustled as a cluster of Storm Casters arrived to get a better look at us newcomers. Marcus chuckled and shook his head before telling them to stop gawking and help out with our horses instead. I patted Silver on the neck before she and the rest of her four-legged friends were led away to a stabling area.

Ydras cleared his throat. "Your horses will be well taken care of by Marcus and the other Ashaana." He shifted his ice-blue eyes to Elaran. "You said the Queen of Tkeideru sent you. Come with me. I will take you to our home where you can live during your stay here. We have a lot to talk about."

Without waiting for Elaran and the other wood elves to reply, he turned on his heel and strode back up the slopes. Keya and Haemir started after him.

"Aw, we're not gonna live together?" Haela drew her lips into a pout while looking at me but her eyes glittered with mischief. "I wanted to watch you flail around like a baby bird and lose Storm Caster fights."

"I agree." The ghost of a smile blew across Elaran's face. "Watching Storm get her ass handed to her would've been a lot of fun." He jerked his head at the other elves. "But we have work to do."

"If you want to," Marcus broke in before I could spit out the snarky remark I had loaded up in reply, "you could just come back tomorrow morning and watch. We're going to start training then. I know Ydras wouldn't mind."

A satisfied grin spread across Haela's mouth. "Will do!"

Whirling around, she jogged to catch up with her brother while Elaran and Faelar gave the unhelpfully obliging human a nod. I rolled my eyes. Why had he needed to tell them that they could come back? If I had to fail, I very much preferred doing it when no one was watching, thank you very much. However, Marcus seemed completely oblivious to the plight he had caused. He waved me towards the glen with a smile on his face.

I looked to Elaran and lifted my shoulders in a shrug. "Good luck."

"We'll be back tomorrow." The grumpy elf narrowed his eyes at me. "Don't burn anything down."

"You know, you really should've thought about that before you taught me how to make a fire." With an evil grin on my face, I spun around and strode towards Marcus.

Grumbles and muttered curses bounced off my back until Elaran and Faelar finally disappeared into the woods as well. The tall human stood waiting for me with an amused expression on his face. He nodded at where my friends had been only a few minutes ago.

"You know each other pretty well, I'm guessing?"

Finally reaching him, I fell in beside him as we moved further into the compound. "Yeah, we've been through some stuff together."

A chuckle bubbled from his throat. "I can tell." He glanced down at me. "I'm Marcus."

"I know."

The superfluously introduced man drew back and raised his eyebrows. "How did you know that?"

"Ydras called you by your name just now."

"Oh." Drawing a hand through his hair, he let out an embarrassed laugh. "Right. So what's your name?"

"The Oncoming Storm."

Another bout of laughter rippled from his chest. I scowled at him while skirting around a straw dummy used for target practice. People didn't laugh at me. A cloud of confusion drifted over his face when he noticed my withering glare.

"Wait... you're serious?" When I only continued glowering at him, he scratched the back of his neck while breaking into an apologetic smile. "Sorry. I didn't mean to be rude. It's just a... very unusual name." He sent a hopeful nod my way. "But very fitting for a Storm Caster."

Blowing out a sigh, I shook my head. Every time I went somewhere on this bloody continent, I had to explain that the Oncoming Storm actually was my real name. They accepted ridiculous names like Nimlithil without question but were tripped up by something as easily pronounced as mine. Such nonsense.

Marcus cleared his throat. "Anyway, this is the longhouse. It's where we eat all our meals."

He swung a muscular arm to point at a building that really lived up to its name. It was a long one-story house. The same dark wooden logs that made up all the other structures in the clearing had been used for this one as well. Smoke drifted from the chimney at the far end.

"They're getting dinner ready so I'll show you the inside soon." My tall guide nodded at a cluster of buildings further away. "But I'll finish showing you around first and then let you get settled in a room."

My stomach grumbled as if on command. Marcus tried very hard to suppress a chuckle but failed miserably, making it incredibly difficult for me to keep the corner of my mouth from quirking upwards as well.

Our tour of the compound took us by the stabling area where Silver and the rest of our horses had found some new friends. I smiled at her satisfied snort before turning my attention back to Marcus. He pointed out the well they drew water from and which cabins held food storages, weapons, and other gear before realizing that he had skipped the training grounds. Waving in the direction opposite us, he tried to show it to me from a distance. I squinted at it in the fading light.

"Yeah, I can't really see anything," I said.

Putting one hand on his hip, he used the other to scratch his head of thick dark brown hair. "I suppose not. I'll just show it to you in the morning then."

"Alright, that works," I said lightly as if I wasn't planning on spending a good portion of the night skulking about and mapping this whole area in my head.

He gave me a satisfied nod. Very trusting, this one. We moved towards a cluster of wooden huts at the back of the clearing. Trees dressed in yellow, orange, and red stood guard behind them in a dense line that marked the end of the wide glen. I swept scrutinizing eyes over the buildings.

Hut was definitely the right word. Compared to the other rather large houses and storage spaces, these looked to be simple one-room cabins. Light flickered in the window of the closest one.

"This is where we all live," Marcus explained. "There aren't all that many of us so there's more than enough room for everyone."

"So everyone has their own cabin?"

"Yeah. Living like this can be challenging as it is, always having other people around, so it's important to have a place where you can be alone if you want to."

At that, my opinion of these people shot through the roof. I definitely agreed with that. If I didn't have someplace I could go to shut the door and be alone, I would go crazy.

"That's good to hear." I looked up at him. "So, where will I be staying?"

"You can have any of these." Marcus pointed out a few different cabins. "Any preference?"

Of course I had a preference. As soon as we had gotten here, I'd started assessing all the huts based on their location and the possibility for extracurricular sneaking they offered. A grin spread across my mouth when he motioned at a cabin situated by the tree line. That was perfect for disappearing unnoticed if trouble came calling.

"That one," I said.

"You sure? Most people usually want one in the middle."

No surprise there. Living in the middle made people feel safer, but I was more concerned with privacy than a false sense of security. And besides, since when had I ever been *most people*? However, instead of voicing that, I just settled for a nod to confirm that I was sure.

"Alright." Marcus shrugged and led me towards the one I had chosen.

Here, the twang of bowstrings and grunts from sparring matches were no longer audible. Instead, faint rustling sounds filled the area as chilly fall winds grazed the trees. I adjusted the pack on my shoulder and drew my cloak tighter around me.

"Here we are." My guide pushed down the handle and pulled the door open. "There is fresh linen in the closet, some candles on the nightstand, and the key to the door is in the top desk drawer."

I peeked through the doorway. It was dark inside in the waning light but I could make out a bed with a pile of neatly folded covers and pillows on top, a nightstand, closet, desk, and chair all made of the same dark wood. Stale air drifted across the threshold. I would have to start by airing it out but at least the sturdy walls appeared to keep the cold out.

"Looks good," I said with a nod while stepping inside.

"I'll let you get settled in and then I'll take you to dinner." I turned back to him just in time to see red flash over his cheeks. He coughed and cleared his throat. "I didn't mean *take you to dinner*, take you to dinner, I just meant..." Letting out a rueful chuckle, he shook his head. "You know what I meant."

"Yeah, I know what you meant." I couldn't stop the corner of my mouth from drawing into a smile. "Thanks, Marcus."

After flashing me a grin, he spun around and strode back across the grass with long steps. He seemed so genuine and trusting. I wondered if it was because he had grown up here, far away from hurt and struggle. Shaking my head, I closed the door on his retreating back. Maybe I'd ask him at some point.

The next half hour was spent sweeping the cabin for hidden traps, and then when I was satisfied, unpacking all my tools and weapons and putting new sheets on the bed. I had just barely finished and sat down by the desk when a knock sounded from the door. Heaving a tired sigh, I pushed off from the chair and approached the thick slab of wood.

Marcus' wide smile met me when I opened it. "Ready?"

"Yeah." Stepping across the threshold, I drew the door shut behind me and locked it before falling in beside him. "So, will everyone be there at the dinner?"

"Yes. Well, no." He let out a brief chuckle. "Some people keep strange hours and some prefer solitude but the rest of us eat dinner together at least."

Dusk had fallen over the compound while I'd been inside but torches mounted on poles had been lit along the different paths to guide the way. A thin coat of mist crawled in from the woods.

"Are you nervous?" Marcus asked, peering down at me.

"No," I lied.

I *was* nervous. When we reached the door to the longhouse, my pulse smattered in my ears and I was worried that my heart would leap out of my chest. This was it. After all my searching, hoping, and wondering, I was now only one closed door away from actually meeting the other Storm Casters.

What if they didn't like me? What if I didn't like them? What if they didn't have the answers to all the questions I wanted to ask them?

Drawing a deep breath, I gave my head a quick shake while Marcus pushed down the handle and pulled open the door. Warm light spilled onto the ground before my feet while I tried to steady my slamming heart. Trying to guess was pointless. There was only one way to find out. I had to go inside.

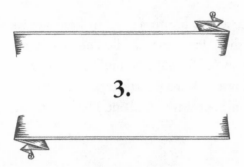

3.

Heavenly scents of roasted game drifted through the room. It was packed with tables and chairs in no particular pattern, and wide dishes full of grilled meat and vegetables stood haphazardly placed on different surfaces. The roaring fireplace set in the middle of the long wall on my left cast the room in warm orange hues. I stared at the people seated on the sturdy wooden furniture.

It was not at all what I had expected. I don't know why but I'd somehow gotten it into my head that the Storm Casters would be a serious bunch. Kind of like a highly exclusive secret society who sat in darkened basements smoking pipes and discussing grave matters. Instead, laughter and boisterous voices filled the room. Some people sat by themselves and seemed content to eat alone while others joked and laughed around crowded tables. It was more like a very large family than a select club.

"Come on." Marcus nudged my arm and motioned towards an unoccupied table by the opposite wall.

While we wove our way through the mess of furniture, he stole platters from other tables. The previous owners of the dishes called out in mock outrage and lobbed breadcrumbs at him but the tall food thief only laughed and scooped up a couple of clean plates and utensils before setting them down on the empty table by the wall. A bowl of grilled carrots and potatoes wobbled precariously by the edge. I reached out and pushed it back on the table before sitting down.

"Is it..." I hesitated.

Marcus slid a plate towards me. "Is it what?"

"Well, is it always like this?"

"Pretty much." He chuckled. "Not what you expected?"

"Not even close."

Another laugh rumbled in his broad chest while he shoveled food onto his plate. After watching him for another few seconds, I did the same. Warm meat tasting of wood smoke and spices melted on my tongue as I took a bite. By Nemanan, this was good. For a few moments, we both simply savored the food but once my immediate hunger had been sated, I placed my fork on the table and met Marcus' gaze with serious eyes.

"Okay, so I have like a million questions," I said.

"Figured you would." He skewered a piece of carrot and popped it in his mouth. Talking around the orange blob, he said, "Shoot."

All this time, I would've given anything to interrogate other Ashaana but now that I finally could, I didn't even know where to start. I took a large gulp of water. It tasted faintly of iron. Placing the mug back on the scratched table, I decided to just go with the first thing that popped into my head.

"Are these all the Ashaana there are?"

"No, only the ones we've been able to get through to." Marcus started sawing off a large ribbon of meat. "We have to keep our location secret because..." He looked up from his cutting. "How much do you know about the star elves and their plans?"

While he devoured his steak, I filled him in on my experiences with the star elves.

"By Werz," my meat-loving dinner companion said.

He swore using the God of War. That was interesting, but not surprising considering that he looked like an archetypical warrior. I wondered if he used to be a soldier.

"Yeah, it was an experience." I had only given him a very shortened and censored version of what had happened in the City of Glass but he seemed to get the idea anyway.

"Glad you made it out."

"Me too."

Shouts rang out as an elf in a green cloak entered the longhouse. The huge group to our right whistled and waved him over with smiles on their faces.

"So you were saying?" I prodded.

"Right!" Marcus took a swig from his mug. "So you already know that the star elves want us to give up our magic so they can feed their crazy spell. We of course want to keep our magic. So that's why we have to keep our location a secret." He lifted his muscular shoulders. "Unfortunately, that also makes it difficult for other Storm Casters to find us."

"Don't I know it," I muttered. When he raised his eyebrows at me, I just waved a hand in front of my face. No need to recount my disastrous stay in Travelers' Rest. "You say *our magic*. So what we have *is* magic?"

"Yeah."

"Where does it come from?" I pursed my lips. "The star elves tried to make me think I sold my soul to a demon for it."

Uncertainty crept into my mind again and I narrowed my eyes. "It's not true, right?"

The brown-haired warrior shook his head. "Yeah, that's their usual play. But no. It comes from the dragons."

My eyebrows shot up. "The dragons?"

"Or at least that's what Morgora says." He nodded at a lump of gray sitting alone by the fire.

I squinted at it. Upon closer inspection, I realized that the lump was actually an old woman. Her large gray sweater matched both her pants and her hair, as well as her eyes, hence my initial impression of her being a unicolored heap. Deep creases furrowed her brow. Orange firelight flickered over a face that appeared to have developed a permanent scowl. With her arms crossed and that disapproving look on her face, she glared at the rest of the room.

"She seems... nice."

Marcus let out a light laugh. "She likes to pretend that she's a sour old lady but she's really a softie at heart."

Given the steel in her eyes, I had a very hard time believing that, but I raised my eyebrows and nodded anyway.

While I continued firing off questions about the Storm Casters, the longhouse started to empty of people. Before they left, some of them came by to introduce themselves. They didn't appear to be plotting to stab a knife between my ribs as soon as my back was turned so I replied and greeted them as well. That is, when I could spare a breath between bombarding Marcus with questions.

He didn't know the answer to everything I asked but he answered when he could. Among other things, I learned that they used to have a large network of contacts in place who could refer other Ashaana here but the star elves had dealt a heavy blow to it some years back. However, when I'd started interrogating him on how our powers actually worked, he would just wink and tell me we would get into that tomorrow.

"We really have to go back and get some sleep now," Marcus interrupted my next question and motioned at the almost empty room around us.

"Fine." I blew out a sigh through my nose. "I still have like half a million questions left, though."

"I bet you do." Furniture scraped against the wooden boards as he stood up. "But there will be lots of time for that later too."

Conceding that he was right, I stood up as well and followed him out the door. My breath left silver puffs in the air when we stepped outside. The fireplace inside the longhouse had kept it warm but out here, fall made itself known again. Leaves crunched under our feet as Marcus followed me back along the torch-lit path. Once my cabin came into view, he stopped and turned to me with a wide smile.

"Get some sleep." His golden-brown eyes twinkled as he winked at me. "Because tomorrow, we start training."

With that satisfied smile still on his face, he strode away. I watched his muscled back disappear into the darkness. That had gone surprisingly well. I had met the Storm Casters. They appeared to like me. I could definitely learn to tolerate them. And they did have answers to most of my questions. All three of my previous worries had been dealt with. Good. Slinking towards my own hut, I let a grin spread across my mouth while excitement sparkled in my chest. And Marcus was right. Tomorrow we would train. And I would finally learn how to be a Storm Caster.

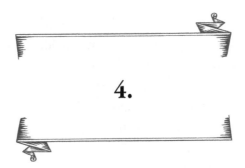

4.

A thin coat of fog clung to the grass. I shifted my weight and glared impatiently at the tall Storm Caster taking his time chatting with another group further down the field. Would he hurry it up already? I'd waited all night for this. Well, the hours I hadn't spent skulking around the darkened camp, scouting the area, that is.

"Ready to flail around like a baby bird?" an excited voice called.

I whipped my head around to find five elves watching me from the wooden fence of a horse pen that wasn't currently in use. Haela had climbed up and sat atop it with a wide grin on her face. Her brother and Keya had taken up position next to her and both were shaking their head in exasperation while Elaran and Faelar leaned against the fence. How long had they been standing there? I hadn't even heard them come out of the woods.

"Damn elves and their damn forest skills," I muttered.

"We heard that!" Haela called, that grin still on her face.

Grumbling even louder, I narrowed my eyes at them. "Don't you have some important diplomatic shit to take care of?"

"Yeah but there was no way we were gonna miss this."

On her right, Elaran and Faelar motioned between me and each other while saying something that I couldn't hear. Suspicion crept into my mind. They shook hands.

"If that's you making bets on this, I'm gonna stab you." I wasn't carrying any knives because I didn't want to accidentally skewer myself or someone else if they got lose in a storm wind but the elves didn't know that. "Remember what happened last time you bet against me?"

Elaran snickered. "I think I'm going to get my money's worth this time."

While I was busy rolling my eyes at my annoying elven friends, Marcus detached himself from the group of Ashaana and jogged across the clearing. A pale fall sun peeked through the trees and made the water drops decorating the grass sparkle. The brown-haired Storm Caster sent a cheerful wave in the direction of the elves before skidding to a halt in front of me.

"Ready?" he asked.

Flicking my gaze between my friends at the fence and Marcus, I nodded. "Yeah."

"Alright, I figured it's best to just push you in at the deep end and see what you can do." He motioned at me. "Go ahead and call the storm."

"What do you mean?"

"Just call it up."

I narrowed my eyes at him. "I can't just call it up. It doesn't work like that, at least not for me." Shrugging, I spread my hands. "It doesn't always respond and sometimes it kind of just shows up on its own."

"Hmm." Marcus ran a hand over his chin while studying me closely.

His golden-brown eyes roamed my body for another few seconds. Then, they stopped and went pitch black. Dark clouds shot out all around him. I blinked in surprise as he raised his arms and drew them in sweeping patterns around his head, but I didn't realize what was happening until it was too late. The blast slammed into me with the force of a boulder.

Air rushed out of my lungs at the sheer force that had hit me. Red, orange, and green flashed before my eyes as the world spun up and down repeatedly while I flew through morning mist. I hit the damp grass with a heavy thud. For a moment I just lay there, blinking rapidly to stop my spinning vision.

"Is she okay?" Keya's concerned voice said somewhere to my right.

Sucking in a deep breath, I finally got my mind working again. Anger surged through me. That bastard. I shot to my feet right as the darkness ripped from my soul.

"What the hell was that?" I bellowed and leveled eyes that had turned black as death on the Storm Caster before me.

Another blast hit me square in the chest. I flew another couple of strides and slammed back first into the dirt again. A howl tore from my throat. Rolling to my feet, I sprinted across the grass while black smoke whipped around me. Marcus drew his arms in an arc but I darted to the side just in time to avoid the next storm wind. Yellow leaves trembled as it hit a tree behind me.

When I was almost upon him, my attacker raised his arms again. Black clouds bloomed around us. I screeched to a halt in anticipation of my vision disappearing but drew back in surprise when I realized that I could still see rather well. It only cast my surroundings in a slight dark haze. Strange. They had looked solid from the outside. I wondered if I could see through it because of my own powers.

Strong winds smacked into my side. I tumbled to the ground but managed to roll with the motion and get to my feet swiftly. Marcus had pulled back the dark smoke so that it only twisted around his limbs. I shot forward. He raised his arms to throw another gust at me but I was faster. As I closed the final distance, I reached for a knife only to discover the sheath empty. Damn. I had left them all in my room.

Pain vibrated through my knuckles as I drove my fist into his side. It was as if I had punched a stone wall. Marcus swung at me. His hand sailed through the swirling black mist around me as I ducked away. I aimed another strike at his stomach.

A large hand closed over my fist. I tried to yank my arm back but his grip was like iron. Lightning crackled over my skin as I screamed in frustration and twisted my whole body around to throw a punch into his back where I estimated a kidney to be. He let out a grunt and his hold on me loosened. I snatched my hand from his grip and kicked at the back of his kneecap.

His left leg buckled but he managed to stay on his feet. Thunder boomed around us as Marcus tried to send me sprawling again using another blast of wind. It bent the grass around us but most of it missed me. I aimed another strike.

Strong fingers locked around my wrist. I sucked in a breath between my teeth as Marcus flashed around me and twisted my arm behind my back. His other hand took a firm grip on my throat from behind. Trapped against his muscled body and breathing only by his grace, there wasn't much I could do except raise my free hand in surrender.

"You're a skilled fighter. That was a really good start." Marcus peeked over my shoulder, looking for eye contact. "You're not going to try to kill me when I let you go, are you?"

I came very close to informing him that if I'd brought a knife today, he would've been dead several times over by now, but in the end I just shook my head. By Nemanan, I really hated losing.

"Good."

His grip on me disappeared and he took a step back. Instinctively, I ran a hand over my throat while the darkness withdrew into the deep pits of my soul. When I turned around, I saw that his eyes were back to their normal color as well.

"Oh come on, Storm, what are you doing?" Haela called from the fence. "I've seen you create clouds and lightning ten times that pathetic display you gave us just now."

Drawing my eyebrows down, I turned to face her. A teasing smile decorated her beautiful face and her eyes glittered mischievously when she met my gaze. Next to her, Elaran twitched his fingers at Faelar who dropped something in his palm while shaking his head.

"Shut up," I muttered, more by force of habit than actual irritation, because she did have a point.

Marcus cleared his throat. "Sorry about that. It was just the easiest way of getting you to call up your powers." He gave me a sheepish grin and lifted his shoulders in an apologetic shrug. "You don't hold grudges, do you?"

Oh, I was the queen of holding grudges. But I decided not to voice that because if this led to him actually teaching me how to control my powers, I just might let it slide. This once.

"We're good," I said.

"Storm," Haemir called across the grass. He and the other elves were moving away from the fence. "We have to go."

"Yeah but we'll be back tomorrow for some more entertainment," Haela filled in, face beaming.

"Morons," I grumbled at the twins as they jogged to catch up with Elaran and Faelar.

"We heard that!"

Keya had lingered by the fence for another minute and now she met my gaze. "Be careful."

"Always am," I replied even though we both knew it was a lie.

She gave me a small smile before following the others into the woods. I shook my head. Elves.

"How are you still standing?"

Whirling around, I found Marcus staring at me. I glanced around the area, looking for hidden threats. "What do you mean?"

He jerked his head, motioning for us to start moving. I fell in beside him as we made our way through the busy compound. Two blond humans were sparring with longswords close to our edge of the training ground while an elf with long red hair fired arrows at a target that was impossibly far away on the other side.

"Here." Marcus motioned at a cluster of benches and tables close to the well. After we were seated opposite each other, he turned pensive eyes on me and picked up the conversation from before. "I mean, why have you not passed out?"

Oh. That's what he meant. Usually, after I'd used the darkness a lot, I would lose consciousness for a while but I hadn't had that problem lately. I felt a bit tired, of course, but it wasn't that overwhelming.

When I didn't reply immediately, Marcus went on. "It's just, our powers don't come for free. As with all magic, it comes at a cost. When we use our powers, it also drains our energy. The more we use, the more it takes. That's why most Storm Casters pass out after using up a lot."

"Yeah, I've had that problem too." I clicked my tongue. "Very inconvenient."

"Right? It doesn't matter that it helps you defeat someone, if you pass out on the battlefield afterwards, you're as good as dead anyway."

"I'm aware." I narrowed my eyes at him. "But you didn't pass out either."

"No, because it's possible to train your endurance so you can use more power without getting to that point." He matched my own scrutinizing gaze. "Which brings me to the strange part of our fight. Almost all new Storm Caster recruits pass out after that first fight. But not you. You have fantastic stamina. How come?"

A cold breeze blew across the area and rustled the colorful leaves all around us. I rubbed my arms to get some heat back. Without a cloak or a fight to keep me warm, the chill was creeping into my bones.

"I used to pass out often," I said at last. "But then I spent a few months with my powers constantly out and after that, it hasn't been that much of a problem."

The crease in Marcus' forehead deepened. "What do you mean, a couple of months with your powers constantly out?"

"I mean, they came out one day and then I had black eyes and dark smoke swirling around me for months before it withdrew again."

"Wow." He stared at me with wide eyes before raising his eyebrows and giving me a slow nod. "That's a bit extreme but great stamina training. How did that even happen?"

Breaking his gaze, I glanced down and instead occupied myself with picking at a splinter sticking up from the table. I shrugged. "It was a rough period."

My table companion was silent for a moment. Clanking swords drifted through the crisp fall air and mingled with the distant twang of bowstrings. I pulled the splinter from the table and flicked it onto the grass.

"Our powers are tied to our emotions," Marcus finally said. "It's how we call them up. And how we awaken them in the first place."

Glancing up at him, I furrowed my brows. "We get our powers from our feelings?"

"No, not exactly. Being Ashaana is hereditary. It lies dormant in the blood until something awakens it. Sometimes several generations can go without powers because they never experience anything strong enough to call the powers out. And sometimes it just skips generations all together."

I stared at him. Wow. So somewhere in my family tree, there had to have been other Storm Casters. Had my parents developed their powers? Was that why they had died? Or were they even dead? Countless questions exploded in my mind but unfortunately, it was questions that neither Marcus nor I could answer.

"You okay?"

Giving my head a quick shake, I pulled myself together. "Yeah."

"What happened that made your powers come out?"

Sharp pain jabbed into my heart at the thought of Rain. The hurt had lessened over the years but I wondered briefly if it would ever go away completely. Probably not.

"I don't wanna talk about it," I answered. "What about you?"

A range of emotions flickered over Marcus' strong features. He sucked his teeth. "Someone died."

He pushed off the chair and stood up. When I tilted my head up to meet his eyes, that open kind look was back on his face again but I thought I could detect something else burning in his eyes as well.

"Let's continue training tomorrow," he said. "Just because you didn't pass out doesn't mean you're not tired. And I already had some previous commitments before you showed up so I have some things to get done. I'm sure you want some time to think too." After firing off a bright smile, he turned to leave. "I'll see you in the longhouse later."

"Yeah," I said to his retreating back.

It appeared as though neither of us was ready to share personal details. Placing my hands on the table, I rose from the bench as well. And Marcus was right. I did want some time to myself so that I could process everything I'd learned today and figure out how I could use it to my advantage. Black sleeves rumpled under my palms as I rubbed my arms while striding towards my cabin. Plus, it was high time to get out of this damn cold.

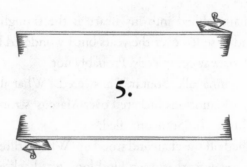

5.

"You seriously don't have anything better to do?"

Leaning against the fence, Elaran raised his eyebrows. "Better than watching someone finally teach you that you're not as good as you think? No."

"Elaran," Keya chided before turning back to me. "We are here to support you, Storm."

"And to watch you fly across the grass." Haela drew her arm in an arching motion. "Like a spinning stick someone threw too fast."

Laughter rang out by the wooden barrier. While the amused twin jabbed an elbow in her brother's side, I threw them all a withering glare. Idiots.

Morning had brought clear blue skies and a brilliant sun that made the iridescent leaves gleam like colorful jewels on the trees. Drawing a deep breath, I filled my lungs with crisp fall air laced with musky earth tones.

"If you're going to watch, you might as well help," Marcus said and waved the elves forward.

The five wood elves exchanged a glance but then hopped over the fence with effortless grace. While they approached us on the field, another elf came striding across the grass. It was the red-haired mountain elf I'd seen practicing archery. She took up position next to Marcus.

"Everyone, this is Cileya," Marcus said. "Cileya, this is... well, you can introduce yourselves because to be honest, I don't remember all of your names either." He let out a short chuckle.

While the rest of our group introduced themselves, I studied the mountain elf. Red hair streaked with gold cascaded down her back and set her ice-blue eyes in stark contrast. Her face didn't betray a lot of emotions but that did nothing to detract from her looks. She was gorgeous. I moved my gaze across the wood elves and found Faelar openly staring at her. Suppressing a chuckle, I glanced between the two of them. Apparently, I wasn't the only one who thought so.

"Great, now that we've gotten to know each other, let's get started." Marcus turned to me. "We need to figure out which emotion it is that triggers your powers and the easiest way to do that is to just test it."

"What kind of tests?" My eyes narrowed in suspicion as I flicked a hand to the others. "And why do we need all of them?"

Marcus cleared his throat while a sheepish grin descended on his face. "It doesn't really work if I tell you beforehand." He motioned between Elaran and a spot on the grass a bit further away. "If you could stand here."

Elaran moved to the indicated place, which was a few strides from me, and drew himself up with a frown on his face. The others took a step back. Having no idea where he was going with this, I simply flicked my gaze between the grumpy wood elf and the tall Storm Caster. Marcus' eyes went black.

A strong current slammed into Elaran. Auburn hair whipped in the wind as he flew across the grass in a flailing of limbs before skidding to a halt further down the field. I doubled over with laughter. Alright, if that was how I'd looked, I understood why they'd laughed at me too.

Marcus studied at me with furrowed brows and a barely hidden smile. "Okay, that rules out any hero triggers."

"What the hell did you do that for?" Elaran bellowed while stalking back across the clearing, flicking dirt and grass off his clothes.

"Sorry about that." The offending Storm Caster turned to the pissed-off elf and sent him an apologetic look. "I needed to test it on someone she cares about and you looked like someone who could take it."

"Oh." Elaran stopped next to Faelar and crossed his arms while puffing up his chest but he didn't look angry anymore. He almost looked a bit proud. "Well, a little heads-up next time would be nice."

Admiration colored my eyes as I turned to Marcus. Not a lot of people could get away with sending that grumpy elf flying across the grass without climbing to the top of his hate list. Whatever else he was, this tall Storm Caster was good with people.

"You said this ruled out any hero triggers," I said. "What does that mean?"

"We like to divide the emotions that trigger our powers into two main branches." He held out his hands and moved them up and down like scales. "We jokingly refer to them as hero triggers and villain triggers. The hero triggers are emotions like love, a desire to protect people, and things like that. The villain triggers are hate, pain, rage, and other stuff."

"And Storm has a villain trigger?" Elaran butted in. "What a surprise."

Narrowing my eyes, I threw him a scowl while simultaneously staving off a chuckle because I'd been thinking the same thing. I wasn't a hero? What a surprise indeed.

"Yes, she does. But to be fair, most people do." Marcus nodded at Elaran. "Thank you for helping us confirm that. Now, we just need to narrow it down further to see which specific emotion it is." Sweeping his gaze over the wood elves, he gave them a smile. "I won't be needing any more help but you're of course welcome to stay and watch."

Haela grinned. "Oh, we're not missing this."

Uneasiness spidered up my spine as they all retreated a few steps while Marcus raised his arms. This couldn't be good. Black clouds shot out around him and enveloped both of us. Thunder boomed around me while lightning danced in the dark haze. Just standing there doing nothing went against my every instinct. At my sides, my fingers twitched. I wanted desperately to draw one of my currently nonexistent knives so that I would be ready for whatever was about to come, but I forced myself to remain still.

Blinding light flashed before my eyes. I only had time to suck in a gasp before the lightning bolt hit me full on. A stabbing force crackled through me with enough power to make my bones vibrate. My legs gave out.

Kneeling on the ground, I tried to blink away the pain bouncing around inside my body. My ears rang in tune with the thrumming inside. I pushed air in and out of my lungs while bracing myself on the damp grass. Eventually, the throbbing stopped and my surroundings came back into focus.

"Ow," I heaved. Still on my knees, I had to crane my neck to meet Marcus' eyes that were once again golden-brown. "You bastard. That hurt."

"I know. I'm sorry." He reached down to help me up. "But now we can rule out pain."

Taking his calloused hand, I climbed to my feet just in time to see Elaran snicker contentedly. I glared at him. Keya looked at me with worried eyes but the rest of them had facial expression that seemed to have gotten stuck somewhere between amusement and sympathy. Someday, I'd get back at them. By Nemanan, I would.

Shifting my gaze to Marcus, I raised my eyebrows in response to the stunt he'd pulled a minute ago. "You can actually direct lightning?"

"*We* can direct lightning," he corrected. "Black clouds, wind, thunder, lightning, all the elements of a storm, we can manipulate it all."

"Wow."

A wide smile spread across his face. "Right? But getting lightning bolts to strike where we want is a pretty advanced skill so it'll be a while before we get to that part of the training." He shrugged. "Ready for the next test?"

"I guess."

"Cileya," Marcus said and motioned at the mountain elf. "It's time for your part."

My legs still wobbled slightly from the lightning strike as I straightened. "What are we testing now?"

"Can't say."

He shot me an apologetic smile before twisting away to whisper something in Cileya's ear. She drew back and blinked at him. When the brown-haired Storm Caster only nodded in confirmation, she shrugged and squared up against me. I heaved a deep sigh. I didn't like the look of this at all.

Cileya spread her hands in a helpless gesture. "I'm sorry about this."

Strong winds hit me in the side and knocked me off my feet. *Again? Really?* I rolled to a stop a couple of strides away and started climbing to my feet. A gust slammed into me again. Hitting the ground with a thud, I let out a huff. Grass and dirt coated my palms as I pushed myself into a sitting position, but no sooner had I sat up than yet another force struck me down.

"Seriously?" I bellowed. "Can't you at least let me get back up again before you do that?"

I shot up but only made it to my knees when the next wind smacked into my chest and leveled me with the ground again. Anger ripped through me.

"Would you stop that!"

Another blast flattened me against the grass as soon as I lifted my head. The darkness exploded out of me. Black tendrils snaked around my arms and lightning crackled over my skin as I flashed to my feet. Leaves crunched under my boots. I advanced on the infuriating mountain elf just as she lifted something in her hands.

Rapid twangs echoed through the clearing, followed by faint hissing sounds. My eyes widened as I noticed the arrows descending on me from above. I threw up my arms over my head. Thuds sounded as a smattering of arrows rained down on me.

When I opened my eyes again, I found a perfect circle around me. The wall only reached slightly above my knees so it didn't trap me as such, but the sheer amount of skill it took to do something like that stopped me in my tracks and made the darkness retreat. Raising my eyes, I stared at Cileya and was just about to open my mouth but someone beat me to it.

"Wow," Faelar blurted out. Baffled admiration glittered in his eyes. "That was incredible."

The redheaded mountain elf appeared to be a woman of few words but she gave him a nod in acknowledgement. Clapping drifted across the clearing.

"Ding, ding, ding, we have a winner," Marcus said. "Your trigger emotion is rage."

After carefully stepping out of the ring of arrows, I turned to the satisfied Storm Caster and crossed my arms. "Couldn't you have figured that out after our fight yesterday?"

"I had my suspicions but it was impossible to isolate the emotions yesterday." He strode across the grass until he was right in front of me. "It could've been any of the emotions pain, hate, and rage. Since we had already ruled out pain and you knew that Cileya wasn't doing it because she wanted to, the only emotion left this time was anger."

Flicking my gaze between him and the group of wood elves further away, I lowered my voice. "So, what about that hero or villain thing at the beginning? You must've already known the answer to that."

"Yep." A mischievous grin lit up his face. "But no harm in confirming. And I figured you might want Elaran to experience that flying feeling too."

Right there and then, I decided that I liked this muscled Storm Caster.

A hearty chuckle shook my chest as I gave him an impressed nod. "You know, you're alright, Marcus."

"So are you, the Oncoming Storm."

I held his gaze. "My friends call me Storm."

He gave me a warm smile. "Storm. Well then, Storm, now we just need to keep training so you can get your powers to come out without having to get someone to beat you up every time."

"That would be preferable."

"Marcus!" a voice called.

We both looked up to find a cluster of mountain elves standing at the tree line. Ydras strode across the grass with a determined look on his face while Marcus and I joined the five wood elves on their way towards him. He stopped before us and gave me a quick onceover before turning to Marcus.

"Looks like you have another hothead on your hands." Ydras shifted his gaze to Cileya. "You handled that well."

The taciturn mountain elf nodded in response. I didn't know how I felt about being called a hothead, regardless of how true it was, but I managed to stop the snarky remark on my tongue. Clanking weapons in the distance filled the silence while the leader of the mountain elves turned back to Marcus.

"It's the fall equinox today," he announced. "As always, you and the other Ashanna are welcome to join."

"Thank you," Marcus replied. "I can't speak for Morgora and some of the others, but I'll be there."

Ydras huffed. "Morgora. That discontented old grump. Does she ever do anything other than sit around and complain about stuff?"

The muscular Storm Caster chuckled. "Not these last couple of years."

"I thought so. Well, you can tell her that she can come if she behaves."

"Will do."

Ydras motioned between the wood elves and the hills leading up into the mountains. "Shall we?"

When Elaran gave him a nod, he turned on his heel and strode back towards his people. Faelar and the grumpy archer followed him without a second look back but Haemir and Keya at least shot me a smile before leaving.

"See you tonight, Storm," Haela called and fired off a salute before jogging to catch up.

I watched their retreating backs. A gust sent Haela's raven ponytail flying over her shoulder and I just had time to see her throw it back before the multicolored trees swallowed her. I wondered what they were doing. What did people do on a diplomatic mission? Given that diplomacy wasn't exactly one of my stronger suits, I hadn't a clue.

Marcus cleared his throat. "Ready to train?"

Whirling around, I found him studying me with a wide smile on his face. Cileya was nowhere to be seen. Man, I really hated being out in the woods with elves. Their ability to sneak up on me or away from me without me noticing was unnerving.

"Yeah."

"Alright, the anger that triggers your powers, where does it come from?"

Still reluctant to share too much, I shrugged. "Stuff."

Marcus shook his head with an exasperated look on his face. "Alright, wherever it comes from, it's time to feed it. When you want your powers to come out, you reach into that pit of rage and you fuel it." He gave me a wave of his hand. "And then when you want it to go back, you smother it. Can you do that?"

After an initial second of hesitation, I nodded.

"Good. Then get ready."

Golden-brown eyes turned black in front of me. I closed my eyes for a second and felt that simmering anger deep inside me. Carefully, I imagined adding oil to a fire. Sparks flickered inside. I dumped a whole barrel on them.

Dark clouds shot out around me and my eyes went black as well. A grin spread across Marcus' face. He slowly raised his arms into the air, gathering the storm. Anticipation bounced inside me. It was on. I darted towards him.

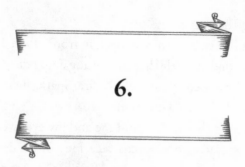

6.

Torches created a line of flickering fire up the mountainside. Craning my neck, I tried to see where it led but only moonlit rocks met my gaze further up. Pebbles came loose under my feet. I threw out both arms to steady myself as they tumbled down the hill. A strong hand shot out and kept me from falling. Sending Marcus a grateful nod, I continued towards the home of the mountain elves.

Marcus and I had spent most of the day training. Now that I finally knew what to look for, it was much easier to reach for the rage that called up the storm. It still didn't come every time I wanted it to, but it was improving.

"Have you ever celebrated the fall equinox before?" the tall Storm Caster asked.

I frowned up at him. "I didn't even know what an equinox was until this morning."

He chuckled. "Then you're in for a treat."

The trail of light ended as we crested a hill and instead turned into a whole carpet of fire. I stared down at it. Torches and bonfires lit up the whole valley. If I didn't *know* what I was looking at, I would've had no idea what I was looking at.

Buildings made of the same gray stone as the mountain dotted the gorge and blended in so well with their surroundings that they were almost entirely camouflaged. If not for the firelight and the fact that I knew there was supposed to be a city here, I would've missed it.

Marcus smiled at the astounded look on my face before placing a light hand on my back and nudging me forward. "It's kind of cool, right?"

"Yeah."

We wove our way through the stone houses that appeared to have been cut straight from the mountain. They were elegant yet practical. And very easy to defend. I wasn't sure it could be classified as a road but we followed some kind of level path towards the heart of the city.

Several fires had been lit on low circular beds in the open space at the middle. Benches made of stone surrounded them. Marcus led us towards the one where Ydras and my friends were seated.

"Storm, you made it!" Haela called and waved me towards the empty seat beside her.

I plopped down next to her while Marcus skirted around the fire and sat down closer to Ydras and his people.

"So this is where you spend your days doing..." I glanced at Haela. "Whatever it is that you do?"

"Yep, this is where we discuss partnerships, trading possibilities, networks." She nodded at the brown-haired wood elf with the leaf decorated braid. "Oh, and Keya is grilling them about history."

"Sounds like just your kind of thing."

Haela draped an arm over her face in a dramatic gesture. "Oh, you know me too well." Letting it drop again, she leaned in and continued in a conspiratorial whisper. "It's all terribly boring. I want to spar and shoot and explore the mountain but Elaran says we have work to do. Can you believe that? Work." She shook her head. "Who has time to work when there's so much adventure out there waiting for me?"

I let out a long chuckle. "I've missed you."

"It's only been two days, Storm."

Bumping her shoulder with mine, I shook my head ruefully. "You know what I mean."

She winked and flashed me a grin that told me she understood. When I'd left last time and had been taken to Tkeister, I had been gone a long time. A lot had happened in the City of Glass during my stay there and things would've been so much easier if Haela had been there with me. Her constant cheerfulness and excitement brightened everything she came into contact with. I truly was lucky to call her a friend.

"The equinox is upon us," Ydras said in a voice that carried across the stones. He stood up and spread his arms. "The day and the night are equally long. It is a great day of symbolism and one we should continue to embrace."

A dull thumping spread across the area as the mountain elves at our fire, as well as the other fires around us, stomped their boots into the stone.

"Balance is the key," Ydras continued. "Light and dark, day and night, are equally important. May our lives be filled with both of them. May we always have both light and darkness in equal amounts in our life."

The stomping feet grew louder until it blanketed the whole valley. Fire flickered over serious faces all around me. Ydras slashed his arms through the air and the thudding stopped.

"To light and darkness!" he called.

A cheer rose from the mountain elves and within a matter of seconds, the ceremonial atmosphere had been replaced by festive excitement. Mugs started appearing in people's hands while others placed slabs of meat on the metal net that covered the fire. It sizzled as juice dripped into the flames.

Haela rubbed her hands, her yellow eyes glittering in the firelight. "Now this is my kind of party."

Ale and grilled meat were handed around while the people around our fire told stories of the past year. Apparently, Ydras, who I learned was the mountain elves' *elder*, had fought off a bear with his bare hands, and Cileya was their top archer. Flames played in her red and golden hair as she shared stories of her exploits in the woods across the mountain. It was the most I'd heard her talk since I arrived but this seemed to be a night of storytelling.

"When we arrived," I interjected before someone else could start a story, "you said that there was no Tkeideru. What did you mean by that?"

"It's not our story to share but..." Ydras looked to Elaran, who nodded. "Alright, then." He moved his ice-blue eyes to me. "These wood elves must have a lot of faith in you if they agree to share their history with you in this way."

That took me by surprise so I just blinked in reply. I didn't usually deserve people's faith in me but maybe my friends felt differently. However, before I could ask about that, the mountain elf elder continued.

"Have you thought about why wood elves are a common sight in human cities across this continent? Why only them? Why not all elves, or no elves?"

Furrowing my brows, I tapped my lips. "I hadn't thought about it that way."

"It's because they don't have a home. Not anymore." Fire flickered over Ydras' serious face. "Thousands of years ago, there was a Tkeideru, a home for the wood elves, on this continent. There was a great forest north of Tkeister, between Frustaz and Sker, in the place that is now known as The Plains."

The Plains was located a little further south of Travelers' Rest. I remembered the flat area from when the star elves transported us towards their lands. Well, before they knocked us out, that is. There had not been a tree in sight when we traveled through it.

"What happened?" I asked.

Ydras blue eyes grew cold. "The star elves happened. They had some grand notion that it would be better for all elves if we became one nation that answered to one ruler. The wood elves thought it was bullshit." He scrubbed his hands over his face. "The queen of the star elves flew into a rage and razed the whole forest to the ground."

I stared at him, aghast. "What?"

He gave me a grave nod. "She forbade them from rebuilding their home and they were forced to live as nomads in other cities after that. When she finally died and her ashes had been thrown to their precious stars, the wood elves were so used to living like nomads that they never rebuilt." A brief smile cracked his serious face as he looked to the wood elves present. "Or so I thought."

"Our ancestors apparently had a stubborn streak," Keya added with a smile. "It appears as though they refused to be told that they could not rebuild so they settled on what became the Lost Island."

"Wow." I looked between my friends and the leader of the mountain elves. "That's awful."

"Yes." He turned pensive eyes on me. "From what I understand, the star elves shared some of their plans with you when you were a prisoner in their city."

After a quick glance at Elaran, I nodded. "Yeah."

More ale and grilled meat appeared around the fire while I shared what I knew about the star elves and their plans. Clouds blew across the moon but the warm food and the fireplace helped keep the cold away. When I was finished, Ydras and the other mountain elves looked at me with somber faces.

"That damn Nimlithil," a voice muttered loudly on the other side of the fire.

We all whipped our heads around to find an old woman with gray hair and eyes of steel glaring at us from across the flames.

"Glad you could join us, Morgora," Ydras said.

"Bah! We both know that's a lie." She turned her hard gaze on me. "She's really planning on expanding across the whole continent now?"

"Yeah."

Morgora clicked her tongue in disgust. "She's just like her grandmother. Gets this great idea that she's going to fix things, save the whole damn world, and then she just barrels down that road like a blind bull." Joints snapped as she flicked her hand. "What everyone else wants be damned. She's going to fix things and her way is the only right way."

"Sounds like you know her," I commented.

"Her grandmother is the one who wiped Tkeideru from existence."

Stunned silence descended on the area. Only the logs in the fire popped and broke the quiet. I studied the old woman from behind the dancing flames. She looked pissed off. Really pissed off.

"Last time that damn family decided to save the world they destroyed a nation." Morgora glared at the glowing embers in front of her. "This time her granddaughter and that damn Aldeor the White has drained magic from the world and decided that no one should feel pain."

"What do you think will happen?" Keya asked in a quiet voice.

"Only the skies know," she muttered, and burrowed into her clothes. "I should've left when I had the chance. Damn Athla and his damn speeches for making me stay."

Leaning towards Haela, I lowered my voice to a whisper. "Who's Athla?"

She lifted her toned shoulders in a shrug. "No idea."

The grumpy old woman appeared to have nothing more to say because she glared at the fire with furrowed brows, completely ignoring the rest of us. A collective shrug went through the ring. I reached for my mug. Lukewarm ale wet my parched mouth as I drained it in one fell swoop. Whatever spices they used for this meat, it left me very thirsty. I placed the empty mug on the ground while Haemir got the conversation started again.

"I've been meaning to ask," he began, "you've known about what the star elves have done for quite some time. Don't take this the wrong way but why haven't you done anything about it?"

Ydras squared his shoulders. "We don't like to get involved in the mess that is the outside world. We leave it alone and it leaves us alone."

"That's not entirely true, is it?" I narrowed my eyes at him. "You're hiding the Storm Casters from the star elves. I wouldn't call that being neutral."

The leader of the mountain elves glanced at the redhead next to him. "Cileya is Ashaana. But she's also one of us." He met my gaze head on. "And we always back our own people."

My mouth twitched into a smile and I gave the fierce elf a slow nod. I could definitely understand his reasoning since I was exactly the same. There was nothing I wouldn't do for the people I love. The rest of the world, however, was on its own.

"Seriously?" Haela heaved a dramatic sigh. "Every time I go to a party with you lot it always turns into talk of gloom and doom. What is wrong with you people? Wasn't this supposed to be a celebration?"

Laughter rippled through the ring of elves and humans around the fire. I could've sworn even Morgora's stern lips curled into a smile deep inside her gray clothes.

"Quite right." Ydras stood up and swept his gaze across the valley. "It looks like everyone has finished eating." Climbing up on the stone bench, he raised his voice. "Bring out the music!"

Another enthusiastic cheer rose from the gathered elves. Heavy beating of drums vibrated off the mountain and mingled with softer tunes of flutes drifting on the cool night air. All around us, people left their seats and took to jumping and dancing around the fires.

Haemir let out a yelp as his sister pulled him up and dragged him over to join the celebrating mountain elves. Shaking my head, I let out a chuckle. Typical Haela.

"Are you not going to join?" Keya said as she moved around the fire and sat down next to me.

I lifted one shoulder in a lopsided shrug. "I don't dance. You?"

"I prefer watching too."

Next to us, Elaran's face turned sad. Following his gaze, I found him watching a couple of mountain elves who danced and laughed in each other's arms. Of course. Illeasia. My heart ached for him and the star elf princess he loved and that he'd had to leave behind when we escaped the City of Glass. I wish I knew the right thing to say but before I could figure it out, he pushed off from the bench and stalked away.

"Wait," Keya said as Faelar made a move to follow him.

The blond elf turned to face us. Keya beckoned him closer while toying with a leaf in her braid. Taciturn as always, Faelar simply looked at us with furrowed brows once he had closed the distance between us.

"Cileya was asking about you just now," Keya said and motioned to where the redheaded mountain elf was standing a little further away.

Faelar raised his eyebrows. "She did?"

"Yes. You should go and talk to her."

For a moment, he just remained standing there, glancing between us and Cileya but then he nodded slowly. Pushing his flowing blond hair back behind his ears, he made his way towards the elven Storm Caster. I turned to Keya with surprise on my face.

"You lied," I stated. "You don't usually lie."

"It was a harmless deception. And for a good cause."

I chuckled. "I think I'm rubbing off on you."

A sly smile spread across her beautiful face. "Perhaps."

Shaking my head, I let out another soft laugh. Keya and I continued watching the celebrations that lasted well into the night. Rhythmic drumming beat in tune with my heart while ecstatic elves danced and laughed like there was no tomorrow. I smiled as Faelar and Cileya snuck away from the party. Gloom and doom might await us when the night was over but at that moment, it felt very far away.

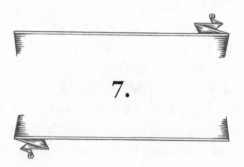

7.

Rage burned in the blackened pits of my soul. I fed it. The dark clouds around me spun faster and lightning crackled over my skin. Feeling the anger coursing through my body, I raised my arms. Now, all I needed to do was to take all those emotions, that fiery rage, and direct it. That was what Marcus had said. Give in to the feelings, focus them, and then make them do what I want. I drew a deep breath. Willing the fury to turn into a blast of wind, slammed my arms forward. Nothing happened.

A frustrated groan ripped from my throat. As the darkness snapped back into my soul, I picked up a pine cone and hurled it across the field in a fit of rage. It sailed through the air before bouncing across the grass. Without a second look back at Marcus, I stalked away.

We had spent the past two weeks training but I wasn't improving much. Granted, I had gotten better at calling up and pushing down the darkness but it was still a bit of a hit and miss at times. When it was out, black clouds of only mediocre size swirled around me and I still couldn't summon any wind.

"Don't beat yourself up." Jogging to catch up with me, Marcus grabbed my wrist and spun me around. "You're doing fine."

I yanked my arm from his grip while suppressing the urge to stab him. "I'm not doing fine! I'm not getting any better. You know it. I know it."

Whirling back around, I continued stomping away. Haela had been right before, the smoke and lightning I created now were pathetic compared to what I had summoned before. And it wasn't even close to what Marcus could do. Man, I really hated being mediocre.

"Morgora!" the annoyingly optimistic Storm Caster called all of a sudden. Taking my wrist again, he pulled me towards the old woman seated outside the longhouse. "Come with me."

The grass in front of her had been flattened by all the times Morgora had sat in that chair, glaring at the rest of the world. She swatted an orange leaf from her face as a brisk wind stirred up a whole cluster of colorful projectiles, and then crossed her arms again.

"What?" she demanded.

"You need to help her train. It's because of you all the rest of us got so good at it." He gave her a hopeful smile. "It would mean the world."

Morgora drew down her eyebrows. "I thought I told you three recruits ago that I was done with this nonsense." Wiggling her body, she placed herself more firmly in the chair. "I'm done teaching people how to be Storm Casters. It never leads to anything anyway."

"Please. Just watch her once."

A smile that could've melted the blackest of hearts radiated from Marcus' face. Morgora grumbled into her collar. Birds chirped above us while that incredible smile worked its magic on the grumpy old lady. At last, she shot up with surprising speed and stalked towards the training area.

"Fine!" she snapped. "Just this once."

Marcus sent a victorious grin my way before jogging after her. Flicking my gaze between the two of them, I shook my head. I wasn't sure what I thought about that old grump but if she could help me get better, I was pretty sure I could tolerate her snide remarks without throwing knives at her. Probably. Letting out a soft chuckle, I strode after her as well.

When Marcus and I had taken up position opposite each other on the grass, we both looked to Morgora. She appeared to be weighing something in her mind but then blew out a breath and stomped towards us.

"If I dragged my ass over here, I might as well get my time's worth," she huffed before stopping in front of me. "Come here."

Eyeing her suspiciously, I stepped forward. A strange surge shot through me as Morgora slammed her palm into my chest. I stumbled back, whipping my gaze between my body and the old woman.

"What the hell was that for?" I muttered while massaging my ribs.

"Now," she said as if I hadn't commented, "call up the storm and then fight."

Silence descended over the clearing as Marcus and I squared up against each other. He flashed me a smile and then his eyes went black. I dove to the side right before his blast swept through the place I had just vacated. Rolling to my feet, I darted forward and threw out my arms. Huge black cloud exploded around me. Lightning flashed through the smoke, followed by deafening thunder. I almost stumbled in surprise at the sheer force I had created but I only blinked at the scene around me while continuing my dash towards my opponent.

On a whim, I swung my arm the way Marcus did when sending a strong gust flying. Air blasted off before me. Since I hadn't thought it would work, I hadn't even bothered trying to aim so the blast went high over his head. Branches snapped and crashed towards the ground as the whole top of the closest tree broke off. Yellow and red leaves rain down.

Screeching to a halt, I stared in shock at the falling chunk of tree. A boom rang out as it hit the ground. Panic flashed through me and the darkness snapped back into my soul right before a strong wind hit me square in the chest. I flew through the air and slammed into the grass further down the field.

My ears rang. I tried to sit up but everything was spinning so much that I just slumped back on the ground again. While blinking away the pounding in my head, I tried to figure out what had just happened. Had I really created a blast strong enough to break a tree? Dread spread through my body like poison. What if I had hit Marcus with that? He could've died.

"You okay?"

Opening my eyes, I found said Storm Caster standing over me. He reached down to help me up. After heaving a deep breath, I took his offered hand and climbed to my feet. Morgora stood glowering at us from a few strides away.

"You have a lot of raw strength," she announced. "But you're terrified of your own power."

"What–"

She cut me off with a flick of her wrist. "Until you stop being afraid of your own power, you won't get any better. There,

I helped." Spinning on her heel, she stalked back towards the longhouse.

My fingers twitched. I desperately wanted to throw a knife at that rude old woman and scream at her that she was wrong. Afraid? I wasn't afraid. But the reason I only remained staring helplessly as her strong back disappeared across the field was that deep in my heart, I knew she was right.

Marcus stepped in front of me and opened his mouth, but whatever he saw in my face made him close it again. Blowing out a long breath, he jerked his head.

"Come with me."

Despite not being in the mood for more surprises, I followed him towards the tree line on the far side of camp. Neither of us spoke as he led me further into the woods. I focused on the beautiful nature around us because I didn't want to deal with the nest of snakes that was my feelings.

Earthen aromas drifted up from the moss and fallen leaves while brisk fall winds added a crispness to the air. Birds too stubborn to seek better weather chirped on the branches above our heads. I watched the light play across the colorful canopy as we followed a slight trail in the root-covered ground. Something glittered between the trees.

A vast lake sprawled before us. I let out a low whistle as we finally cleared the trees and could see it properly. Sunlight glinted in the still water while red, orange, and yellow trees decorated the rim like a frame. It was stunning.

Wood groaned as Marcus sat down on a fallen tree trunk by the shore. He waved me forward. Brushing off some stray pine needles, I sat down beside him.

"Look, I know she can be a bit... intense," Marcus said. "But she's usually right." Golden-brown eyes peered down at me. "Are you afraid of your own power?"

And just like that, the nest of snakes was back. I glanced away.

"Okay, let's try a different approach," he said. "What was it that awoke your powers?"

Picking up a thin twig, I started winding it around my finger. "I don't wanna talk about it."

"It would be so much easier to help you if I actually knew what we had to work with."

"Easy for you to say." I pitched the twig towards the lake. It landed in the water with a faint plop. "Given everything I've seen, your trigger is probably a hero emotion, like love or protecting people. Am I right?"

Soft winds rustled the leaves around us as Marcus fell silent for a few seconds. Then he expelled a forceful breath and turned to face me head on.

"My trigger emotion is hate."

Drawing back, I blinked at him while my mouth dropped open.

"That surprises you?"

"Yeah."

Marcus let out a humorless laugh. "My dad was an ambitious man. He was determined to climb the ranks and become an important person, someone people looked up to and obeyed. He rose fast and high. But..."

"But?"

"But my mom fell in love." A tired smile spread across his lips. "With a smuggler, of all people. They planned to run away together." Sadness crept into his eyes. "My father found out. He couldn't have her indiscretion ruin his career so he killed her. Killed them both. Then he pinned it on some lowlife and used it to garner sympathy that furthered his career."

"By Nemanan," I breathed.

"I was there when it happened. I saw him do it. He killed my mom because she fell in love." Wood vibrated as he slammed his fist into the tree trunk. "My hate eventually summoned a storm that blew up our house. I left that night and haven't been back since but if I ever see that bastard again, I'll kill him."

Heavy silence fell around us. By all the gods, did all Ashaana have childhoods this difficult? I glanced at the muscular man next to me.

"I'm sorry. I shouldn't have assumed." Leaning back on the trunk, I raked my fingers through my hair. "Alright, you really wanna know what made my powers come out?"

If he was honest with me, I might as well afford him the same courtesy. When he nodded in response, I released a slow exhale and told him the story of how I'd gotten Rain killed that night in the darkened alley. I left out most of the gruesome details of what happened afterwards but I think he got the gist.

When I was finished, Marcus gave me a long look. "Have you ever forgiven yourself for that?"

"No. And I don't think I ever will." I shrugged. "But I've learned to live with it."

"And what happened afterwards, is that why you're afraid of your powers?"

A slight chuckle slipped from my lips. "No, I'm not losing any sleep over that. I've already accepted that I'm a villain, so we're all good on that front." Bracing my arms on my knees, I blew out a breath. "It's just... there have been times when I've lost control after calling up my powers and almost killed people I care about. And *that* scares me."

Back in the City of Glass, the star elves had tricked me into believing that I had killed Elaran and put Shade in a coma. I had spent weeks thinking I had killed my friends. Again. Just because I had eventually found out that it was a lie didn't mean that all those mind games hadn't messed with my head. After all, I *had* summoned a storm strong enough to smash up a building. It hadn't actually fallen down on top of Shade and Elaran. But it could have. What the star elves had done had left me hesitant and second-guessing my powers so that every time I told myself that I *hadn't* hurt my friends, my mind kept adding: *yet*.

"I get it," Marcus replied. "We've all been there." His lips quirked upwards in a rueful smile. "Morgora helped us all get through it."

"But she won't teach me."

Marcus pushed off from the tree trunk and held out his hand. "No, but I'll help you as best as I can. Come on, we're going to try something."

Letting him help me to my feet, I gave him a nod. "Alright."

Boots hit the ground with a thud followed by shirts and pants. I gaped at him.

"*What* are you doing?"

He chuckled and jerked his head towards the lake. "Getting in the water."

Pale rays of sunlight played over his chiseled abs and strong arms. The muscles in his broad back flexed when he turned around and strode towards the shoreline with confident steps.

By Nemanan, he was fit. Shaking my head, I pushed down the stupid blush that had crept over my cheeks.

"Are you coming or what?" he called as he waded into the water and stopped at knee height.

Once I had pulled off my boots, I rolled up my pants and followed him. The freezing water sent a spike through my body.

"Man, it's cold," I hissed.

He lifted his toned shoulders in a shrug. "Everything is cold in the mountains."

Dark smoke appeared around him and he pushed his arms outwards. The gust created violent ripples across the calm lake. With eyes still black as the night, he turned to me.

"There's nothing here except the water," he said. "The trees on the other side are too far away to snap. No one can get hurt." Motioning at the vast expanse of water, he gave me an encouraging smile. "Try it."

Reaching into the deep pits of my soul, I managed to call up the darkness. Black tendrils whipped around me. While trying to concentrate on the emptiness in front of me, I pushed my hands forwards. Nothing happened. Irritation bubbled through me. I jammed my arms forward again. The dark clouds around me grew but still no wind.

"It's okay," Marcus said. "We have all afternoon."

I flicked my eyes up and down his muscular body. "You know, if this is the only thing we're doing, you didn't need to take your shirt off."

"I was taking my pants off so I had to take off my shirt too. Otherwise it would've looked weird."

Barely hidden amusement flashed over my face as I pointed downwards. "Or you could've just rolled up your pant legs."

A teasing grin spread across his face as he winked at me. "What would be the fun in that?"

Shaking my head, I let out an exasperated chuckle. Men.

The half-naked man and I spent the next couple of hours by the lake, trying to get my powers to work. Though not all of it was in the water because after a while, I complained that I couldn't feel my feet so we went back to shore and kept working from there. Marcus looked relieved when I suggested it and I swore he was stopping his teeth from chattering by sheer force of will. I repeat: *men*.

Our only interruption was when Faelar and Cileya accidentally stumbled out of the woods. The usually stone-faced wood elf looked uncharacteristically embarrassed and pulled me aside while Marcus and Cileya exchanged a few words. When he told me not to tell Elaran about this, I almost laughed out loud. In the end, though, I promised him I wouldn't.

I smiled as the two taciturn elves disappeared into the woods again. At least someone was making progress. If I didn't start getting better soon, I didn't know what to do. The elves had talked about leaving soon because their diplomatic mission was coming to an end. What was the point of staying here in the woods while all my friends left if the one person who could help me get better refused to teach me?

Heaving a deep sigh, I swept my arms in another unsuccessful attempt at creating wind. Maybe I was better off leaving too.

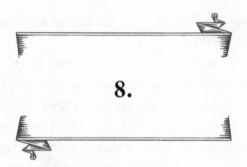

8.

Horses snorted and stomped next to us. The twins were busy saddling them all while Elaran stared down at me with that customary frown on his face. A crowd had gathered by the horse pen.

"Last chance," he said. "We're leaving so you need to make a decision. Leave or stay."

Glancing from him to the tall Storm Caster behind me, I chewed my lip. Was there any point in staying? I didn't like wasting time on futile attempts but if I'd traveled this far, maybe I should stay and continue trying to convince Morgora to train me.

I blew out a deep sigh and straightened. "I'm staying."

If he was surprised by my decision, he hid it well. He just gave me a curt nod before turning to the blond elf a short distance away. "Faelar, let's go."

The elf in question jerked his head up but didn't approach straight away. Instead, he stepped closer to Cileya. Raising a hand, he pushed back a few strands of red and gold hair behind her pointed ear. She placed her hand over his and leaned against his chest for a moment.

"Oh, Elaran," Keya said in an exasperated voice. "Do not be so blind."

"What do you mean?" Elaran turned to her with a frown.

"Can you not see it? Faelar is in love."

"Faelar? In love?"

Elaran turned towards his blond friend and was about to protest, but when he saw Faelar stroke a hand over Cileya's hair, the grumpy elf's face softened. It was a softness I had only seen back in Starhaven when he looked at Princess Illeasia.

"Faelar!" he called again and jerked his chin.

Keya pursed her lips in disapproval but said nothing while the blond wood elf tore his gaze from Cileya and shuffled over. Elaran locked eyes with him.

"We need someone to stay here and coordinate this newfound partnership." Elaran nodded at his friend. "And I want someone I can trust so I need you to be the one who stays behind."

Surprise, disbelief, and hope blew past on Faelar's handsome face. Both Keya and I had to twist away to hide the smiles spreading across our lips. Who would've known Elaran had it in him? Actually, I did know that.

"You want me to stay?" Faelar finally blurted out.

"Yes."

Smiles tugged at the lips of both wood elves as they looked at each other with true love and admiration in their eyes. Still holding his gaze, Faelar held out his arm. Elaran clasped it.

"Thank you."

The auburn-haired ranger nodded. "Be safe, my brother. I'll see you again soon."

While Faelar made his way to the other wood elves of Tkeideru to say goodbye, I shot Elaran a wide grin.

"When did you become such a softie?"

He drew his eyebrows down and replied with a somewhat halfhearted glare because we both already knew the answer to that question. "Shut up."

Twigs snapped and leaves rustled in distress as a blond human I hadn't seen before came crashing out of the forest a few paces away. Whipping his head around, he caught his breath until his eyes fell on Marcus. Dirt sprayed into the air as he sprinted forward again.

"Marcus," he panted, doubled over with his hands on his knees. "Bad news."

Panic flashed over the tall Storm Caster's face. "What?"

"The star elves are on the move. They're marching on Sker!"

"*What?*" Marcus repeated with even more force.

Distressed murmuring broke out all around us as the crowd shifted nervously. Everyone nearby clustered in to hear the news.

"Why would they do that?" someone called from the back of the group. "They haven't expanded their territory in years. Did something happen?"

The scout gulped down more air before answering. "People are saying the Queen of Tkeideru and the King of Keutunan have boarded a ship to Pernula to sign a triple alliance and that the star elves felt threatened. Apparently, something about some prisoners finding out what they were up to and then escaping made them jumpy and now this alliance pushed them over the edge."

Across the trampled grass, Elaran and I exchanged a look.

"Shit," Marcus swore. He whirled around and snapped his fingers at an elf in a long green cloak. "Send word to whatever's left of our network. If any Ashaana surface, they need to get them clear ASAP."

A ripple went through the cluster around us as several people took off in different directions. White clouds blew across the sun and cast the area in temporary gloom. Elaran flicked his gaze between the twins and Keya.

"We have to move. The Queen's coming and there's an army on the loose. We have to make sure she's safe."

"Elaran," Faelar interrupted. "Should I...?"

"No." He shook his head. "I meant what I said. I need you here."

While the four wood elves renewed their efforts to leave, and I tried to battle my even more conflicted feelings about staying, an irritated figure stomped across the grass. The crowd parted as Morgora stalked up to Marcus.

"What's this nonsense about star elves attacking Sker?" she demanded.

"They're not attacking yet," Marcus answered. "But yeah, they're marching on Sker."

A violent string of profanities rolled off the old woman's sharp tongue while her gray eyes hardened even further. Then she fell silent. For a moment, it looked as if she was calculating possibilities in her head until at last, she straightened. She was short but powerfully built so when she drew herself up, her body appeared taller than it actually was. Eyes of steel fell on me.

"You're a thief or some kind of assassin, aren't you?"

I narrowed my eyes at her. "Yeah, how did you know?"

"So you'd know how to sneak in the shadows and get someone out of a city undetected?" she pressed on, completely ignoring my question.

"That would be within my skillset, yes."

"Good. Then I have a proposition for you." Morgora raised her chin. "If you go to Sker and get a man called Malor out before the star elves take complete control, then I'll train you."

"For real?"

She gave me a curt nod. "Yes."

Marcus and the remaining Storm Casters had watched the exchange with wide eyes. From their looks of surprise, I figured that Morgora wasn't usually this concerned about other people. Keya's brown horse neighed inside the pen as she finished saddling him. I shot Silver a look before turning back to the grumpy old lady.

"Alright, deal." I nodded back. "So I'll just bring him back here?"

"No! Don't bring him here. And don't tell him I'm the one who sent you." She muttered curses into her shirt collar. "That ridiculous old fart will never let you help him if he knows I'm the one behind it."

Furrowing my brows, I studied her. "Alright, Pernula it is."

"I'm going too," Marcus announced.

"Over my dead body," Morgora snapped. "You're not cut out for this kind of work. You have no experience of it. Skulking and scheming in the shadows of a city." She swept hard eyes across all Ashaana present. "None of you do. You're forest people. Mountain people. You will only get yourselves killed and I did not put all that work into training you just so you could throw it all away by getting yourselves killed. You're all staying well clear of this."

The ring of Storm Casters shrank back and averted their gaze. All except one. Marcus. He took a step forward and placed a large hand on Morgora's shoulder.

"I know what you're trying to do, Morgora. But I'm going." He squeezed her shoulder. "This Malor obviously means a lot to you, which means that he also means a lot to me. So I'm going to help get him to safety whether you like it or not. I owe you that. After everything you've done for me."

"You owe it to me not to die," Morgora muttered.

"Hey, Storm!" Haela called as she led her horse from the pen. "We're leaving."

"Wait up, I'm coming too."

A frantic state descended on the whole camp as people milled about like stressed ants. After getting all the information Morgora had on her friend Malor, I darted to my cabin to retrieve all my stuff. Elaran stalked restlessly back and forth while I got ready to leave. One final rushed goodbye to Faelar later, our party of six grabbed our horses by the reins and hurried into the woods.

When I came back, I would finally get the Storm Caster training I needed. Well, if I accomplished my mission, that is. All I had to do was sneak into a non-allied city that was about to be occupied by another hostile force, find some mysterious man who didn't want to be rescued, convince him to let me rescue him, and figure out a way to get him out without anyone noticing. Piece of cake. I let out a chuckle as we raced up the hill. But first I needed to make a pit stop in Pernula. I had a certain Master Assassin to see.

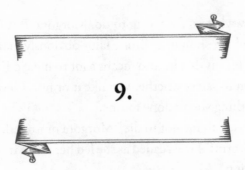

9.

Halls of black and red gleamed in the candlelight. The whisper of soft voices drifted from somewhere around the corner further down the corridor. Staying on the soft red carpet, I snuck forward.

We had arrived at Blackspire just in time. Queen Faye and King Edward had signed the alliance and were leaving again the next morning. Parties and ceremonies had already been hosted the previous evenings so they had planned on having one last intimate dinner together before they had to say goodbye. When our group of six had arrived at the gates, dusty and out of breath, we had of course been invited too. While the three rulers finished up whatever politically important stuff they were up to, and while we waited for the other two last-minute additions to the dinner to show up, I skulked around the castle because... well, do I really need a reason?

Rippling giggles bounced off the smooth obsidian walls. I drew up by a twisting arch set into the stone and peered around the corner. A stunning woman in a midnight blue dress stood in the middle of the wide room beyond. She appeared to have pulled back slightly at whatever comment had caused the giggling but now she leaned forward again and put a hand on the chest of a man in a black suit. I narrowed my eyes. Politically important stuff, huh?

While the blond lady in the blue dress batted her long lashes at Shade, I slipped into the room and took up position behind one of the numerous pillars in the otherwise empty room. She traced her fingers down his toned chest. The infuriating assassin was standing with his back to me so I couldn't see the expression on his stupid face but I could imagine the satisfied smirk present there.

Since the flirtatious lady only had eyes for the General of Pernula, she didn't see me sneak further in. Coolness seeped through my shirt as I rested my shoulder against an obsidian column and glared at the couple a short distance away.

"When will I see you again?" the blond lady said.

"Soon," Shade replied.

She pouted her lips and looked up at him with sad eyes. "I wish we didn't have to keep it a secret."

A flash of irritation burned through me when the Master Assassin reached up and cupped her cheek. "Me too. But it's for the best. At least until you can sway your father's opinion of me."

"I will continue working on him."

"Good."

Rising to her tiptoes, she planted a quick kiss on his cheek before gliding across the room. I glowered at her until the last of her midnight blue skirts had disappeared through the arch on the other side. Shade whipped around.

Steel whizzed through the air as a blade flew straight at me. Twisting around, I hurled two throwing knives. The one in my right had spun at an angle towards the projectile aimed for me and knocked it out of its path, while the one in my left hand sped towards the man who had thrown it. Shade yanked out another blade. Metal clattered all around us as he batted it away while the other two knives bounced off a column nearby before skidding across the floor.

In the time it had taken me to twist and throw, Shade had closed most of the distance between us. My body hit the stone with a soft thud as he pushed me back against the wide pillar I had used as my hiding place. The edge of his blade rested against my throat.

"Been spying on me, have we?"

I grinned up at him. "Oh, but you make it so easy." Shifting my gaze, I nodded at where the lady had disappeared to. "That your strategically important daughter?"

"One of them."

"*One* of them?"

Tilting his head to the right, he studied my face. "Yes."

Since I had a feeling that he was watching my reaction, I wiped any trace of emotion from my face and changed the subject. I motioned at the knife in his hand. "Don't you ever get tired of putting blades to my throat?"

"Oh, but you make it so easy," he repeated back at me while his lips curled upwards in a teasing smile.

I pushed forward ever so slightly. He stiffened. His eyes widened as I continued drawing my stiletto blade up his stomach, lifting his shirt as the sharp point grazed his skin.

"Easy, huh?"

He flicked his gaze between my smirk and the knife positioned right above his vital organs before letting out a soft chuckle and shaking his head. "Why are you here? I thought you were staying with the Storm Casters."

With blades still in place, we stared each other down for another few moments. Outside the room, soft footsteps rose and fell as someone passed by our room, completely oblivious to the two knife-wielding underworlders inside. At last, I lifted one shoulder in a lopsided shrug.

"I'm going to Sker."

"Now?" He raised his eyebrows. "There's an army of star elves heading there."

"I know. That's why I'm going. I've gotta rescue the senior advisor to the king and queen before the star elves take over completely because if I do that, the Storm Caster boss will train me. I'll be bringing him to Blackspire after I get him out so you need to get the High Priest and Master of Knowledge on board with giving him sanctuary here."

Shade's dark eyebrows stayed up for another few seconds before he narrowed his eyes at me. "It sounds like you're *telling me* that you'll be bringing a politically risky refugee into my city. Shouldn't you be asking my permission?"

"Have you ever known me to ask anyone for permission?"

"I bet you asked your Guild Masters."

"In the Thieves' Guild? Of course. But see, there's one big difference between them and you. Them, I called Master. You, on the other hand..." I shot him a challenging grin. "Have you ever heard me call *you* Master?"

His black eyes glittered and a sly smile spread across his lips as he pushed the knife higher up under my chin. "Not yet."

Grabbing his belt with my free hand, I drew his hipbones closer to me so that the stiletto pressed harder against his exposed skin. "Keep dreaming, bastard."

Footsteps echoed against the black walls somewhere behind us. The Master Assassin and I kept our eyes locked on each other even though the person approaching walked right into our room. A cough sounded.

"I hate to interrupt your little power showdown," Haela announced with poorly hidden amusement that told us she wasn't sorry at all. "I know it's been like a minute or so since you last had a chance to threaten each other, but Liam and Norah have arrived so save all that tension for the bedroom and let's go eat."

Red flashed over both our faces as we snatched our hands and weapons back and put some distance between our bodies. Haela let out a cackle.

"Come on then, kids," she called before winking at us and striding out of the room.

Shade stared at her retreating back with complete bafflement written all across his handsome face. "How has she survived this long? Saying things like that to people would've earned anyone a dagger to the heart years ago."

"I've thought about that too." I retracted my stiletto and went in search of my two missing throwing knives. "But I'm pretty sure it's because the God of Death doesn't want her. She's way too cheerful. Might mess up the doom and gloom of being dead, you know."

While retrieving his own missing blade, Shade nodded. "Probably."

Once we were both fully armed again, we started after the black-haired twin. Haela might be a complete tease but she was also incredibly perceptive. I cast a glance at Shade from the corner of my eye. Both of us jerked our heads forward again when we realized we'd been doing the same thing. Heat crept into my cheeks again.

Save that tension for the bedroom? How ridiculous. What tension? There was no tension between us. We had already gotten past that silly notion when we decided that love was not for people like us. And what in the world would we be doing in a bedroom? Sparks shot through my body as my hand accidentally brushed the side of his ripped stomach. Yanking my arm away, I stalked forward so that I was walking two steps in front of him instead, and gave my head a vigorous shake. There was no tension between us.

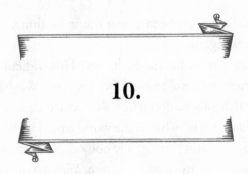

10.

Candlelight glinted off the finely polished silverware and cast glimmering shadows on the walls. Shade lifted a bejeweled goblet. Smiling at the room of friends, I did the same.

"To the new alliance between Pernula, Keutunan, and Tkeideru," he said. "And to a wise queen and a resourceful little brother."

King Edward chuckled. "To family."

"And friends," Queen Faye filled in.

"Family and friends!" the rest of us echoed.

Everyone in this cozy dining room that was nestled in the residential part of Blackspire knew each other. Except Marcus. We had started by introducing everyone, and though the tall Storm Caster seemed slightly intimidated to be meeting kings and queens in such an intimate setting, he took it mostly in stride.

"Speaking of friends," Faye began and looked to me before nodding at Marcus as well. "I heard that you and your new friend are going to Sker to rescue someone."

"Yeah, we are," Haela called from down the table. When the whole room turned to stare at her with raised eyebrows, she threw her hands out in a surprised gesture. "What?"

Keya's mouth drew into a smile. "I believe everyone is surprised, Haela, because we did not know that you would be going as well."

"Of course I'm going." She gave a short shake of her head as if that should've been obvious, and then flicked a hand at me. "Last time, you went on an adventure without me and you ended up meeting a dragon. This time, I'm going too."

I chuckled at the simultaneously offended and determined expression on her face. "And I have no say in the matter?"

"And neither do I?" Queen Faye shot her a pointed look.

Haela raised her chin and crossed her arms. "No." Her attempt at a stern mouth failed miserably and she broke into a wide grin before turning to her queen. "Alright, but please. I really wanna go and we've already finished that mission with the mountain elves so I don't have anything else to do."

"Fine." The Queen of Tkeideru let out an exasperated sigh followed by a hearty chuckle. "But be careful."

"Yes!" The excited twin pumped a fist in the air just as a group of servers arrived with the food.

Fragrant herbs and grilled meat filled the small dining room. The heavenly food almost melted on my tongue when I put it in my mouth. We had all missed the other stately dinners that the kings and queens had enjoyed these last few days since we'd been away. And even if I'd been here, I probably wouldn't have been welcome anyway. But now that it was just us, my shady underworld self was welcome to experience the expertly prepared food as well.

Utensils clinked on my left as Liam shoveled food into his mouth with a satisfied expression. Norah giggled next to him.

"Can I just ask?" Marcus said, speaking up for the first time since the dinner started. He turned his golden-brown eyes on Shade. "Why don't you just send an army to Sker to help them scare off the star elves? Surely that would be smarter than just letting another nation fall to Queen Nimlithil?"

I wasn't sure if the others could tell, but I could almost feel the temperature in the room drop several degrees as Shade narrowed his eyes before locking them on the Storm Caster. Marcus frowned slightly but met his gaze head on.

"You think I hadn't considered that too?" The Master Assassin ran his thumb over the silver knife on the table. "As soon as I heard the star elves were marching, I sent word to the King and Queen of Sker and offered my assistance. They turned it down. In no uncertain terms."

"I can imagine that," Liam added around mouthfuls of spiced meat. Gulping it down, he took a swig of ale. "Relations between Sker and Pernula have apparently always been strained. Our trading contacts down the coast are saying that the Stagheart siblings are an odd pair."

I turned to stare at my friend. "The king and queen are brother and sister?"

"Yeah."

"Wow. That *is* odd."

Shade cleared his throat. "To bring us back on topic, yes, it would be much better if we could prevent Sker from falling to the star elves." He swept serious eyes around the table. "Which is why I'm going with you to Sker."

"What?" Edward exclaimed and stared at his older brother. "Last time you left, you almost died."

A lopsided smile spread across Shade's lips. "I know. But we need this. Pernula and Keutunan need another ally, or at least one less enemy, if we're going to win this war. And I'm the General. Securing allies is my job."

Only the soft hiss of the candles sounded for a moment while everyone thought about the war that would reach our three homes one day. The stillness was broken by a creaking chair as Faye shifted her weight.

"Tkeideru could use another ally too." She tapped her fingers on the table while plans swirled in her eyes. "I have a proposition."

As if she already knew what Faye was going to say, Haela clapped her hands in excitement before elbowing her brother in the ribs. Suspicion filled Elaran's yellow eyes as he turned from Shade to his queen.

"Why do I have a feeling I'm not going to like this proposition?" he said.

The queen flashed him a grin before turning to me. "Shade is right. It would be in all our best interests if Sker remained free from Nimlithil and her army. But we can't send a large party to make that happen without it being interpreted as an act of war on our part. And that, we're not ready for. That's why we should send a small team."

"Oh, no," Elaran spluttered as realization dawned. Shifting his gaze between me and his queen, he shook his head. "I've said it before and I'll say it again: you *do* remember that last time I went on an adventure with that one, she got us captured by the star elves and I ended up having my death faked?"

"Yeah, I remember." Faye's smile widened. "You're still going, though." She motioned at Haemir. "And you're going too. I need at least one reasonable person who can keep the rest of you out of trouble."

"She can't be serious," Elaran muttered into his plate. "We're leaving again? With *her*?"

Shade didn't say anything but gave him a sympathetic clap on the shoulder. Meeting Keya's eyes across the table, I exchanged a smile with her. So, Marcus and I wouldn't be going to Sker alone.

Liam and Norah would of course be staying in Pernula, and Keya would be heading back to the Lost Island with Faye and Edward. But now there were six of us taking part in this crazy scheme instead of just two. Since this had started as my own personal mission to get Morgora to train me, I hadn't thought anyone else would be joining. After everything that had happened these last few months, though, I found that I was actually glad for the added company.

"Well, we're leaving tomorrow, so you'd better be ready," I said.

"Of course we're ready." Haela grinned. "I've been ready for adventure since the day I was born."

Rueful laughter erupted around the table. Leave it to Haela to raise everyone's spirits. Shifting my eyes from her to the Master Assassin, I found him watching me with a strange look in his black eyes. When I frowned at him, he just threw me a quick smirk before turning back to his little brother.

It had been wonderful to see the two Silverthorn brothers reunited again. When they parted ways in Keutunan last year after Edward was forced to banish Shade, their eyes had been filled with pain and unshed tears. But now that they finally had an excuse to spend time together again, their souls seemed to sparkle with renewed life.

Queen Faye lifted her cup again. "To more new friends!"

"And to not getting captured by the star elves again," I added. Another bout of laughter broke out. "Hear, hear!"

The rest of the dinner continued in much the same way. Eating, drinking, and simply enjoying each other's company. I filled my starving soul with every single minute of joy and companionship. Soon we would have to say goodbye again. I wondered how long it would be before I saw Liam and Norah again. Not to mention Faye, Keya, and Edward who would be heading back to the Lost Island.

Shaking off the somber mood, I ate a piece of pearl cake that the servers had brought in. Now was not a time for sadness. After all, we still had tonight.

"THIS IS IT, THEN?" King Edward asked, all too soon, when we were at last standing outside in the corridor after a night filled with food, drink, and friends. "This is our last chance to say goodbye before the grand formal one tomorrow?"

"I guess it is," Shade replied.

Haela flapped her arms. "Oh for Nature's sake, just hug already!"

Chuckling echoed through the obsidian corridor. While Queen Faye and the rest of the wood elves gathered to exchange final words, I watched Shade approach Edward. The ice around my heart melted a little when the assassin drew his little brother into a tight hug. He whispered something in his ear while the young king nodded against his shoulder.

I let out a yelp as I was pulled into a hug as well. Faye shot me a satisfied grin when she finally let me go.

"Take care of them," she said. "And yourself."

"I will." I nodded at the silver-haired queen. "I'll see you soon."

After a nod back, and a hug from Keya, the elves of Tkeideru wandered off. Shade and Edward were studying me from across the hall, both their heads tilted to the right in that telltale Silverthorn mannerism, and I had the strangest feeling that they'd been talking about me. Shade flicked his gaze over Marcus before locking eyes with me again.

"I'll see you tomorrow, then," he said.

"Yeah."

"Take care of yourself, Storm," King Edward said. "And my brother."

The Master Assassin gave him a shove and shook his head. Pulling his little brother back again, Shade draped an arm over his shoulders and started leading him away. "Come on."

"You too," I said to the king's retreating back as he disappeared down the hall with Shade's arm still around his shoulders.

Liam took Norah's hand and nodded at me and Marcus. "Are you coming?"

After a glance at the tall Storm Caster, I nodded back. "Yeah."

Marcus and I would be sleeping at Norah's school tonight so the four of us started down the corridor in the other direction. I was glad for that because that meant I could spend some time with Liam. Just the two of us. I wanted to tell him all about what had happened in the White Mountains without anyone else listening.

Warm night air met us as we exited Blackspire. Thankfully, dawn was still hours away so I would have time for that. Then, we would be leaving again. Riding out the gates and towards another impossible mission. Crazy, I know. Tilting my head back, I grinned at the bright moon above. But then again, crazy really did seem to be my natural state.

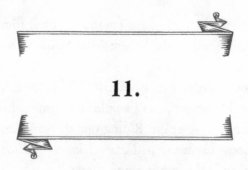

11.

Gigantic walls made of red stone rose from the dusty ground. Silver let out a snort as I pulled on the reins and slowed to a walk. My five companions did the same. As we drew closer to the gate, we dismounted and clustered together a few strides from the main road so that we wouldn't be blocking it.

"How do we get inside?" Haemir asked and nodded at the guards stationed by the open portcullis.

Shade ran a hand over his jaw. "We could always threaten or bribe them but depending on how dedicated they are to their job, it might turn ugly." He shifted his gaze to me. "How about you and Marcus here create some black smoke as cover so we can just slip inside?"

"Absolutely not!" Marcus protested. "We can't do anything that will draw the star elves' attention to any potential Ashaana hiding in this city." Serious eyes met mine. "You understand that, right, Storm? As long as we're here, we can't use our powers."

To be honest, I didn't really understand it. So what if the star elves found out about us? But I guess he was right that it might complicate stuff for any civilian Storm Casters who lived here, so in the end, I nodded in acknowledgement. Since Marcus was busy looking at me, he thankfully missed the assassin's eye roll.

"How do we get in then?" Elaran demanded.

"We could just *walk* in!" a voice called from down the road.

Whipping my head around, I realized that Haela was missing. Close to the gate, a group of traders pulled a heavy cart towards the opening while laughing children ran around it. And there was Haela. Striding after them with her horse in tow.

"For Nature's sake," Elaran grumbled. "We'd better go after her."

Horses snorted and neighed in surprise as the five of us scrambled off the side of the road and jogged to catch up with the black-haired twin. The elf in question shot us all a beaming grin when we fell in beside her. I kept my face carefully neutral as we reached the bored-looking guards at the portcullis.

"Halt," the dark-eyed one said in a language that sounded like Pernish except with a slight accent. He barely looked at me, Shade, and Marcus but spent a good minute studying the elves. When he was satisfied, he waved a lazy hand. "Go on then."

"Thank you," Haela chirped.

Barely audible mumbles sounded from the guard before he returned his somewhat lacking attention to the road outside. I suppressed a chuckle. Once we were all clear, Haela swung around and fired off another wide grin.

"See! You scheming underworlders might be a sneaky bunch but you always go for the complicated solutions." She tapped her temple. "Sometimes, just walking through the front door is the best move."

I gave her upper arm a shove. "Whatever."

"Those guards are a disgrace to their profession." Elaran cast a disapproving look at the two men leaning against the stone on either side of the gate. "No discipline. What if we'd been spies or assassins?"

"We *are* spies and assassins," I pointed out.

Jutting out his chin, Elaran crossed his arms. "I am a ranger."

"Not right now."

"Maybe we should save this argument for when we're indoors," Marcus interrupted. Adjusting his grip on the reins, he turned to Shade. "You said you had somewhere for us to stay?"

"Yeah. I inherited Pernula's spy network and according to the ones who've been stationed here, *The Broken Wing* is a no-questions-asked, don't-wanna-know-your-name kind of tavern." He jerked his head. "This way."

Shade and Elaran took the lead, followed by the twins, while Marcus and I brought up the rear. Tall three-story houses made of the same red stone as the city walls followed us as we moved deeper in. Sker was a strange city. It wasn't exactly ugly but there were no decorations, flowers, or anything that could be called pretty either. Everything, from the biggest houses to the dusty road of packed dirt, had that faded reddish color, and the further in we walked, the more I had a feeling that the whole city was made up of identical square blocks. Some of them were filled with buildings and some had been left as open spaces. And everything smelled like dry sand and warm stones.

"Is he always this..." Marcus began but then trailed off.

Following his line of sight, I found him studying Shade's back. "Is he always this what?"

"I don't want to say dictatorial but... actually yeah, he has all the dictator vibes."

A genuine laugh shook my chest. "Oh you have no idea." I raised my hand over Silver's back to motion at the buildings around us. "Are you alright? With this? We're a long way from your camp in the White Mountains."

"Yeah, I guess. I haven't been back in a city since... well, since I blew up our house." He lifted his broad shoulder in a shrug before reaching over to pat his horse on the neck. "Don't like cities much, to be honest. Lakes, woods, mountains, that's more my thing."

"But you came anyway."

He nodded. "Morgora needed me. And I owe her a lot. She's the one who took care of me when I first arrived at camp, terrified, angry, and starving. I meant what I said. She likes to pretend that she's a mean old grump but she really does care, deep down."

"Hurry it up," Shade called from further up the street. "We're here."

Marcus shook his head. "Dictator."

"As I was saying."

Exchanging a glance, we both burst out laughing. The rest of our group had stopped outside one of the numerous three-story buildings we had passed. It was identical to the houses next to it, except for one thing: the faded sign swinging over the door. *The Broken Wing* was written in black letters.

"Something funny?" Shade asked while Marcus and I finished tying our horses next to everyone else's.

"No, I just started laughing for no apparent reason at all." I shot him a challenging grin. "You know, the way people do."

An exasperated glare met me. After breaking my stare, he swept his gaze across our group and jerked his chin. "Let's go."

"You're giving orders again," Elaran muttered but stalked up the stairs nonetheless.

I grimaced as well but followed the arrogant Master Assassin into the tavern too. Tables and chairs made of pale wood occupied most of the floor space while a counter in same material ran along one of the walls. At the back, a narrow staircase led upwards. Shade motioned for us to stay back before approaching the bar.

While our self-proclaimed leader secured rooms and stabling for our horses, I took a closer look at the scattered occupants who were already here. A grim-looking woman with graying hair, a thin man who appeared to be half rat, and a short fellow with nervous eyes. They all sat alone. Yep. This tavern definitely catered to a no-name kind of clientele.

Once the shady tavern keeper with the greasy brown hair had scooped up Shade's payment, the assassin strode back towards us. "We're all set. He's sending out someone to get our horses stabled and we've got the whole upper floor."

Top floor. Perfect. I shot Shade a quick smile. As any underworlder would know.

"Let's go drop off our things and then get out and scout the city so we can figure out how we're going to stop this invasion." The assassin motioned at the stairs.

"I don't mean to be rude, but that's not my mission," Marcus said, stopping everyone in their tracks. He motioned at me. "Our mission. Storm and I are here to rescue Malor."

Shade leveled unreadable eyes on the tall Storm Caster. For a moment, they just stared each other down. I flicked my gaze between them and was just about to interrupt when the assassin spoke up.

"If we stop the invasion, you won't need to rescue him."

Marcus raised his eyebrows and gave him a slow nod. "Good point."

"So, what do we do?" I motioned vaguely at the area around us. "How are the six of us gonna accomplish that?"

The Master Assassin shot me a knowing look while a smirk curled his lips. "We've fought off an invading army before, haven't we?"

"True." I grinned back. "So, we do what we always do. We cheat, lie, and manipulate."

Haela let out a loud cackle and raced up the stairs. "Let's go make some mischief!"

Soft chuckling echoed through the room as we watched her black ponytail disappear to the second floor. Haemir lifted his toned shoulders in a light shrug and waved a hand at the now empty staircase.

"You heard her."

After a rueful shake of my head, I climbed the stairs after the excited elf. We *had* fought off an invading army before so we shouldn't have a problem doing it again. Right? It wasn't as if we'd been running the city last time and had had armies of soldiers and hordes of underworlders at our disposal while this time there were only six of us and we'd never even set foot in the city before. Right. Of course we were going to pull this off. No problem at all.

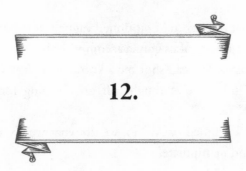

12.

Warm night winds whipped through my hair as I jumped the gap between two buildings. Tucking and rolling, I absorbed the impact and was back on my feet running within seconds. It was incredible how different the climate was on this side of the continent. In the White Mountains, fall had nature in its cold grip but over here in Pernula and Sker, it only felt like late summer. I very much preferred it that way.

When the sprawling castle made of red stone came into view, I slowed down to a trot before finally coming to a halt on the edge of the last building separating the city from the royal palace. We had decided to split up in order to cover more ground and then meet up in front of the castle. I cast a glance at the moon. The others should be here soon but I preferred staying on the rooftops until they arrived.

The air shifted behind me. I whirled around and slammed up a hunting knife. Amused black eyes met me.

"Impressive." Shade glanced from the knife I was pressing into his throat to the blade he had resting against my own neck. "You would've almost survived this time."

I snorted and sheathed the hunting knife again. "Find anything interesting?"

"Yeah, apparently Queen Nimlithil has been granted an audience in the Red Fort." The Master Assassin nodded at the castle in front of us. "Though it'll be more like a general party as far as I heard because the Staghearts didn't want to make her the center of attention."

"When?"

"Two days."

Running both hands through my hair, I pushed back rogue strands that the wind had blown loose. "We need to be there."

"Agreed."

"Any thoughts on how we're getting in?" I pursed my lips in annoyance. "We don't exactly have a secret entry point like we do in the Silver Keep and Blackspire."

Shade arched an eyebrow at me. "You have a secret passageway into Blackspire?"

"Of course I do." I smirked at him. "Who do you think I am?"

Blowing out a breath, he shook his head. "Right."

"But as I was saying, we don't have one into the Red Fort and if it's going down in two days, we're a bit short on time if we're gonna find one."

The black-eyed assassin was staring at something across the open plaza. I snapped my fingers in front of his face.

"Hey, you listening?"

He gave me a sidelong glance until I removed my hand. "I think I have an idea."

Following his gaze, I squinted at the cluster of people moving across the dusty ground and towards the red palace walls. Clouds had obscured the moon for a few moments but when they blew clear, the figures were illuminated by silver light.

My eyebrows shot up. *Oh*. Tipping my head from side to side, I considered. *That could work.*

"That could work," I repeated out loud before a grin stole across my face. "Elaran is gonna hate this."

Shade chuckled. "That he is."

"I HATE THIS," ELARAN muttered.

The Master Assassin and I exchanged a glance, both of us trying to suppress a smile. We had met up with the rest of our group earlier and then spent the next few hours waiting for the figures we'd spotted to return from the Red Fort. Once they had, we'd followed them to their base of operation.

"This is indecent," the grumpy elf continued. "No honorable man would go near a place like this."

His strong sense of honor and the fact that a profession like this didn't exist in Tkeideru had been a dead giveaway that Elaran wouldn't like this plan. I looked up at the nondescript red building. A sign with a pink lily swung gently in the breeze. He was right about one thing, though. There would be no honorable men found inside this building.

"We're not here as customers," Shade pointed out. "We're here because they can get us inside the castle."

While Elaran and Marcus appeared to be engaged in a competition to see who could scowl the deepest, the twins regarded the building with a healthy amount of skepticism. I blew out a breath and stalked up the stairs. Whatever feelings we had about this kind of profession, we needed their help. Warm air filled with perfume and incense hit my face as I strode into the Pink Lily Pleasure House.

A small bell tinkled repeatedly as the six of us pushed open the door one after the other to get inside. Drapes and decorated cushions in red, pink, and gold crowded the room. I drew up next to the dark wooden wall in order to give the rest of my party room to gather.

"Welcome," a sweet voice said as a woman with long blond hair swayed into the room. "Oh." She drew up short and blinked at our large group but recovered quickly. "Welcome to the Pink Lily. What are you in the mood for today?"

Shade took a step forward. "We're not here to buy. Tell whoever's in charge that we have a proposition."

"Uhm," she began. Nervous blue eyes flicked across the multitude of weapons peeking up over our shoulders. "Okay. Please wait here."

Feet thundered up the stairs as she ran to get her boss. I drummed my fingers on my thigh. The twins seemed mostly curious as they wandered around the room studying the different decorations, but Elaran and Marcus were still scowling. Shade's passive eyes glided over a man in a well-tailored vest as he was led up the stairs by a half-naked young man covered in gold glitter. A girl wearing only a see-through robe followed them. I raised my eyebrows but didn't comment.

Red drapes were pushed to the side as an older woman with thin lips and a tight bun on her head stalked through. Suspicion swirled in her gray eyes. "I'm Madam Cordina, the owner of the Pink Lily. I was told you're not here to buy and that you have some kind of proposition for me."

"Yes." Shade lifted a large sack of pearls in the air.

Greed pushed out the suspicion in her eyes and she gave us a curt nod. "You'd better come upstairs then."

Without another word, she turned and strode back up. After a collective shrug, we followed her. The dark wooden stairs creaked under my feet as I brought up the rear. A long hallway filled with doors met us. While we moved towards the one at the back, I couldn't help glancing inside the open rooms.

As I passed the men and women in various stages of undress lounging on couches in the open spaces and the muted grunts drifting through the closed doors, I suddenly felt very thankful for my messy life full of violence and bloodshed. I would take fights and blackmail over this kind of existence any day of the week.

"Now then, what's this proposition?" Madam Cordina said after I'd closed the door to her office.

"You supply the Red Fort with whores," Shade said without preamble.

"Whores? Whores!" Cordina pressed a hand to her chest in affront before lifting her chin. "My boys and girls are *escorts*. Escorts."

"My apologies," the assassin said smoothly. "You supply the Red Fort with *escorts*. Will you be doing that for the party the day after tomorrow as well?"

She narrowed her eyes. "Yes. Why?"

"We would like you to smuggle us in."

"No."

Shade lifted the pouch again. "We pay very well."

Madam Cordina pursed her lips. Twisting away, she made her way towards the large oak desk at the back. Glittering jewelry and fine silk robes along the walls gleamed in the firelight as a gust from the open window caused the candles to flicker. Plopping down in the chair, she rested her elbows on the sturdy wooden slab and leveled determined gray eyes on us.

"I'm afraid the answer is still no. The Red Fort is my best customer. I can't afford to risk their goodwill." Resentment drifted over her stern face as she looked at the bag of pearls. "No matter how well you pay."

"Then perhaps it's not money you seek." When Madam Cordina's eyes flicked to the side for a second, Shade pressed on. "What is it?"

She cleared her throat. "I might be persuaded to risk it if..." Waving a hand in front of her face, Cordina shook her head. "No. It would never work."

Clothes rustled as Shade moved closer and leaned his hip against the desk. "Try me."

"There is a man," she began. "People just call him *the Trader*. He's very powerful and very dangerous. A few days ago, he..." Pure hatred blazed in her eyes. "He *took* one of my girls. Milla. She's twelve years old. Twelve!"

Marcus took a step forward and raised his voice in shock and anger. "You have a twelve-year-old working here?"

"No! What kind of monster do you think I am?" Cordina glared at him. "She's not an escort. She cleans the house. But the Trader wouldn't take no for an answer so his goons knocked me out while he took her to a room." She lifted her hand to touch a fading bruise on her cheek. "When I came to, the room was completely trashed and Milla was gone. I can only assume he took her but no one in this city dares go against him."

"I'm sorry," Haemir said.

"So am I." The madam raised her chin. "So there you have it. My price. Get Milla back and I will sneak you into the party at the Red Fort."

The Master Assassin glanced back at us. Once he'd seen us all nod, he turned back towards Madam Cordina. "Done."

While Cordina filled us in on everything she knew about this lethal man called the Trader, I tried not to think about the scared kid he kept prisoner in his house for reasons I wasn't even sure I wanted to know. I wasn't even close to being some kind of hero who rescued lost people but that thought managed to tug at even my cold black heart. No child deserved that fate.

As we made our way out of the perfumed-filled building, my mind was already spinning with schemes. Some of them I liked better than others but after everything Madam Cordina had told us about the Trader, it appeared as though I would have to do things I didn't like regardless of which plan we decided on. Milla's scared face popped into my mind again. But maybe just this once, I could bear those unpleasant things. For all our sakes.

13.

"**A**re you sure you can handle this?" Haemir's concerned eyes drifted over my face.

Tugging at the ridiculously short hem of my dress, I gave him what I hoped was a determined nod. "Of course."

"It's just," Haela added, "I think we all have a bit of a hard time believing you can pull off being submissive and charming someone."

I raised a finger. "I'll have you know that I successfully pulled off flirting back in the City of Glass."

"Wasn't that with Niadhir, though?" Elaran frowned at me. "That lunatic who wanted you to think the two of you were in love so he could drive you insane?"

"That's entirely beside the point." Straightening, I threw out my arms and met their gazes head on. "Alright, fine! I don't like this any more than you do but do we really have any other choice?"

Last night at the Pink Lily, Madam Cordina had explained that the Trader had several different houses in the city. Finding and breaking into them all in the span of a day and a half without tipping him off would be impossible.

Shade's plan to ambush and torture the information out of him had been voted down since the information we got from it might be unreliable and we wouldn't have time to fix it if it was. And I think also because Marcus turned a pale shade of green at the thought of torture.

That had left one option. Bait. A runaway escort that we were almost certain he would take to the same place as Milla. The Trader preferred his escorts female and human, and since I was the only one fitting that description, it was down to me. The only problem was that he also preferred his women submissive and charming. Out of the two, I fell firmly in the *neither* category.

"We'll be following you from only a short distance away." Strange emotions swirled in Shade's black eyes. "You'll be protected the whole way."

Elaran backed him up with a nod. "As soon as you have eyes on the girl, signal us and we'll be there in seconds."

"And if anything, *anything*, goes sideways, you call us in straight away even if you haven't found the girl. This guy is dangerous." Shade leveled eyes of steel on me. "Clear?"

Four more heads nodded their agreement. Their worry was making me nervous so I shrugged and made my tone light as I replied.

"I have dealt with dangerous people before, you know." When my friends only continued looking at me expectantly, I heaved a deep sigh. "Alright, yes, clear." I flapped my arms at them. "Now scram. He'll be here in a few minutes."

It had taken us the better part of the day to locate the Trader, figure out where he would be this evening, and get my costume ready. I couldn't exactly pretend to be a runaway escort while wearing pants and shirts in black and gray along with an army of knives. While the rest of my companions disappeared into the shadows, I tugged at the hem of my dress again.

The smooth garment made of dark green silk was beautiful but way too short and low-cut for my liking. My hair had been left in its customary braid because if it came down to a fight, I couldn't have waves of loose hair obscuring my vision, but I was barefoot to really sell the helpless runaway bit.

Clanking weapons echoed from up the street. I transformed my face into that of a scared young girl and cowered my shoulders slightly right as a group of people became visible between the red stone houses. Two burly men with long swords flanked a third one. He wasn't as muscled as the other two but was still fit and he walked with the confidence of someone who firmly believed that he owned the world. His light brown hair and narrow nose fit Madam Cordina's description. This was the Trader. *Showtime.*

"Excuse me, sir," I said in a soft voice and stepped out of the shadows.

His bodyguards reached for their swords at the sudden sound. Raising my hands, I stopped a few strides away.

"Please don't." I flicked nervous eyes over their weapons. "I don't mean any harm."

The knife strapped to my thigh under the green dress would disagree but they didn't know that. Shifting his weight, the Trader studied me. Then he nodded at his guards and twitched his fingers at me, beckoning me closer. I lowered my hands and slid forward, still keeping my shoulders hunched.

"What do you want?" he demanded once I'd come to a halt before him.

With my head slightly bowed, I glanced up at him briefly as if I didn't dare meet his eyes. "I'm sorry to bother you, sir, but I heard that you're the one who helped Milla escape from the Pink

Lily." I kept my eyes on the ground in front of me and shuffled my feet. "I was hoping you'd do the same for me."

A hand shot out and grabbed my chin in a strong grip. It took all my considerable self-control not to stab him when he forced my head up and then proceeded to scrutinize me. His roaming eyes lingered on my cleavage for a moment but then he released my chin with a jerk.

"You're not pretty enough," he stated.

That insult would've hurt if not for the fact that I actually prided myself on my incredibly unremarkable looks. The Trader snapped his fingers at the two burly men next to him and made as if to stride away. *Crap.* Maybe I had overestimated my abilities just a tiny bit. That had never happened before. Well, perhaps once or twice. But that wasn't the point. My heart pattered in my chest. This was our only shot.

"Please, sir," I called. "Please, I ran away from the Pink Lily. I can't go back. Madam Cordina won't take me back now even if I begged her." I looked up at him through my eyelashes with pleading eyes. "I'll do anything."

That stopped him in his tracks. His brown eyes took on a sharp glint as he scratched his jaw. "Anything?"

I nodded eagerly. "Yes, anything you want."

A smirk spread across his face before he shifted his gaze to the goons. "How's the sale coming?"

Sale? What sale?

"We're meeting them tomorrow at the party," the one on the right replied.

"Good." The Trader nodded. "Maybe we'll throw in this one too. She can keep an eye on the girl so we don't have another incident like the one at the Pink Lily."

Oh. And now I suddenly knew why people called him the Trader. He was going to sell Milla. Greed glittered in his eyes as he looked at me and beckoned me forward. And me. He was planning on selling us both.

"Come on then, girl," he said. "I'll make sure you end up with good employers."

Giving him a hopeful smile, I tiptoed over to him. "Thank you."

Thank you for bringing me to Milla. A villainous grin threatened to spread across my face so I pushed it down and instead concentrated on his boots as I trailed demurely behind him. But in the safety of my mind, I was cackling. Inviting me into his home would be the last mistake he ever made.

The trek to his house was long and uneventful. Buildings of pale red stone stared down on us like silent sentries and the people moving in the streets weren't much better. The whole city felt muted. Empty. I'd noticed it as soon as we arrived. No one was strolling around just for the fun of it. They all walked with purpose, as if the only reason they were outside was because they had to, and they avoided eye contact with people they passed. The usual chatter that was normally present in big cities shone with its absence and instead, apprehension hung like silent storm clouds over everyone. Maybe that was what happened to a city when there was an army of star elves camped outside the gates.

"No one in or out," the Trader ordered his two guards once we arrived at a wide house with only two stories instead of three.

Grabbing me by the upper arm, he shoved me inside before barreling in after me. Wood vibrated as he slammed the door shut behind us. A spotless hall ended in grand double stairs that occupied the whole back half of the room while delicate wooden tables, tall candelabras, and huge paintings in red and beige decorated the side closest to the door.

My mind was busy mapping potential exits while I swung back around to face the Trader. "When will I see Milla?"

I had barely finished turning around when someone backhanded me across the mouth. Taking a step to the side to steady myself, I blinked black spots from my vision. The Trader was staring at me, his hand still raised, while anger and suspicion flared in his eyes. *Shit.* I was supposed to be a normal person. Civilians who weren't as used to getting beaten up as I was would've collapsed by that surprise strike.

When he drew back again, I just stood there and braced myself for the impact. Pain shot through my face as his knuckles connected with my cheekbone. I made a show of dropping to my knees.

"You will only speak when spoken to," the Trader growled.

Narrowly preventing myself from rolling my eyes, I instead put a hand to my cheek and dropped my gaze while giving him a nod.

"Say it!"

My fingers twitched by the hidden knife on my thigh but I forced myself to keep cowering on the floor. "I'm sorry, sir. I will only speak when spoken to."

His hand shot down. Yanking me back up by my throat, he leveled hard eyes on me. "That's right. You belong to me now. Don't ever let me catch you being insubordinate again or I'll make you wish you were back at the Pink Lily."

Oh, I so desperately wanted to stab him. Just once. Or maybe twice. One flick of my wrist and I'd ram that cold hard steel right into his heart and watch the light dim in his smug eyes. But I couldn't. Not until I was certain that Milla was here. So instead of skewering the Trader like the rat he was, I averted my eyes and gave him a terrified nod.

"Yes, sir."

"Good." Releasing my throat, he shoved me towards the stairs. "Now get a move on."

As we made our way up the curving stairs, I studied the thick walls around us. Would Shade and the others even hear me from all the way in here if I called out? I felt the comforting weight of the knife shift against my thigh as I climbed. Hopefully, I wouldn't even need to call them.

The stairs emptied into a wide hallway filled with more delicate wooden tables and large paintings. Tall vases, wrought silver candlesticks, and painted bowls filled with dried flowers littered the side tables. At the end of the hall was a gigantic mirror. I avoided my reflection in it as we moved towards a room about halfway down.

"This will be your job for two days until you will move to your new employers." The Trader pushed down the handle of a nondescript door and shoved it open. "Make sure she doesn't do anything stupid."

A small girl with shoulder length black hair sat cross-legged on a bed inside. Her dark eyes watched us warily.

"Is this Milla?" I asked.

As soon as the words were out of my mouth, I realized my mistake. Silence descended on the corridor as the Trader turned to me with suspicion written all over his face.

"I thought you said you already knew each other."

Shit. How was I supposed to save this? I desperately cast my gaze around for something that would explain my strange comment. A lone candle flickered on the nightstand inside the room.

"Of course we do," I began. "It's just, the room is so dark so I can't really see who it is from here."

But the damage was already done. The Trader took a threatening step towards me.

"Who are you?"

"Are you Milla?" I called over his shoulder.

"You're not an escort from the Pink Lily," the brown-haired man in front of me said. He kept advancing on me. "Whoever you are, you'll regret this."

Retreating into the corridor, I locked eyes with the girl in the room and raised my voice. "Answer! Are you Milla?"

"Yes," a soft reply sounded.

Malice glittered in the Trader's eyes as he stepped closer to me. *And now we fight.* I let out a loud scream in a prearranged pattern. Any second now, my backup would come storming through the windows. The seconds dragged on. My heart slammed against my ribs as nothing happened. *Shit.* They couldn't hear me through whatever these walls were made of so there would be no help coming. My fingers brushed the knife under my dress as I continued backing away. I was on my own.

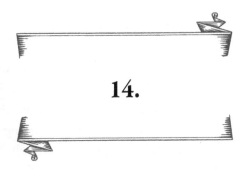

14.

Wood vibrated as a door slammed open and footsteps thundered out. I whipped my head around to find a heavily muscled man looking from me to the Trader with confusion swirling in his eyes.

"Boss?" he said, still flicking his gaze between us.

The Trader didn't take his cold eyes off me. "Take her."

Crap. My friends hadn't heard the scream but his guard sure had. Precious seconds ticked by as I tried to figure out how I was going to survive this while the muscled man stalked towards me. I yanked out my hidden knife and hurled it across the corridor.

A dull thud sounded, followed by a grunt. The advancing guard stopped and stared dumbfounded down at the knife sticking out of his chest. I sprang forward.

If I could only kill one of them with a surprise attack, it had to be the guard. The Trader might be athletically built but I still had a chance of winning against him even without a knife. That goon, on the other hand, could've crushed my spine with one hand.

Roaring bounced off the stone walls behind me as I dove for the blade in the dying man's chest. If I could just get it before the Trader caught up with me, I would win. Blood rushed in my ears as I landed on the floor, my fingers almost brushing the hilt. I let out a yelp.

Strong hands around my bare ankle yanked me back before I could reach the weapon. Rolling over on my back, I kicked at the Trader's face. He jerked to the side, making me miss, and my heel instead connected with his collar bone. Sucking in a sharp breath, he drew me towards him in one forceful pull.

Stone scraped against my back as I slid across the floor. As soon as he was forced to let my ankle go in order to move his hands higher up, I made my move. Tense muscles met me as I drove a knee into the side of his chest. He flipped to the side. Launching myself up, I made another attempt to reach the knife.

Hands snatched at my dress. I whirled around and grabbed the closest object I could find. Ceramic shattered and shards flew across the hall as the red painted vase broke against the Trader's defending elbow. Using his already raised arm, he backhanded me across the face. Still trying to recover from the force of swinging the vase, I stumbled to the side and crashed into the delicate table next to us.

Dried flowers sailed through the air as I snatched up the bowl and heaved it towards him. He ducked. More broken ceramic hailed towards the floor as it hit the stone wall behind him. While he shot forward and grabbed the heavy candlestick from the side table, I dove for the buried knife again.

Wet squishy sounds drifted from the guard's corpse as I finally succeeded in getting the knife. I rolled to the side. A silver candleholder slammed into the ground right in the space I had just vacated. Jumping to my feet, I whirled around to face the candlestick-wielding man. I lunged.

He swung his makeshift weapon with such force that I was forced to dart away again to avoid getting my arm broken. Pressing the advantage, he sprung forward. I tripped over the dead man's arm in my hurry to get away and stumbled towards the top of the stairs.

A frustrated howl tore through the room as the Trader charged right at me like a crazed bull. *Shit*. I had to risk it. Adjusting my grip, I threw the knife. If this missed, I was dead. Metal clanged against metal as my attacker batted away the blade using the candlestick. Hopelessness washed over me as I watched it fly across the railing behind me. Gods damn it.

His whole weight crashed right into me with enough force to send us both tumbling down the stairs. Pain shot through me with every sharp edge of the steps. Eventually the jutting stones evened out into the smooth floor downstairs and I came to a stop a short distance from the wall. My mind spun. I was busy heaving deep breaths and trying to push out the pain and dizziness when something rattled a few steps away. Another scream sounded.

My eyes shot open just in time to see the Trader swing a walking stick towards my chest. I rolled to the side. The metal handle smacked into the ground, sending chips of stone flying. *Shit*. If he landed a hit with that, he would break my ribs. Placing my palms on the floor, I pushed myself up and twisted while kicking out a leg. My shin slammed into the back of his knee. He crashed to the floor.

Using the second of grace, I shot to my feet and snatched up the huge candelabra next to me. The Trader climbed to his feet while baring his teeth at me. I twitched my fingers, telling him to get on with it. He swung.

I pushed out the candelabra. It vibrated in my hands as the silver arms absorbed the impact. Shoving it outwards again, I tried to get him to back away. Somewhere behind me, a side door opened and then closed. While I kicked myself for missing a chance to call for help, two men had strolled into the wide hallway. They blinked in surprise at the mess around them.

"Uhm...?" the blond one said, flicking his gaze between his boss and me.

"Get her!" the Trader screamed.

Crap. With the two of them advancing from behind, and my main opponent doing the same on the other side, I was forced to keep turning in a slow circle to keep them all in sight. The two guards drew their swords. I swung the candelabra at them with every smidgen of strength I had. The twisted silver arms caught the looped sword hilts and sent them flying across the room. Steel clattered against stone as they bounced across the floor.

Air rushed out of my lungs. While I'd been busy with the two guards, the Trader had snuck up behind me and slammed the whole length of the wooden walking stick across my stomach. The candelabra fell from my grip as I gulped in a desperate breath. A fist connected with my side. I stumbled backwards a step before my knees buckled and I collapsed on the ground.

The two swords were so close. If I could only reach them, I'd be okay. Still trying to get my breathing working away, I stretched my arm towards the closest blade. One heavy boot trapped my wrist against the floor while the other kicked my chest. Gasping, I flipped over on my back. Another foot appeared on my other wrist. I pulled at the forces keeping my arms pinned to my sides but against the weight of the two muscled goons, I was defenseless.

"You are not an escort from the Pink Lily," the Trader repeated for the second time that night. "Who are you?"

Black spots still swam before my eyes. Pushing the pain to the back of my mind, I managed to clear my vision enough to see the man standing above me. The Trader ran a hand over his mouth, wiping blood off his lips, while his hard eyes bored into me. He spun the walking stick in his hand a couple of times before jabbing it forward. The metal handle pressed into my throat.

"Who are you?" he screamed.

Anger burned through me. Gods damn it. If I'd had all my knives with me, this fight would've been over before it even started. I was so sick of fighting at a disadvantage.

Bending down over me, the Trader pushed the handle further into my throat. "Who are you?"

A scream so full of rage and frustration that the ceramic vases vibrated tore from my throat. *Enough*. Black cloud exploded around me. Startled shrieks rang out in the hall and the forces keeping me pinned to the floor loosened slightly. I yanked my arms free and shot across the room. Lightning crackled around me as I snatched up the two dropped swords. A few strides away, the Trader and his two guards were blundering backwards to escape the dark mist. With eyes black as death and tendrils of smoke whipping around me, I stalked towards them.

Cries were interrupted by wet gurgling as I threw out both arms, simultaneously slashing the throats of the two guards. Their bodies hit the floor with dull thuds.

"Who are you?" the Trader demanded in a trembling voice as he retreated towards the front door.

He never made it. Warm blood pooled over my hand as I rammed a sword through his heart.

"I am death," I whispered into the darkness.

The blade made a wet sliding sound as I withdrew it. I let the black clouds continue to billow around me until the light had dimmed in the Trader's eyes. Then I pulled it back. Tiredness washed over me but didn't drown me in its dark embrace. Tipping my head back, I let out a long exhale.

"Is he dead?" a soft voice said.

I snapped my head back down. Up on the landing, a small girl with short black hair peered through the railing. She watched me with curious eyes.

"Yeah," was the only reply I manage to press out.

"You saved me." She gave me a smile that was tinged with something I couldn't quite place. "And you got revenge for me."

Frowning at the strange girl, I wasn't sure how to respond to that. Instead, I stumbled over to the front door. Throwing it open, I yelled into the night.

"Get in here!"

Metal scraped against stone as I dragged the swords on the ground while making my way back towards the stairs. Feet smattered behind me.

"What's going on here?" a distraught voice called.

I whirled around. The two bodyguards who had been with the Trader when I'd first approached him stood staring at the carnage around me. The ones he had ordered to guard the door.

"Oh for Nemanan's sake!" I snapped. "Can I never catch a break?" My knees wobbled but I raised the swords anyway.

Blood dripped from the gleaming edges. With my dark green dress slipping down one shoulder and hair that had come undone hanging around my face in thick tresses slick with blood, I spun the blades once in my hands and raised my chin in challenge. "Come on then."

Strangled gasps echoed through the room. Squinting, I stared at the blood-smeared metal now sticking out of their chests. The sharp points disappeared and the guards collapsed to the floor, revealing Shade and Elaran who were standing behind them with bloody swords in their hands. My knees buckled. Thuds and clanks rang out as my blades and I hit the pale red stones.

"Better late than never," I mumbled.

"What the hell happened?" Shade stalked across the floor littered with blood and dead bodies. Crouching down, he ran his eyes over the torn dress and my battered body. "You were supposed to call for backup if shit went sideways."

"I did." I blew out a long breath. "You didn't hear me."

Soft fingers appeared on my skin as Shade tilted my chin up to inspect my face. Fury and something that looked a lot like guilt flickered in his black eyes. "They did this to you?"

"Yeah."

"Is there anyone still alive?"

"Don't think so." My arm was heavy when I lifted it to motion at the mess around us. "We were pretty loud."

Nodding, Shade released my chin right before three more people barreled into the room. Marcus and the twins came to a screeching halt just inside the door. I jerked my chin to indicate the landing above us.

"Milla is up there." Meeting Shade's gaze, I gave him a tired smile. "Mission accomplished."

He replied with a lopsided smile and stood up. "Good job."

While the Master Assassin and Haela wove through the corpses on the floor and made their way towards the black-haired girl upstairs, Marcus approached me. His concerned eyes found mine.

"You okay?" he asked, reaching down to help me up.

"Yeah," I replied but made no move to take his hand. "But I need a minute."

The Trader and his goons hadn't gotten in that many hits but the ones that had landed, had been more than enough. Marcus knelt next to me while I let the waves of pain roll off my body.

"I'm sorry we weren't here for you," he said.

"It's alright." I lifted my aching shoulders in a shrug. "I can take care of myself."

A soft chuckle escaped his lips as he glanced around the room. "I can see that." He cupped my cheek and moved it so that I looked straight into his golden-brown eyes. "But still, I'm sorry."

Three pairs of feet sounded on the stairs as Shade, Haela, and Milla moved towards us. Haemir started towards them while Elaran kept guard at the door. When the Master Assassin looked over to where Marcus and I were seated, that unreadable mask of his descended on his face. I was just about to open my mouth but he beat me to it.

"We should go." He broke my gaze and instead stared straight ahead as he made for the door.

Straightening, Marcus took his hand from my cheek and made another attempt at helping me up. This time, I let him.

After drawing a deep breath, I followed the rest of them out the door.

Milla said nothing at all as we walked across the city. She only kept stealing glances at me when she thought I wasn't looking. As if I'd miss that. I was a thief; I was very well aware of when people were watching me.

When the bell finally tinkled to announce our arrival at the Pink Lily, I was well and truly tired. I was going to need a long sleep after this.

"Milla!" a voice called.

Madam Cordina shoved aside a cluster of red drapes and ran towards the black-haired girl currently holding Haela's hand. After giving the elf a small smile, Milla let go and walked over to the madam. Utter relief washed over Cordina's face as she took the girl in her arms. She met our eyes over Milla's slender shoulder.

"Thank you."

We all nodded in acknowledgement. Once Madam Cordina had let go of her young ward, she straightened and swept her gaze across our group again.

"You held up your end of the bargain. I will hold up mine." She motioned at me, Shade, and Marcus. "I can get the three of you inside the party tomorrow." Before anyone could protest, she held up a hand to silence it. "The Pink Lily only employs humans. Sorry."

"Fine," Shade said. "It will have to do."

She gave us a curt nod. "Come back here tomorrow at midday so we can get you ready."

"Midday." The Master Assassin nodded back. "We'll be here."

With that, he spun around and strode back out into the night. Elaran followed close behind while Haela waved goodbye to Milla. The girl's dark eyes were trained on me. I gave the strange girl a shrug before disappearing out the door as well.

That hadn't gone exactly as planned but it hadn't been a total disaster either. I massaged my sore shoulder. Now I just had to cram in some sleep and hope the bruises weren't too bad when I woke up in the morning because tomorrow, another mission awaited. Sneaking into the Red Fort with the help of escorts and spying on the star elves without anyone recognizing us. What could possibly go wrong?

15.

A cloud of perfume hung heavy over the room. The midday sun filtered in through the translucent red curtains and painted everything in a deep pink color. I let my eyes glide over the multitude of velvet couches and divans as we waited for the girl who had shown us in to fetch Madam Cordina.

"I did tell you that I could only sneak in the humans, didn't I?" the straightforward madam said as she swept into the room in a flurry of rustling skirts.

Elaran crossed his arms. "Yes."

When Cordina realized that no other explanation for the three elves present was forthcoming, she pressed her lips into a thin line and simply turned her back on them. Shifting her eyes to the human half of our group, she waved her hands.

"Well then, if we're going to have time to get all three of you dressed up as escorts, we'd better get started."

Surprise flashed over Shade's face as he blinked and drew back slightly. "Excuse me?"

"What?" Cordina demanded.

"I'm afraid you've misunderstood. You will sneak us in as guards *to* your escorts. Not *as* escorts."

"I have misunderstood nothing." She crossed her arms. "You will be disguised as escorts."

The Master Assassin leveled hard eyes at the madam. "Not going to happen."

"Suit yourself. There's the door." Madam Cordina flicked a hand to the other side of the room. "The Red Fort doesn't allow external security for my boys and girls. You get inside as escorts or not at all."

Because I was a girl, I had already pieced together that I would have to be dressed as an escort to get inside, but Shade and Marcus had apparently both been taken by surprise by this news. A lightning storm flashed in the assassin's black eyes. Next to him, Marcus was shifting wide eyes between the two arguing humans while his mouth had been left gaping.

"What's it going to be?" Cordina raised her eyebrows. "If you don't want my help, then I have other things to do today."

"Fine," Shade pressed out. We'll do it."

After giving the assassin a curt nod, she motioned at him and Marcus. "Good. Then take your shirts off. I need to see what I have to work with before I send for people to help you."

If she'd have asked me to do something like that, I would've protested loudly but both Marcus and Shade pulled off their shirts without complaint. It took all my self-control not to gawk. Madam Cordina, on the other hand, appeared unaffected by the rather impressive display of muscle before her. She simply narrowed her eyes and proceeded to walk around them while scrutinizing their appearances.

"Hmm." Stopping before Shade, she looked up at him. "Handsome face, lean muscles. I can work with that." She clicked her tongue. "But you have a lot of scars. That brings down your looks quite a bit."

The smug arrogance that had been present in the assassin's face when Cordina had praised him was slapped right off his sharp cheekbones by that last comment. I stifled a chuckle. It was so much fun to see someone put that smirking bastard in his place.

"We'll have to find a workaround for that," Madam Cordina finished before striding over to Marcus. Her eyes practically glittered as she took in his muscular form once more. "You, on the other hand. You have a body sculpted by the gods. This will be perfect."

Lightning flashed in the Master Assassin's eyes again as he glared at the tall Storm Caster. When Marcus shot me a beaming smile, Shade's scowl deepened. In the corner, a grinning Haela was elbowing Haemir in the ribs and nodding at the pissed-off assassin while even Elaran's mouth quirked upwards slightly.

"You I saw when you borrowed that green dress yesterday," the madam said and turned to me. "But I still don't know what to do with you. As if all your awful scars and those fresh bruises weren't enough, you're also just so..." Furrowing her brows, she waved her hands over my body. "Average."

Once again, that insult would've stung if not for the fact that I prided myself on being incredibly average-looking. It had helped my career as a thief tremendously.

"Fortunately, we have a few hours to figure it all out." Raising her voice, she called for backup.

While men and women with serious faces filed into the room, the three elves got comfortable on the sofas. Dust swirled in the sunlight as Haela flopped down on a divan.

Shade narrowed his eyes at them. "You really don't have to be here for this."

"Oh, I'm not missing this." Haela's whole face glowed with mischief. "Not for anything."

Haemir gave us an apologetic shrug but motioned at his sister as if to say: *what she said*. From atop a dark red couch, Elaran met Shade's glare while his lips twitched in amusement. I rolled my eyes. Elves.

Once Madam Cordina had finished giving the employees of the Pink Lily their instructions, she herded us out the door. Shade and Marcus were shown into different rooms by a couple of dark-haired men while the madam and two beautiful women in pale dresses ushered me into a third one.

If I'd thought getting ready for balls in Starhaven had been bad, it was nothing compared to the fuss that Madam Cordina made. I was forced to try on endless outfits before she finally decided on a black and gold dress that would cover up the majority of the scars on my chest, stomach, and back. Though, *dress* wasn't quite the right word. It was more like a corset with sheer lace flowing down my legs. When she laced it up, I complained loudly about not being able to breathe until she finally relented and loosened it a little. As much as I liked breathing, I actually did it so that I'd be able to fit a blade in there. But she didn't need to know that.

Afterwards, she and the two other women went about pulling my hair in all different directions, drowning me in perfume, and shoveling mounds of makeup over me. With every layer of shimmering powder, Cordina's mutterings about my scars grew fainter.

"There," she finally said and steered me towards the mirror.

My hair had been pulled back from my face by golden pins but then cascaded down my upper back to hide the scars there.

The black and gold corset did the rest. I squinted at my body. The powder on my skin made it smooth and gave it a slight golden shimmer. Turning slowly, I studied the translucent skirt. The fabric might be black but it was too see-through to strap any knives to my legs. Pity.

"You're still not nearly beautiful enough to be an escort from the Pink Lily," Madam Cordina announced. Pulling out a decorated mask in black and gold, she tied it behind my head. It covered the area around my eyes and the bruises there. "But this is the best I can do."

"I'm sure my winning personality will distract them from my looks."

She answered my snarky comment by pressing her lips together and whirling around. "Come with me."

While her back was turned, I snatched up a knife from the pile of my belongings and stuck in down my cleavage before following her out the door. The black flats I was wearing produced no sound as we moved back to the large room that the elves waited in. Good. Perfect for sneaking.

"Wow," Haela said as I stepped across the threshold. "Storm, you look great!"

Throwing her an embarrassed smile, I scratched the back of my neck. "Thanks."

"It suits you better than the white poofy dresses at least," Elaran muttered. When he saw me raise my eyebrows in surprise, he drew his down in a scowl. "But it's still way too little fabric to count as clothes."

I snorted. "Tell me about it."

Right as Elaran and the twins stood up and drifted over to inspect the outfit further, Marcus entered the room. He was wearing a gold-trimmed white garment around his hips that ended at the knee, and leather sandals. Two golden armbands wrapped around his bulging biceps. I stared at his gleaming skin. Had they oiled his whole body?

"Wow," Haela repeated. A mischievous grin spread across her face as she ran her tongue over her teeth and flicked her eyes over his muscled body. "Now that's a view."

A furious blush spread across Marcus' cheeks and he suddenly didn't know where to look. However, he was spared an awkward reply as a third person stalked across the threshold. My mouth dropped open.

Shade was wearing boots and pants made of black leather and stark black lines accentuated his eyes, but that wasn't what made my eyes widen. His upper body was covered in golden glitter.

Elaran burst out laughing. Not a discreet snicker either. He was doubled over, chipping for breath, laughing. It was so rare to hear the grumpy elf express such unbridled amusement that it was impossible for the rest of us not to chuckle as well. Shade swept murderous eyes across the room.

"If any of you *ever* breathe a single word about this to anyone," the Master of the Assassins' Guild said in a voice as cold and deadly as poison, "I will have you killed. Violently. Am I making myself clear?"

Marcus looked worried as he wiped all trace of merriment from his face but Elaran just crossed his arms and shot Shade a smug smile.

"Your threats are much less scary when you're covered in glitter."

The Master Assassin narrowed his eyes at him. "I will beat you up."

"No, you really won't. Because all that glitter will give away your every move from a hundred strides away."

"It was the only way to cover up all your scars," Madam Cordina interrupted before Shade could make good on his threat. "Besides, now all three of you match the theme for tonight, which is gold."

Shade blinked at me and Marcus as if he hadn't realized that we were there until now. When he tilted his head to the right and ran his eyes over my body, heat crept into my cheeks. I had a sudden urge to trace my fingers over his muscled chest and abs. Or throw a knife at him. Either of the two would be fine.

"What exactly are we expected to do tonight?" Marcus asked.

He shuffled his feet while adjusting the armband on his left bicep. For someone with the looks and physique of a sculpted god, he looked surprisingly uncomfortable. His golden-brown eyes flitted nervously through the room.

"You're worried someone will demand you sleep with them," Cordina stated. "I've already told you, my boys and girls are escorts. At least the ones I'm sending to the Red Fort tonight."

"What does that mean?"

A soft wind fluttered the red curtains. The thin layer of dust in the air swirled and caught the light as the gust disturbed the peace. I pushed a loose strand of hair back behind my ear.

"Consider yourselves eye candy." Madam Cordina knitted her fingers. "You will move through the crowd carrying trays or filling drinks while the party guests ogle your bodies." She shifted her gaze to me and shook her head. "Though how you will pass for one of mine is beyond me."

"I think you look beautiful." Marcus gave me a wide smile. "Striking."

Flicking my gaze over his muscular body, I returned the smile. "You're not so bad yourself."

It was a ridiculous understatement. He looked like one of those golden heroes of old that were depicted in paintings in rich people's houses. I had stolen several paintings like that, so I would know.

"The rest of my boys and girls should be ready and waiting downstairs by now," Madam Cordina announced. "So let's get going."

Her pale skirts fluttered around her as she whirled towards the doorway. Turning in that direction as well, I found Shade watching me with an unreadable mask on his face. However, before I could ask what was wrong, Elaran stepped in front of the assassin.

Clapping a hand on his shoulder, he steered Shade towards the door. "Come on then, glitter boy."

"I will stab you in your sleep," the Master Assassin grumbled in reply but followed the smirking elf into the hallway.

I chuckled. Oh, I was so not going to let Shade forget about this. Ever. Death threats or not. While I gazed after them, Haela curled a finger at Marcus and then cackled when alarm and embarrassment flashed over his face. The tall Storm Caster fled out the door while Haemir distracted his sister with a backhanded swat and a shake of his head. Having had her tormenting of the muscular human cut short, Haela sidled up to me and threw an arm around my back.

A wide smile decorated her beautiful face as she peered down at me. "This is so much fun."

"You think everything is fun," I pointed out as we made our way downstairs.

"Yep." She grinned at me. "But especially this."

I let out another chuckle. A mass of beautiful people in gold glittering outfits that barely covered their bodies crowded the hallway downstairs. While Madam Cordina gave last minute instructions, I studied my two human friends on the other side.

Shade was scowling at the gathered crowd. When Marcus took up position next to him, dwarfing the assassin's lean muscles with his own bulging ones, Shade's glare darkened. After shooting an irritated look at the well-built Storm Caster, he crossed his arms and took a half step to the side. I smirked at the flustered assassin even though he didn't see it. Haela was right. This really was fun.

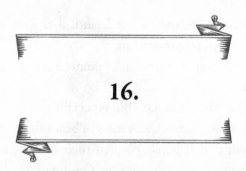

16.

Flutes and string instruments filled the vast chamber with cheerful tunes. Men and women wearing well-tailored outfits were mixed in with high-ranking soldiers in spotless armor. I wove between the groups that had formed on the pale red floor. Casual chatter hung in the air. Shifting the tray filled with delicate glasses to my other hand, I edged closer to the corner that held the only star elves in the room.

Queen Nimlithil stood with her back straight and head held high. Pale violet eyes gazed across the hall full of guests and large red columns as if she already owned the place. Though, I thought I could detect a hint of annoyance in the rigid set of her shoulders. It looked as though the Staghearts' play in making it a general party instead of a grand reception in order to shift the focus from the star elves had worked.

An elf in silver-decorated white armor flicked his gaze in my direction. I ducked behind a ridged pillar. Captain Hadraeth's dark eyes passed over me without recognition as he continued scanning the room. I glanced down at the black corset with gold trimmings and the black lace skirt I was wearing. Yeah, I wouldn't have recognized me either.

Something sparkled in the corner of my eye. "Illeasia is here."

"I know." I glanced at the assassin covered in golden glitter who had appeared next to me. "What do we tell Elaran?"

"The truth. She's probably here because the queen made her." Shade shrugged. "Or because she's trying to stop this."

I shifted my gaze back to the cluster of white and silver in the corner. Princess Illeasia stood a few strides away from her mother. While her face betrayed nothing, her eyes had that distant look in them that someone gets when they're here but not really here. When Hadraeth leaned over to ask her something, she just brushed a speck of dust from her white dress and nodded before going back to staring at the crowd with empty eyes.

"She looks annoyed," Shade observed while nodding at Queen Nimlithil.

"I noticed that too."

"It's probably because the Staghearts haven't paid the star elves any attention since that first short greeting," Marcus said as he came to a halt on my other side.

"Yeah." A malicious grin spread across my lips. "And she really hates that."

"Heads up," the Storm Caster hissed.

Two redheads were striding towards the group of star elves. Heavy crowns made of gold and studded with crimson jewels rested atop their heads and fur-lined capes billowed behind them. Kristen and Kristian Stagheart.

The three of us exchanged a glance before splitting up and sneaking closer. I pretended to serve drinks to a group close by while turning my back on the gathering of royals so that I could eavesdrop without them spotting me.

"Queen Nimlithil. Princess Illeasia," Kristen Stagheart said in a controlled voice somewhere behind me.

"Queen Kristen. King Kristian," Nimlithil replied in a tone dripping with honey and unspoken resentment. "This was not what I had in mind when I sent word for us to meet."

"Your army camped at our gates was not what I had in mind either," the redheaded queen said. "And yet, here we are."

I dared a peek over my shoulder. The two queens were staring each other down while the king and the princess next to them both looked like they would rather be anywhere but here. Unconsciously, the groups closest to the royal showdown edged away.

"Now that you have seen for yourself that we will never surrender our country willingly, I suggest you take your army elsewhere." Kristen Stagheart jerked her head in the shallowest of nods. "Goodnight."

In a rustling of clothes, she threw back her cloak and stalked away. After a quick nod at the stunned star elf queen, Kristian followed his sister into the mass of people. Cheerful tunes continued mocking the dismissed group of silver and white.

Drifting away from the corner, I let another grin spread across my lips. I might not have a lot of love for upperworlders in general, but even I had to admit that Kristen Stagheart was pretty cool.

Fingers snapped in front of my eyes. "Hey, over here."

Tearing my gaze from the exiting royals, I found a robust man in a dark blue suit staring at me with eyebrows raised. I was about half a second away from demanding 'what?' when I remembered that I was supposed to be an escort, so instead I plastered a smile on my face.

"Yes, sir, what can I do for you?"

"My friends and I are thirsty." He motioned at a group of men and women in equally fine clothes.

"Of course." I moved towards them while trying very hard to keep the sarcasm from my voice. "It's my pleasure to serve you."

Glasses clinked as the man in the blue suit and the five other members of his party took the drinks from my offered tray. Perfume and tobacco smoke hung heavy over their group. I tried not to breathe too deeply while I waited for them to finish replacing the empty glasses on the silver tray.

"I have never seen this one before," a lady in a pink dress said. She furrowed her delicate eyebrows as she scrutinized my every curve. "Have you?"

The other five people lowered their glasses slightly while inspecting me as well. I fought a very strong urge to stab them all in the eye but managed to push it aside.

"No, I have not."

The lady in the pink dress cocked her head. "She is not very pretty, is she? Look at her body. She looks more like an athlete than a woman."

"You are right." Fingers traced my shoulder blades as the man who had brought me over walked around me. His meaty hand grabbed my chin and tilted it up as he came full circle. "Madam Cordina should know better than to send someone like her to the Red Fort."

And the urge to stab someone was back. My fingers twitched. These people talked about me as if I wasn't even in the room and his possessive touch made my skin crawl. Before I could decide whether it would be worth all the drama afterwards if I killed them all, the man in the blue suit let go of my chin and flicked his hand in a dismissive gesture.

"I will get us a prettier one next time," he said to his companions while I stalked away.

More leering gazes followed me around the room as I made my way towards Shade and Marcus. I hated the hungry glint in the eyes of strangers that I passed. Hated how they either looked at me like I was part of the furniture or as if I was a meal they had ordered. Once I finally put down roots somewhere, I would make sure no one ever looked at me like that again.

"Are you okay?" Marcus asked when I drew up next to them and crossed my arms. "That looked a bit intense."

Looking from the worried Storm Caster to the stone-faced assassin, I nodded. "Yeah, nothing I can't–"

"Citizens of Sker," a confident voice rang out.

The three of us whirled around to find Queen Nimlithil standing on the dais at the back. All around us, conversations trailed off as people turned or shuffled around the pillars in the vast room of red stone in order to see better. Alarm flashed over Kristian Stagheart's face a few groups away while his sister looked completely furious. Oh this could not be good.

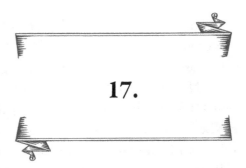

17.

White gems sparkled in the candlelight as the Queen of Tkeister threw her silver hair back, making her headdress clink. The flutes and cheerful strings had come to an awkward halt as the musicians glanced at the surprise interruption while lowering their instruments.

"I have been invited by your kind king and queen so that I might share with all of you why I decided to visit your beautiful nation," Nimlithil declared.

Given the state of Kristen's face, that was a blatant lie, but the star elf queen pressed on regardless.

"I understand that some of you might be frightened but I am here to put those worries to rest." Queen Nimlithil spread her arms in a placating gesture. "We are not here to conquer or bring war to your home. That is a lie that has been repeated so many times by our enemies that people have started believing it."

"Who are your enemies, then?" a brave young man called from the right.

"Our enemies are the wicked greedy people who would seek to destroy our world." She raised her chin. "They are the ones who would keep you shackled in your pain and grief."

A surprised murmur went through the high-ceilinged hall. Next to us, a group of ladies in red dresses whispered among themselves while the most nervous-looking one emptied her whole glass in one swig.

"You see, the reason why we are here is to offer you a world free of suffering." Nimlithil transformed her face into a kind benevolent mask. "I know that all of you carry pain in your hearts. It might be the death of a parent, sibling, or child. The loss of something you hold dear. Broken dreams." Her mouth drew into a sad smile. "There is so much pain in the world. We are here to offer you a cure for that."

An even stronger ripple went through the crowd. Kristen Stagheart had crossed her arms and was glaring at the star elf queen but there was nothing she could do. As soon as Nimlithil had stepped onto that dais and proclaimed that the Staghearts had invited her to speak, there was nothing she could do to stop her. Unless she was prepared to cause a rather embarrassing scene, that is.

"We are skilled in the ways of old scholars and we have uncovered a ritual that will free anyone from pain. You will still experience all the joyous emotions that life has to offer but you will never have to experience grief, hurt, or heartache again. You are all welcome to take part in the ritual. It is completely voluntary and it costs you nothing." She smiled sweetly at the transfixed audience. "All we want is a better world. If you want that too, seek out any star elf here in Sker and we will help you live a happier and more comfortable life." After inclining her head, she stepped back down.

Hurried whispers started back up all across the room. While the confused partygoers tried to make sense of everything they had just heard, the Staghearts stalked towards a side door. With eyes still on Queen Nimlithil, Shade let out a long breath through his nose.

"Oh, she is good."

"Yeah." Tipping my head back, I blew out a sigh as well. "Now the Staghearts can't just declare war on the star elves without making it look like they don't want their people to be happy."

Marcus shook his head. "What a manipulative little schemer."

"You have no idea." I motioned at the restless crowd. "We should make our rounds and try to see where people's heads are at."

When both boys next to me nodded, I grabbed a fresh tray from a linen-clad table nearby and slipped into the mass of bodies.

The next few hours were spent eavesdropping on conversations, dodging the star elves, and fighting the urge to stab anyone who looked at me too long. By far the most difficult of the three was the last one. Fortunately, I made it through the night without getting blood all over my black corset.

"People seem more curious than afraid now," Marcus said as I joined him in the shadows of a huge red pillar. "A lot of them seem interested to know more about this world free of pain stuff."

I leaned my bare shoulder against the cool stone. "Yeah, I've noticed the same thing."

The star elves had left about an hour ago but we had stayed to see what people said once they were gone. Unfortunately, the open and curious mood had remained.

"Maybe we should start heading back?" A mischievous glint crept into his golden-brown eyes. "Before you ram that knife you have hidden in your cleavage into someone's throat."

Raising my eyebrows, I let out a surprised chuckle. "You noticed that, huh?"

Marcus reached out and straightened the mask around my eyes. "How could I not?"

"If you're done taking a break, we have work to do," Shade announced after appearing seemingly out of thin air. He arched an eyebrow at us. "The Staghearts just left through that side door again and it didn't look like they were coming back this time. If we follow them, we might be able to get some really useful information."

Without waiting for a reply, he turned and strode towards the indicated door. Marcus and I exchanged a look.

"Dictator," he whispered, a smile tugging at his lips.

I let out a chuckle as the two of us followed the presumptuous Master Assassin. When we passed an empty table, I discreetly disposed of my silver tray. A few ladies gazed at me curiously but when I shot them a psychotic grin, they jerked back and hurried away. I'd had quite enough of people staring at me, thank you very much.

Hinges squeaked slightly as Shade pulled open the unadorned door set into the pale red stone. After checking so that no one had heard, we all slipped inside. Sudden quiet pressed against our ears once the door to the lively party had been shut. I gazed down a long corridor. Walls and floor made of the same material as the rest of the city led forward until a bend in the hallway obscured our sight. Nothing else occupied the space.

Shade jerked his chin. "Let's go."

The corridor widened the further in we got but there was nothing in it except locked doors. Just as I was about to suggest that we head back, something clanked behind us. We all whipped our heads around.

"Shit," Shade breathed.

He didn't need to explain further because we all knew what that sound had signified. Someone dressed in armor was coming up behind us in the corridor. I sprinted towards the nearest door. If I could just pick the lock before whoever was coming rounded the corner, we'd be alright. More clanking sounded in front of us. Right as I knelt before the door, four guards rounded the corner up ahead.

Shouts rose. Feet stampeded behind us as well as the guards on that side were alerted to the threat. I shot to my feet and whipped out the blade I had hidden in my corset.

"Fight?" I asked as I backed towards my two companions.

"We can't get caught here," Shade said. He had produced a dagger from somewhere in his black leather pants and was gripping it tightly.

Marcus appeared not to have smuggled in a weapon because his hands were empty. "But we also can't kill anyone. If we do, don't you think the already strained relations between your country and Sker might take a turn for the worse?"

The two walls of guards were closing in rapidly from either side. My heart thumped in my chest.

"You're right," the General of Pernula pressed out before shooting me a pointed look. "Put that away. No killing."

"Then how are we supposed to win this?" I hissed but shoved the blade back between my breasts. "We can't take out eight guards in a damn fist fight."

"Use your powers."

"No," Marcus cut in. "I already told you. We can't risk it."

"Then a fist fight it is."

Shade darted forward. The guards on his side yelped in surprise but recovered quickly. I only had time to see the assassin dodge a sword before a suit of armor barreled straight for me. Sidestepping the charging guard, I grimaced as he instead crashed right into Marcus. A hand shot out.

Metal gloves sailed through the air where my throat had been only a second before as I ducked and twisted away. Black lace whirled around my legs. I threw out an arm. Pain vibrated through my bones as my elbow connected with the side of the guard's armor. He whipped around and reached for me again.

The armored hand missed as I threw myself backwards. Solid metal slammed into my back. I jerked my head to the side to find a second guard having cut my escape short. Two huge arms swung towards me. I ducked. They smacked into his own breastplate just as I rolled forward on the floor.

Small stones lodged in my palms as I pushed myself onto my knees. A heavy boot connected with my shoulder blades and sent me crashing back down on the floor. I released a huff. While the weight of one soldier kept me pinned to the ground, another one twisted my arms behind my back. Cold metal clicked in place around my wrists.

With one cheek pressed to the dusty floor, I let out a rather long string of profanities before it was cut short by a yelp when strong hands hauled me back up and ripped the mask from my face.

"Keep quiet," a guard growled in my ear.

Shade and Marcus were still fighting, but unarmed and against three opponents each, it was a losing battle. Once the assassin was handcuffed and held immobile by a blade to the throat, the rest of the guards made short work of the muscular Storm Caster. Irritation flashed in Shade's black eyes, while Marcus looked more worried than angry, but neither of us could discuss how to best play this because we were led forward separately.

The corridor we followed eventually ended in a meeting room that was shaped as a hexagon. Rows of bookshelves covered the walls and a few large tables occupied the far half of the room. Flickering candles cast dancing shadows on the red walls. And on the three people already present there.

"Don't you think we keep track of which escorts the Pink Lily sends to the Red Fort?" Kristen Stagheart said. "Did you really think you could sneak in here and skulk around our party unnoticed?"

The tall queen stood straight-backed and watched us with judging blue eyes while her brother shifted nervous glances between us. If I didn't know he was a king, I would never have guessed it. Of average height and slender built, there was nothing remarkable about the King of Sker. While he shared his sister's red hair and blue eyes, he somehow only looked like a pale imitation of her fierce looks.

"Who are you?" the queen demanded.

I glanced at Shade and Marcus. Since we hadn't had a change to get out story straight, I wasn't sure which lie we were going with. The Master Assassin raised his chin.

"I am Shade, General of Pernula."

Okay, so the lie we were going with was the truth. What was he thinking?

A satisfied smile cracked Kristen's stern face. "I know. I just wanted to see if you would tell me the truth. Which you did. Interesting." She scratched her jaw. "Why are you here, General Shade of Pernula?"

Even with his hands shackled behind his back and a sword to his throat, Shade managed to look imposing as he leveled hard eyes on the redheaded queen. "We are here because the star elves are dangerous. If they take over Sker, it will be bad for all of us. We are here because we can help."

"You and your little band of misfits?" Kristen snapped her fingers.

A hard jab to the back of my knees sent me crashing to the floor. Next to me, Shade and Marcus were forced to their knees as well. When the sharp point of a sword pressed into the back of my neck, I was forced to tilt my head down in a bow to keep from getting skewered.

"You are kneeling at my feet and you will die by my hand if I so wish. You couldn't even infiltrate a party without getting caught." She clicked her tongue. "We don't need your help."

I rescind my previous comment about the Queen of Sker being kind of cool. Kristen Stagheart was a bitch.

"Kristen," a man's voice said. It belonged to the third person who had already been present in the room when we arrived.

"I don't want to hear it, Malor," the queen snapped.

Malor. The man I was supposed to rescue if we couldn't stop the star elves from invading was right here, but I couldn't see his face because the sword to my neck restricted my vision to the floor.

"Escort them outside the gates," Queen Kristen ordered as I was hauled to my feet again. She swept eyes as hard as a frozen blue lake over the three of us. "If I ever catch any of you inside the Red Fort again, I will have you executed."

Spinning on her heel, she strode out the room while Kristian trailed behind her. As the guards shoved us back into the hallway, I got ready to study Malor before we were out of sight but to my surprise, the Staghearts' senior advisor followed us.

Malor was tall and powerfully built. A long sleeveless robe in red and black stretched across his broad chest and showed off his muscular arms while black pants covered strong legs. His long black hair was shot through with gray and had been tied back behind him. Light from the candles flickered in determined eyes that were of a reddish-brown color.

By Nemanan, this was the advisor that Morgora had called *an old fart*? Even after she had explained what he looked like, I had still expected someone who looked a bit more like a wrinkly old man with his nose in a book rather than... well, this. Malor looked like a retired army commander who could make experienced soldiers quiver in fear with one look.

"Keep up," the guard next to me muttered.

When he tightened his grip on my arm and pushed me forward, I shot him a venomous glare but shifted my attention back to the pale red corridor in front instead of studying the advisor behind me. The clanking of our manacles and the guards' armor were the only things breaking the silence as we were led through more empty passageways.

Eventually, they ended before a wrought iron gate somewhere on the side of the Red Fort. While the guards lined us up in front of it, I glanced around the secluded area. This might be a good entry point if we ever needed to get back in.

"Uncuff them," Malor ordered.

Shade and I exchanged a glance. Metal clattered against stone as the assassin and I took off the handcuffs we had already picked and dropped them on the ground in front of us. The approaching guards trailed to a halt. Uncertain eyes flicked between the two of us and Malor.

The muscular advisor barked a laugh. "An assassin and a thief, indeed. I would expect nothing less from the infamous Shade and the Oncoming Storm." He motioned at the guards to approach the still shackled Storm Caster. "Help him out, will you?"

"How do you know who I am?" I asked while Marcus was uncuffed.

"I make it my business to know about the people who are taken to Starhaven." His reddish eyes glittered. "Especially the ones who manage to escape." Once Marcus was free, Malor jerked his head to the guards. "Leave us. I'll take it from here."

"But–" the young blond one began.

"Did I stutter?" Malor snapped.

"No, sir. Sorry, sir."

While the guards beat a hasty retreat and disappeared into the corridor again, I studied the tall advisor. Bold move. He willingly sent his only protection away and now was left with people he knew could kill him. And yet, he didn't look the least bit worried.

Malor shifted his confident gaze to Marcus. "The only one I don't know is you."

"Marcus." The brown-haired Storm Caster held out a large hand.

Surprise flickered in the advisor's eyes at the friendly gesture but then a smile tugged at his lips as he reached out to shake his hand.

"Pleasure to meet you," Marcus said.

Malor studied him curiously as they clasped hands. "And you."

Warm night winds blew across the courtyard, kicking up clouds of dust. I smoothed down the black lace over my legs.

"I will get straight to the point." Malor rested his hands behind his back. "Kristen Stagheart is a strong queen but she is also a very proud woman. She refuses to admit it but Sker is in real danger. Especially after Nimlithil's little charade tonight." He drew his eyebrows down. "Kicking them out without looking like the bad guys just became a whole lot harder."

"We caught that too," Marcus said.

"But..." Schemes glinted in Malor's eyes. "If certain foreigners were to assist, it might be possible." He blew out a breath. "Look, I know that you're not here out of the goodness of your heart. You all have your own agenda for being here. I don't care about that, and I can promise you nothing in return, but we all know that everyone would be better off if Sker remained free."

Shade tilted his head to the right. "Which means...?"

"Which means that Kristen might be too proud to ask for help." Malor drew himself up to his full height. "But I am not. Do whatever you can. Nimlithil has to be stopped."

"Agreed." The Master Assassin locked eyes with the advisor. "Can you keep the Staghearts from having us arrested or killed, then?"

"I will speak to Kristen and make her see sense but as long as she doesn't see you as a threat to her rule, everything is fine."

"And Kristian Stagheart?"

"Not an issue. He loves his sister more than anything so he will do whatever she tells him."

"Good." Shade gave Malor a slow nod. "It's settled then. Keep the queen and her guards off our backs and we'll do what we can to keep Sker from falling to the star elves."

Malor nodded back. "Deal."

After one last look at the determined advisor, I slipped out the gate and into the darkness beyond. Marcus and Shade followed me. This night had taken an unexpected turn and we'd blown our cover but it hadn't been a total loss. We'd had a chance to meet Malor face to face and had gotten him on our side. Or at least, so we hoped.

Casting a glance behind me, I studied the space where he had been standing seconds ago. Only shadows remained. Based on that first meeting, Malor didn't seem like someone who would run. If the city fell, I might not be able to persuade him to leave. I blew out a sigh as we set course for The Broken Wing. So we'd better make sure it didn't.

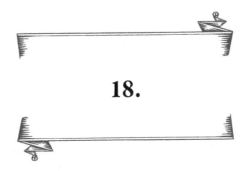

18.

"How many buckets of water did it take to get all that glitter off?" Haela shot the glowering Master Assassin an innocent smile. "Just out of curiosity."

Shade heaved a deep sigh and shook his head. "Stay focused."

When we'd woken up the morning after our stunt as escorts, the elves had informed us that they'd been gathering intelligence as well. Apparently, while Queen Nimlithil was telling the citizens of Sker about her kind and benevolent plans, her soldiers had been sneaking into the city under the cover of darkness.

"This is where they came in." Elaran pointed at a small water inlet set into the outer wall.

The creek had long since dried up but the opening remained. Across it were iron bars that were rusted after years of neglect and could easily be loosened and then put back again as if nothing had happened. I peered at the red dust that had fallen from the wall.

"As far as we can tell," Haemir added, "there are at least nine more grates like these all around the wall."

"Are they using them all?" Shade asked.

"Impossible to tell. But we think so."

Shade straightened and took his hand from the wall. "We need to make them believe that all these entry points are compromised."

"We run interference at all the gates simultaneously when they try to get in tonight, making it look like the whole guard force is onto them." A grin spread across my mouth. "I like it."

Haela rubbed her hands. "Any particular kind of mischief?"

Shade shook his head while a slight smile settled on his lips. "Anything you want."

Cackling bounced off the red stone buildings around us as Haela made her joy known. "Well excuse me while I go plot some mayhem then."

I couldn't help smiling as the excited twin whirled around and raced up the street. Marcus, his mouth hanging open, stared at her retreating form.

"Is she...?"

Haemir blew out a sigh. "Yep."

After watching Haela disappear in a cloud of dust, the rest of us turned to the remaining two elves.

"Alright, show us where the other grates are and then we can get to plotting some mayhem too," Shade said.

Elaran was still staring at the dust swirls Haela had left in her wake with an exasperated look on his face, but then turned to the assassin and nodded. "Yeah. You can all run whatever interference you want at your grate but as soon as the star elves try to slink through tonight, make sure they know they're busted."

I grinned at him. "Got it."

As Elaran waved us forward, my mind was filling with schemes. Haela was right. It was time to plot some mayhem.

THE NIGHT LAY DARK and still around me. Moonlight bathed the rooftop in silver light while the hole covered in iron bars was cast in shadows by the tall city walls. Ordinary citizens had returned to their homes to sleep hours ago and only the people who dwelled in the dark remained skulking about. Me included.

A squeaking sound drifted from the wall. I tensed. Straining my eyes, I stared into the hole in the wall as if I could make the shadows disappear by strength of will. It sounded again. Metal grinding against stone. *They're here.*

Jumping to my feet, I moved into position. I didn't know what kind of mad plan Haela had cooked up for her site but mine was pretty straightforward. For me at least. The wooden barrels and crates I had stacked around the opening had been left alone by people who passed by during the day. Everything was set. Now I just needed to wait for the first white-haired head to pop out and then they'd get the welcome of a lifetime.

"It's clear," someone whispered down below. "Let's go."

A hood-covered figure, crouching under the low stones, crept forward. Clouds drifted over the moon and blotted out the area for a second. I kept my eye on the figure. As the wind picked up and blew the dark clouds clear, white armor glinted in the silvery light. Star elves.

After drawing a deep breath, I yanked out two throwing knives and set my plan in motion. Steel whizzed through the air as I hurled them towards the two unsuspecting elves who had climbed out of the opening. Even before the projectiles had reached their targets, I drew two more. I threw the first one wide.

Once it had sailed off course for a few seconds, I hurled another blade at it. A faint ding sounded as the knife changed course. It sped towards the elves from a different direction while I drew back another pair of knives.

Startled yelps rang out as the first two throwing knives struck the wooden crates next to the two elves.

"Intruders!" I bellowed in as dark and masculine a voice as I could produce. "Surrender to the guards of Sker!"

Inside, I cringed. I had no idea if that was how real Sker guards actually spoke. It sounded ridiculous to me but it was the only thing I could come up with.

Thuds rang out as the other blades I had thrown hit their marks. I hurled another pair. More soft metallic dings echoed through the dark alley as I made the knives change direction, making it look like there were a large number of people attacking.

Armor clanked and cloaks rustled as the two disguised star elves scrambled back through the hole again. I grinned at the empty opening and hurled my final pair of throwing knives at the wooden barricade just to be sure.

Metal squeaked followed by a soft grinding sound as the intruders no doubt screwed back the loosened bars. Ha! Victory. It really was a sweet feeling.

Sitting down on the edge of the roof, I twisted around and began climbing down the side of the building. The warehouse it contained was empty so no one would've heard our little altercation. I dropped the last bit to the dusty ground. Well, it was empty now anyway. While striding over to the crates and barrels I had borrowed from the warehouse, I considered whether I could be bothered to move them back. A wall of wooden boxes rose before me.

"Yeah, nah," I concluded and yanked the closest knife from the wood.

We had decided not to kill anyone tonight because that could set off a whole chain reaction of unintended consequences, so I hadn't wanted to hit the star elves when I threw. But I also didn't want to aim for the stone wall because it would ruin my knives. The boxes had been the perfect middle way. So I had spent a good portion of the afternoon rolling and pushing them out of the warehouse. I returned another knife to my shoulder holsters. Someone else would have to move them back in, though.

Movement by the grate caught my eye. After quickly retrieving the rest of my missing blades, I peered around the edge of the barricade I had built. White swirls snaked out of the grate.

"What the hell?" I blinked at the strange occurrence before stepping around the stack of crates to examine it closer. "Is that...?"

A memory snapped in place. An awful, awful memory. I jerked back and sprinted to the warehouse while cold fear drew its icy fingers down my spine.

Stone chippings lodged in my hands as I scrambled up the building as fast as I could. My heart drummed against my ribs. How could they have brought that here? They couldn't have. Finally rolling over the edge of the roof, I shot to my feet and whirled back towards the alley.

White mist crept along the ground. It looked like normal night fog that often blanketed cities by the sea, such as Sker, Pernula, and Keutunan. Perhaps a little thicker. If you didn't know better, you'd think that was what it was. But I knew better. This was the white mist created by the star elves. The one that produced horrifying hallucinations that drove people mad. The one that had almost driven me mad.

Visions of dead people stabbing accusatory fingers at me pressed against my mind. I gave my head a violent shake to clear them out. As long as I stayed away from the ground, I'd be fine. Closing my eyes, I tilted my head up towards the sky and drew a deep calming breath. It would all be fine.

I opened my eyes and my heart fell into my stomach. Thick white mist crashed over the top of the city walls like a tidal wave and fell rapidly towards the unsuspecting town inside. Panic flashed in my mind. I had to get away.

My feet thudded against the roof tiles as I sprinted away from the red walls. The gap to the next building came up quick so I pushed off with all my strength and flew through the air. That usual sense of freedom and joy I got from jumping between houses was drowned out by the rising fear as the white mist hunted me from behind. I dared a peek at the wall on my right.

A wave of unnatural fog washed over the stones. *Shit*. Not slowing down even a second, I whipped my head in every direction and found white mist billowing over the whole west side of the city walls. *Shit shit shit*. I picked up speed.

Using a chimney to swing around, I changed direction and dashed towards the east side of town. If I could just make it there before the fog, I'd be fine. I kept repeating that same phrase in my head while trying to push out the panicked voice screaming that the mist might reach all the way to the sea.

With my mind distracted, I didn't notice the clothing line on the next roof until I had already jumped. I flew right into the piece of string, snapping it in half, and rolled across the roof in a tangle of limbs and damp shirts.

"Gods damn it!" I yelled while yanking at the mess twisting around my limbs.

Thick white swirls stretched its tendrils over the side of the building. My heart hammered in my chest. Fabric tore as I whipped out a hunting knife and cut the bloody garments to shreds. The wall of white had almost reached me when I finally got myself free of whatever was left of the clothing line. I hurled a slashed brown shirt into the mist and sprinted away.

It was closing in on all sides now, a tidal wave devouring everything in its path. There was no way I was making it all the way across town before it swallowed me in its cloying embrace. The darkened windows of the next building appeared before me. Maybe if I got indoors it wouldn't affect me? I screeched to a halt.

The ground dangled far below me as I wobbled on the edge of the roof. I spun my arms in backwards circles to keep from falling. Thick fog rolled over the chimney behind me. Dropping down, I scuttled down the side of the building until I reached the topmost window. The wooden windowsill groaned underneath me as I landed on it and whipped out a lockpick. White tendrils snaked towards me from above.

After shoving the lockpick between the shutters and lifting the clasp, I yanked open the one on the left and jumped inside. Wood rattled as I slammed it shut behind me.

Shrieks rang out. I whirled around just as a candle flickered to life inside the room. A woman in a white nightdress was backing away with one hand pressed over her mouth and the other pointing straight at me. On the other side of the double bed, a brown-haired man in a long shirt stared at me with wide eyes. *Crap.*

Throwing a quick look at the window behind me, I found white fog starting to trickle in through the cracks in the shutters. I had to seal that up. Just as I took a step towards the bed to grab the sheet, the brown-haired man snatched something up from next to the nightstand.

"Get out!" he bellowed and hoisted a wicked-looking bat in the air.

I wanted to scream in frustration. "Put that away. I need to cover these shutters before the mist gets inside. Or it will be bad for all of us."

"Get out or it will be bad for you." He leveled the bat in my direction and took a threatening step forward. "I mean it."

"I said put it away!" I cast another panicked glance at the mist creeping through the shutters. "We don't have time for this."

The woman had reached the door on the other side but the man stood his ground. He gripped the bat so tightly his knuckles turned white and then advanced on me with determination blazing in his eyes. I let out a howl. Yanking one knife after the other from my shoulder holsters, I hurled them at him. Sharp thuds rang out as each blade struck his raised bat in a long line all the way down to the handle. He dropped the skewered piece of wood as if it had burned him.

"I'm not fucking kidding!" I drew my hunting knives and jabbed one towards the door. "Get out. Lock the door behind you if you want. I'm not gonna go after you and I'm not gonna do anything. I'm just gonna sit here and wait out the mist." Raising my voice, I stabbed in their direction again. "Go! I'll be gone before morning. But don't you dare come back in before then!"

The owners of this house huddled together before escaping into the corridor beyond. Once the door had been slammed shut behind them and a metallic click had sounded, I stuck my hunting knives back in their sheaths and darted to the bed. I snatched up a yellowing sheet and shoved it against the shutters.

Fingers made of white fog poked through the cracks before falling to the floor in heavy drops. I pushed the fabric tighter into the gaps.

Once I had sealed up the window as much as possible, I retreated across the floor. Something round met my heel. I glanced down to find the knife-covered bat rolling a short distance across the dusty planks. Bending down, I took it with me while I walked backwards towards the door.

Light from the candle still flickered over the messy bedroom. A chair had been toppled on the side where the woman had slept and heaps of covers and discarded clothes littered the room. My back hit the door with a soft thud. Still gripping the spikey bat, I slid down the dark wood and drew my knees up to my chest.

White mist still leaked in through the window and the tiny cracks in the walls. I rested my head against the door and heaved a deep sigh. This was going to be a long night.

While I kept myself busy by pulling out the throwing knives I had hurled into the bat, the hallucinogenic fog began working its magic. At first, it was just shadows moving in the corner of my eye but then they started to take shape. And of course it knew exactly which shape would make me feel worst. Or maybe it was because *I* knew that it was my biggest regret. My drugged mind was the one who summoned her, after all.

"Is this all you ever do?" Rain asked. "Get into one mess after another and drag your friends in there with you?"

I studied the girl I had gotten killed more than a decade ago. She watched me with raised eyebrows for a moment before skipping over to the bed. After plopping down on the rumpled covers, she drew her legs up underneath her and rested her elbows on her knees.

"You're not really here," I said.

"Of course I am." She gave short shake of her head as if that had been the stupidest thing she'd ever heard. "Otherwise you wouldn't be talking to me."

A thin coat of pale mist hung over the whole room. I closed my eyes so I wouldn't have to see the visions my drugged mind had created.

"You murdered me," Rain said matter-of-factly.

"I didn't murder you." Keeping my eyes closed, I expelled a deep sigh. "I just made a mistake. One I have never made since."

"You've never made a mistake since then?"

"That's not what I said. You died because I hesitated in killing someone. I have never made *that* mistake again."

"No, you really haven't. Instead you've left a trail of bodies behind you. The Oncoming Storm: mass murderer. And that was by just using a fraction of your powers. Imagine the death and destruction you could bring if you had more power. If you used all of your power."

Dread squeezed my heart. I knew it was only my mind playing painful tricks and using my own guilt and fear against me because the real Rain would never be so cruel. But that did unfortunately not make the words spoken any less true.

Opening my eyes again, I leveled an arrogant glare at the distorted specter of the kind girl I used to know. "Yes, I really am just a cold-hearted mass murderer. So you'd better run and hide before I kill you again."

"False bravado and arrogance." Rain sucked her teeth. "You use that a lot to cover up fear and guilt. But on the inside, you're still just a coward. An unusually cruel coward who just hurts more and more people the more power you get."

"That right?" I mumbled in a disinterested voice. "How about that?"

I wasn't sure if I would ever fully recover from everything that the star elves had put me through in the City of Glass, but at least things like this weren't as jarring anymore. The experiences I'd had in Starhaven had left me incredibly jaded so it was now much easier to shrug off visions of dead people telling me how awful I was.

Tipping my head back, I rested it against the door again. While I closed my eyes and tried to block out her incessant voice, Rain proceeded to list all the people I had killed. Once she had gotten to the bottom of that rather considerable list, she started recounting all the times I had put my friends in danger. Tapping a finger against my thigh, I counted down the minutes. Yep. This was going to be a long night.

19.

"They weren't real, were they?"

Stepping around a deserted cart, I raised an eyebrow at the tall Storm Caster lumbering next to me. "Who?"

Marcus stuffed his hands in his pockets while keeping his gaze fixed on the empty street in front of us. "The people we saw last night in the mist. That wasn't really them, right?"

"You saw someone who's already dead?"

"Yeah. But that's not why..." Pain crept into his kind eyes. "The things she said, I don't think... I hope..." Finally tearing his gaze from the dusty red road, he glanced at me. "It wasn't real, was it?"

"No, it wasn't. It's just the drug using your own mind against you."

Marcus bobbed his head and went back to studying the road ahead.

All of us had been in various states of discomfort when we'd returned to The Broken Wing early that morning. The twins appeared to have been the least affected and I was already jaded after my experiences in Starhaven, so I wasn't that out of sorts. Elaran and Shade had looked shaken but not too bad. Marcus, on the other hand, had been pale as a sheet and his hands had trembled when he opened the door to his room and stumbled inside.

That hadn't stopped us from continuing our mission, though. We'd all been out scouting the city for danger and possibilities when Shade had sent word for everyone to gather at the market square. I'd spotted Marcus down below while I sprinted past on the rooftops and had decided to join him instead. I much preferred running across the roofs to traipsing about the streets like some kind of civilian but Marcus had looked like he could use the company.

I glanced up at him. "You wanna talk about it?"

A group of men in stained workmen's clothes stomped towards us while arguing loudly, but my walking companion stayed silent. The crowd was thickening since we were getting close to the market square. I twisted slightly to avoid getting trampled as they barreled past, still arguing.

"Why should we trust them?"

"Why would they lie about something like this? It doesn't make any sense. Strategically. We should've at least stayed and watched."

"We've got more important things to do. Like actually work."

Their voices grew fainter as they disappeared down the street. For a moment, only the warm glow of the afternoon sun and the sound of our thudding feet filled the alley. Just when I had concluded that Marcus wasn't going to answer, he heaved a deep sigh.

"My mom." Running his fingers through his dark brown hair, he tipped his head up towards the sky streaked with orange and pink. "I saw my mom. She said it was all my fault that she was dead. That if I'd been a better son, she wouldn't have needed to find love in the arms of a smuggler. And that I should've stopped my father from killing her before it happened instead of blowing up the house afterwards."

Remembering all the cruel things Rain's ghost said last night that the real Rain never would've said, I shook my head. "It wasn't really her."

"Doesn't make it any less true, though."

Since I had thought the exact same thing about everything Rain had said, I didn't know how to answer. Motivational speeches weren't really my thing anyway, so instead I just reached out and gave his hand a quick squeeze to let him know that I understood. His eyes glittered in the golden light as he turned to me with a grateful smile.

A whistling sound came from somewhere above us. Tilting my head up, I found a black-clad man standing atop the roof of the three-story building to our right. He jerked his chin. I narrowed my eyes at the arrogant Master Assassin but grabbed Marcus' sleeve and pulled us towards the cracked red wall anyway.

"How are you at scaling buildings?" I asked.

He studied the stone house before us while tipping his head from side to side. "If it's anything like climbing mountains, I'll manage."

"Yeah, I'm not a climbing mountains kind of girl so I have no idea, but the general principle should be about the same."

He let out a chuckle. "Let's give it a try then."

Faint red dust trickled down the side of the building as the mountain climber and I made our way up to the roof. He did actually do surprisingly well. When he reached the edge of the roof only a few seconds after me, I gave him an impressed nod. A satisfied smile tugged at his lips.

"You're late," a voice muttered behind us.

With my back still turned, I rolled my eyes before spinning around to face the grumpiest elf I'd ever met, along with a frowning Master Assassin and a pair of amused twins.

"We were all the way across town," I replied. "It's not my fault that the rest of you just happened to be closer."

Elaran crossed his arms. "You were *strolling* here. That makes you late."

"Sorry," I said in a voice dripping with sarcasm. "Next time I'll just dash through the streets and draw the attention of everyone within a thousand strides." Before that eternal grump could retort, I cut him off by turning to Shade. "What's going on?"

"Don't know yet." Intense black eyes locked on me. "But it can't be good."

Without another word, he spun on his heel and stalked towards the other side of the roof with Elaran close behind. After a synchronized shrug, the twins followed. Marcus and I exchanged a worried look before doing the same.

Long rays from the afternoon sun painted the market square in pink and gold. In the middle of the wide area, the vendor carts had been pushed aside to create an empty space next to the large sculpture of a warrior astride a rearing horse. A considerable group had gathered around it. For a few minutes, they continued shuffling their feet and murmuring restlessly as if waiting for something.

At last, the brass bells in the red clock tower on the far side of the square tolled, marking the full hour. Silence fell over the gathered crowd as two tall figures stepped out of the shadows surrounding the gigantic warrior statue. When they threw back their hoods to reveal silvery white hair, Elaran swore under his breath.

"Esteemed people of Sker!" called the star elf not wearing armor. "I commend you for your bravery in casting off the pain and sorrow of your past and embracing a brighter future."

Shade and I exchanged a glance. They were going to perform the ritual to rid themselves of their pain. This was bad.

"How's this going to go down?" the assassin asked.

Flicking my gaze between him and the scene unfolding before us, I shook my head. "I don't know. I threatened to kill the queen during the first ritual so I never got to this one."

In the square below, the crowd had formed orderly lines in the previously empty space. A strong gust ripped dark brown strands from my braid. I pushed them back behind my ears while the leading star elf raised his arms above his head and called out instructions.

"Now, repeat after me," he said.

The dusty stone buildings all but rattled with ancient power as his voice boomed across the square. Words from a language long dead vibrated through the air. In front of the star elf in his crisp suit, all the gathered citizens of Sker repeated the phrase. I kept my eyes trained on them and barely dared breathe while they finished articulating the strange words.

Everything went silent. For a moment, nothing happened as the crowd quieted down and the leading star elf lowered his arms. Then a surge so strong I felt it in my bones shot across the area. I drew in a sharp breath between my teeth.

"You felt that too?" Haela asked in an uncharacteristically worried voice.

"Yeah," her brother confirmed while the rest of us backed him up with tense nods.

Down by the statue of the charging warrior, the orderly lines were breaking up as people went up to thank the two star elves. The one in armor simply nodded but the leader smiled and chatted with them as they came up and shook his hand while wide grins decorated their features. Panic bloomed in my chest. A few words? That was all it took to complete the ritual? This did not bode well.

As the newly pain-free citizens strolled off in different directions, other people approached the star elves with cautious steps. The leading elf greeted them with a gracious smile.

My friends and I remained rooted in our spots, staring in disbelief as a new group of people formed orderly lines in the empty area. More people were about to perform the ritual.

"We..." I began but trailed off as clanking armor and stomping feet echoed between the buildings a few streets away.

Rank upon ranks of soldiers in gleaming brown and gold armor marched into the square. Curious bystanders who had been loitering by the remaining vendor carts quickly shrank back as the soldiers of Sker advanced on the group by the statue. A nervous buzz went through the air. The armed force snapped to a halt a few strides away.

"By order of the queen, cease this foolishness and disperse," an imposing voice called from the front ranks.

The star elf wearing the white armor rested his hand on the pommel of his sword but made no move to draw it as his companion spoke up. "Do not be frightened, brave citizens of

Sker. We are not doing anything illegal." He turned towards the man who had ordered them to stop. "We have broken no laws. All we are doing here is unburdening ourselves and stepping into a brighter tomorrow."

I let out a derisive snort. Right. As if it were that simple.

"The Queen of Sker has ordered you to stop this. Refuse, and there will be consequences."

"Do you hear that? Your queen tries to prevent you from being happy. She needs your pain and fear to rule and will not let you live a joyful life." The leading star elf raised a fist in the air. "But we will not be bullied! We will never stop fighting for a better life for you."

Shrieks rang out as the soldiers charged. Chaos spread across the red sand as half of the gathered crowd ran to meet them with fists raised while the other half scrambled to get away. While no one was looking, the two star elves slipped away. Armor met unprotected skin as the queen's forces pummeled the angry civilians. Cries of fear and outrage echoed across the whole area as the fleeing citizens were mowed down as well.

"We have to do something!" Marcus snapped and made as if to climb down the building.

Shade grabbed a hold of his shirt before he could start his descent. "Use your head! What's the six of us going to do? Huh? We can't take on an entire army by ourselves. And besides, that army is stopping the ritual, which is what *we* want too. Not to mention that the army is sanctioned by the queen of this nation."

Snatching his arm back, Marcus whirled on him. He drew himself up to his considerable height and squared his broad shoulders while leveling a challenging stare on the assassin. He had about twice Shade's muscles but the Master Assassin didn't back down. The General of Pernula just cocked his head to the right and studied him with unreadable eyes.

"They are beating up civilians," Marcus growled. The muscles in his jaw clenched and unclenched. "You might not care about other people because you're an assassin, but I do."

Lightning flashed in Shade's dark eyes but before he could say anything, Haemir cut him off.

"I don't like this either," he began, glancing between the two of them. "But Shade is right. If we go down there, two things will happen. We will be captured or killed because we are *heavily* outnumbered. And the already angry Stagheart queen has another reason to execute us."

"So we do nothing?" Marcus demanded.

"Yes. If we're going to have any chance of stopping this invasion then yes, right now, we do nothing."

When Elaran backed up Haemir's reasoning with a curt nod, the disappointed Storm Caster shook his head violently and stalked away. I watched the tense muscles in his back shift until he swung himself down the side of the building on the other side and disappeared from view. Letting out a small sigh, I turned back to the chaotic scene in front of us.

Men brawled and women ran for cover as the soldiers broke up the remnants of the group who had been about to perform the ritual. As the last of the gathered crowd fled the scene, I straightened and crossed my arms. Damn the star elves for being so crafty. Kristen Stagheart might have won the brawl but Queen Nimlithil was the one walking away with the true win. She had set this up perfectly to garner sympathy for herself and inflame hatred for Kristen. And the human queen had played right into her hands. I shook my head. We needed to be even smarter.

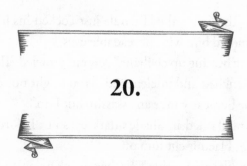

20.

Discontent hung like a wet blanket over the city. Every night, the star elves had sent more mist over the walls and every day, they had performed new rituals. The hallucinogenic drugs people breathed in plagued them with nightmares of their biggest fears and regrets, which increased the demand for the rituals. Kristen's frequent raids might complicate the process but it also added a sense of rebellion to the cause. And people love a good story about standing up to a tyrant.

"We need to talk."

I jerked at the sudden sound. Shooting two stilettos into my palms, I whirled around to face the source of the voice. Eyes of a strange reddish color met me as Malor emerged from the shadows in the deserted alley. I studied him. How a man of such considerable height and build could sneak so quietly was a mystery to me.

"About what?" Retracting my blades, I moved away from the house I'd been surveilling and turned to the Senior Advisor of Sker.

A warm afternoon wind kicked up a cloud of red dust from the ground. It swirled around me before blowing out of the alley mouth and into the busy street beyond.

"You have to find a way to stop these rituals."

Frowning, I motioned at the large house on the other side of the street full of carts and people. "What do you think we've been doing? The list of influential people you sent our way has helped a lot but it's still slow going. Swaying them while keeping the Red Fort's involvement out of it isn't exactly easy. Especially when we've got next to no pull in this city."

"I know. However, until I can persuade Kristen to change her mind, you have to keep her out of it."

Silence fell across the alley. It would've been so much easier to get these influential people to speak out against the rituals if they knew the Red Fort was backing us, but since the stubborn Stagheart queen had refused our help, we couldn't play that card. I gave Malor a quick nod.

"You still have to hurry, though." The advisor let out a heavy sigh and shook his head, making his long black ponytail swing across his broad back. "If this keeps up, Sker will be lost without them ever having to attack the city."

"What do you mean?"

"The people who complete the ritual feel more loyalty towards the star elves than the Staghearts but every time Kristen tries to stop them, she loses even more support. If the people have no faith in the Staghearts, the city is lost."

"And having her soldiers beat up civilians who want to do the ritual isn't exactly inspiring loyalty." I blew out a breath. "She's playing right into the star elves' hands."

Violent swearing broke out behind us. Twisting my head, I cast a glance over my shoulder to find a merchant waving his arms around in distress next to a wide wagon. Wood creaked as four helpful passersby lifted it up so that he could reattach the wheel.

"That's what worries me," Malor said, picking up the thread of conversation. "Kristen Stagheart is a stubborn hothead and this is her default reaction. But... the star elves aren't supposed to know that. It's as if they are intimately familiar with the politics of this city, and yet, they have never been here before."

Turning back from the accident in the street behind me, I narrowed my eyes at the advisor. "Good point."

"How did they know that setting it up like this would end with the Stagehearts losing support regardless?"

"Maybe they were just really lucky?"

"You don't believe that."

Blowing out a long breath through my nose, I smacked my lips. "No."

"Which is why you need to try something else." Malor closed the distance between us in a few long strides. Stopping next to me, he nodded at something behind me. "Lady Beltham might be influential and getting her to speak out against the rituals would certainly help, but it won't be enough."

When I once more turned back to the busy street, the distressed merchant and his broken wagon were gone and a beautiful lady had appeared. Wind blew through her long blond hair as she closed the door to the house I'd been spying on. After smoothing her well-tailored blue dress, Lady Beltham started down the street.

"What did you have in mind?" I asked.

Malor peered down at me with appraising eyes. "The star elves have taken to moving the location of the ritual. If you can somehow find out where the next one is, you can disrupt it before Kristen can send her soldiers and do even more damage to her reputation."

"I'll see what I can do."

After giving me a satisfied nod, Malor spun on his heel and strode back down the alley in the other direction. I watched his retreating back before a sudden thought popped into my mind.

"Hey," I called.

Coming to a halt halfway down, he turned back to me with raised eyebrows.

"You ever think about leaving?" I motioned vaguely at the red buildings around us. "You know, Sker?"

His dark brows furrowed. "Why would I do that?"

"Well, you know, if shit hits the fan and the star elves take over. Wouldn't you wanna get out if that happens?"

Suspicion swirled in his reddish-brown eyes. "Why are you asking this?"

"Contingencies." Lifting my shoulders in a light shrug, I gave him my best innocent smile. "I always have a plan for when things go sideways. Just wanted to know if you wanted to be included in it too."

"Until the day when Sker is beyond saving, I am not going anywhere." He gave me a curt nod. "Good day."

Twisting back around, he continued striding down the alley with confident steps. I shook my head. And he called Kristen stubborn. Why did people always have to insist on fighting for lost causes?

Red dust tumbled from the wall as I gripped the cracked surface and started climbing towards the roof. Lady Beltham would have to wait because no matter how lost I thought this cause was, Malor was right. We needed to do something drastic to interfere with these rituals. I grinned as I rolled onto the roof. And I had just the thing.

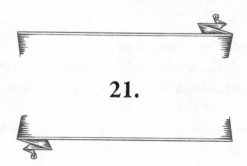

21.

White tents covered the dusty ground outside the city walls like a gleaming sea. Hugging the shadows below the red stone wall, we snuck forward until the fortification curved in the other direction. I drew up next to the still warm stones and gazed across the moonlit area.

"Everyone clear on the plan?" I asked. When my friends nodded, I shifted my gaze to Shade and the twins. "Alright then, go create that distraction."

A wide grin spread across Haela's features as she rubbed her hands. "Distraction is my middle name."

Chuckling, I shook my head. "I thought it was mischief."

"I thought it was trouble," Haemir added.

"Oh shush." Another smile played over Haela's lips as she gave her brother a shove.

Soft laughter echoed over the dusty ground. When the merriment had died down, Elaran locked eyes with Shade.

"Make sure she doesn't..." He waved a hand around. "Get herself or all of you killed or something."

The assassin gave him a lopsided smile. "I'll keep them both safe." When Elaran nodded, Shade shifted his gaze to Marcus. "And you, if anything goes wrong, you cover those two." He nodded at me and Elaran. "In this darkness, a cloud of black smoke will be hard to spot."

"I already told you," Marcus began, "I can't risk using my powers when the star elves are here."

Steel filled Shade's black eyes. "I don't care. You make sure Storm and Elaran get out alive no matter the cost. Or I will hold you personally responsible." Before the Storm Caster could reply, the assassin flicked his gaze to me. "Don't do anything stupid."

A sly smile tugged at the corner of my lips as I shook my head in fake surprise. "When have I ever done anything stupid?"

The Master Assassin shot me an exasperated look before jerking his chin to the twins. "Let's go."

Mischief glittered in Haela's yellow eyes as she took off across the sand. I watched all three of them disappear into the darkness before turning my attention back to the white tents. We were well into the night so most of the camp was silent and still. Only guards in gleaming armor patrolled the perimeter. Earlier in the day, we had spent a few hours spying on the star elves' temporary home so our target had already been marked. Now, all we needed to do was get there.

A clamor rose from the far side of camp. All attention shifted to it as soldiers hurried towards it or cast worried glances in that direction. I exchanged a look with my two companions. *Showtime.*

We sprinted towards the closest tent. With their attention otherwise occupied, we managed to slip inside the rather loose ring of perimeter guards without notice. Fabric rustled faintly in the wind as we skirted around a small white tent and made for the next one.

Boots thumped against the packed dirt. Throwing my arms out, I stopped Elaran and Marcus from running straight into a couple of star elves. While the soldiers thundered past, I pushed the three of us back into the shadows. Marcus let out a soft breath. Once the threat was gone, we started back up again.

Only a pale moon illuminated our path but I had memorized the route beforehand so we moved forward without hesitation. Since most of the guards on duty were watching the outer ring, we didn't run into any more of them as we made our way further in. Queen Nimlithil had a couple of guards stationed outside the entrance to her tent but we weren't heading there anyway.

I skidded to a halt. Apparently, our target had a star elf protecting it as well. After putting a finger to my lips, I jerked my thumb towards the back of it. Elaran nodded and took the lead. Sneaking on soundless feet, we made our way towards the other side of the decorated white tent. It let out a soft rustling sound as we lifted open the back cloth wall and rolled under.

The glinting head of an arrow nocked in a large white bow greeted us. Pushing myself onto my knees, I tilted my head up to study the elf attached to the drawn weapon. Glossy silvery white hair tumbled down in loose curls over a white nightgown. Pale violet eyes set into a determined face lost their hostility when they flicked over us. Incredulity filled them instead.

"Elaran?" Princess Illeasia breathed.

All his usual grumpiness melted away as the wood elf straightened in front of the princess. "Hello, Illeasia."

Wood clattered as Illeasia threw the bow and arrow onto the bed next to her. They bounced precariously but remained on the rumpled white covers. The princess didn't even bother looking at the discarded weapons as she and Elaran closed the distance between them. I smiled at the two elves lost in each other's arms.

After a while, Illeasia drew back from the ravenous kiss and rested her head in the crook of Elaran's neck while he stroked a hand over her flowing hair.

"I wasn't sure I would see you again," she whispered.

"Me neither," Elaran answered.

Marcus shuffled his feet and appeared to be studying the tent walls in detail while an awkward blush crept up his neck and onto his cheeks. My heart, on the other hand, was too busy fluttering with happiness at seeing the grumpy archer and the joyful princess reunited to care much about the awkwardness of just standing there watching them have a moment.

At last, they stepped back from each other. Elaran ran a soft hand down her cheek before taking that last step back to signal that Marcus and I now had permission to exist again.

"It's good to see you, Storm," Illeasia said as she tore her gaze from the man she loved and turned to me and the tall Storm Caster. "And...?"

"Marcus," he filled in.

"Nice to meet you." She flicked her pale eyes between me and Elaran. "But what in the world are you doing here?"

I sent her a smile. "Here in your tent or here in Sker?"

"Both? Either?"

"We're trying to stop your mother from taking over the city," Elaran supplied. "If she does, our cities will be in danger."

Sadness blew over Illeasia's beautiful face. "I know. I've been trying to get her to leave it alone but after you escaped, she's become uncharacteristically nervous. And then there is that new alliance." She shook her head. "When my mother feels threatened, she attacks. I can't stop this. All I can try to do is mitigate the damage she does."

Elaran and I exchanged a glance.

"We're actually trying to swing public opinion so that the city bands together to kick her out," I said. "Which is why we're here. We need your help."

"We need to know where the next ritual will be," Elaran filled in. "So we can stop it before it happens."

The tent walls snapped in the wind as a strong gust blew through camp. It almost drowned out the sound of something else. Almost. I jerked my head up. Footsteps.

"Someone's coming," I hissed.

Panic flashed over Marcus' face but Illeasia was already moving. She grabbed a hold of Elaran's shirt and pulled him towards the bed.

"Get under there," she whispered while snatching up her weapons and shoving them into his arms.

Elaran blinked in befuddlement but dropped to floor and rolled under the bed while still clutching the bow and arrow. The footsteps drew closer. Marcus darted back and forth across the room but when he couldn't find anywhere to hide, he just stopped and stared at the princess. There was no closet to hide in and no doors to take cover behind.

Shooing at us, Illeasia directed us towards the large chest in the corner while yanking a large fur blanket from her bed. Confusion filled Marcus' eyes but I had already worked out what she was doing so I just grabbed him by the arm and pulled us both down on the ground. The heavy blanket blotted out the light as the princess threw it over us. It was a very crude plan, but it was all we had.

"Princess Illeasia," a voice called from outside the tent barely a second after our flimsy cover was in place. It was a voice I knew very well.

A mattress creaked as Illeasia no doubt jumped onto the bed as if she had just woken up. Next to me, Marcus drew a shallow breath that send a soft poof of warm air against my neck.

"Yes?" Princess Illeasia answered at last.

Cloth rustled and boots trampled into the tent as the owner of the voice strode inside. "Are you alright?"

"Yes, Hadraeth, I'm fine. Why wouldn't I be?"

Hadraeth, the Captain of the Guard, was silent for a moment before replying. "There was a disturbance at the edge of camp. I just wanted to make sure that you were alright."

"I'm fine," the princess repeated. "Though as you can see, I'm a bit indisposed."

Captain Hadraeth cleared his throat. "Right. Yes, of course. I apologize. I will leave you to it."

Silence fell across the room. My heart pattered against my ribs but I stayed pressed against Marcus under the white fur blanket. Heat from his body mingled with mine where our skin touched.

"Thank you for checking on me," Illeasia said. "Have you checked on my mother?"

"No, I wanted to..." He trailed off. "I will do that now. But I'll send over a couple of extra guards to your tent just to be sure."

"Thank you."

Another awkward silence fell and the sound of shuffling feet drifted through the fabric around me. At last, Hadraeth cleared his throat again.

"Goodnight, Princess Illeasia," he said before striding out of the tent again.

The flap rustled faintly as it fell back in place.

"It's clear," Illeasia whispered.

Marcus rose, taking the blanket with him when he drew up to his full height again. I gave my body a quick stretch while he dropped the white fur on top of the chest and Elaran rolled out from under the bed.

"You heard him," the princess continued. "There are more guards coming so you have to hurry." She flicked her eyes to me. "The next ritual will be tomorrow afternoon down by the docks. So if you want to stop it, that's where you have to be."

"Got it. Thank you." After nodding to the princess, I put a hand on Marcus' arm and pulled him towards the back of the tent. "Come on."

While we moved towards our exit, Elaran and Illeasia strode towards each other. The princess reached up and grabbed a hold of the ranger's shirt. She pulled him towards her and planted her lips on his. Elaran wrapped his arms around her. While the two of them lost themselves in another kiss, another couple of footsteps approached.

"We need to go," Marcus hissed.

It was with great reluctance that the two elves withdrew from each other's embrace. Elaran lifted a hand and cupped Illeasia's cheek.

"I'll see you soon."

A small moan escaped the princess' throat. "Be careful."

"Elaran," Marcus whispered again.

The guards were almost there so we both dropped to the ground and rolled out of the tent. A second later, Elaran crawled out from under the white cloth wall as well. Armor gleamed in the moonlight a short distance away. *Shit*.

Not bothering to even ask Marcus, I reached deep into my soul to find that simmering rage. Orange sparks flickered inside it. Now that I knew what to look for it was so much easier to find it. Getting the darkness to come out, however, was still hit and miss sometimes. *Please work*. I pulled on it.

Black cloud shot out around me. Elaran jerked back in surprise but let me yank him into the dark smoke anyway. I could feel Marcus' eyes burning holes in my back but I ignored him as all three of us moved away from the tent under the cover of darkness.

Once we had put some distance between ourselves and Illeasia's tent, I let my powers disappear into the deep pits of my soul again. No need to waste energy.

"Please, Storm," Marcus said as we drew up behind a white tent towards the edge of camp. "Don't do that again. We can't draw attention to our people."

Swatting red dust off my clothes from our roll on the ground, I drew my eyebrows down. "What's the point of having powers if we can't use them to help us survive? And besides, the star elves already know that I'm Ashaana so it doesn't matter."

"But they don't know that it's you. They don't know you're here, remember?"

Damn him and his logic. I blew out a forceful breath.

"Fine. Only as a last resort."

Marcus looked only partly satisfied but nodded anyway. Turning away from him, I peeked around the edge of the tent. There appeared to be more guards present now than there had been when we snuck in. If we moved across an area bathed in moonlight, they'd see us now that the distance between each guard was closer. I tilted my head up.

Glittering stars covered the dark blue sky above but thick clouds were sweeping across them at a quick pace. Huh. If we couldn't use artificial darkness, then a cloud-based one would have to do.

Snapping my head back down, I pointed at the large one approaching the moon. "Get ready."

Elaran and Marcus flicked a quick gaze at it before nodding. It was moving fast, which was good because we wouldn't have to be standing in camp for much longer. But on the other hand, it also meant that it would only be covering the moon for a short period of time. We would have to be quick. I crouched down and got ready. Seconds ticked by.

"Now," I hissed.

We sprinted forward. Heavy darkness blanketed the area as the fast-moving cloud covered the moon. I could barely see more than a few strides in front of me but it didn't matter because we only needed to run straight ahead.

With their long legs, Elaran and Marcus were getting further ahead with every passing second. The looming city walls had to be getting closer. I stole a quick glance at the sky. Moonlight started peeking out on the side of the thick cloud.

Panic welled up in my chest. Soft silver light began illuminating the area around us again as our protection blew clear and revealed that the city walls were much further away than I had hoped. We weren't going to make it.

My heart slammed in my chest as I pushed myself to pick up speed. Dust puffed into the air behind me with every stride. We had to make it. We had to. I threw a hurried glance over my shoulder. Any second now, the star elves would see us and raise the alarm. Gods damn it.

Dark smoke erupted around us. I tripped and almost tumbled to the ground in surprise but managed to stay on my feet. Whipping my head around, I met Marcus' eyes. They were black as death. I blinked at him in surprise but he just motioned for me to keep moving.

"Guys, I can't see anything," Elaran breathed from a few steps to my right.

Of course. When I'd use the darkness inside camp, I'd had to lead Elaran as well since he wasn't Ashaana and couldn't see through the dark haze. I closed the distance between us and took his hand. Once he had knitted his warm fingers through mine, I led him forward.

When the grumpy elf broke into a trot, a surprised but sparkling feeling went through my body. Apparently, he was so sure that I would steer us to safety that he was comfortable running even though I was the only one who could see anything. I had no idea he trusted me that much.

Marcus kept the black smoke swirling around us until we had reached the safety of the city walls. Letting go of Elaran's hand, I turned to peer at the Storm Caster as he withdrew the dark clouds.

"I thought you said we weren't supposed to use our powers," I said.

He lifted a hand to scratch the back of his neck. "Yeah, I know. But you were right too. If we can't use them to survive, what even is the point of having them?" A rueful smile spread across his lips. "Also, Shade made it very clear that he would hold me responsible if anything happened to you. And I figured having a pissed-off Master of the Assassins' Guild coming after me would be pretty bad for my health."

I let out a soft chuckle. "True."

While the night winds continued blowing clouds across the moon, the three of us waited for our mischief-making team to get back. Marcus leaned back against the stones and closed his eyes and I pretended to do the same so that Elaran could stare at the darkened camp in peace.

One day, I truly hoped he and Illeasia could be together. This war had to end at some point and when it did, they could both follow their hearts. My mind went back to the harbor on the other side and the schemes I had already started to plan. But first we had a ritual to crash. Good thing I specialized in hurting, destroying, and burning things to the ground.

22.

Damp wood and seaweed filled the air that drifted through the harbor on strong fall winds. People chatted in hushed tones while trying their hardest to make it look like they were there to inspect the freshly caught fish or to simply stroll along the water. Slinking through the throng, I let out a chuckle. Amateurs.

We needed to plant some surprises before the ritual started so the task had naturally fallen on the two sneakiest members of our group. The thief and the assassin. Shade's dark eyes met mine from across the adjacent pier. I gave him a nod. After returning it, he slipped behind a stack of crates while I bent down in a show of inspecting the merchandise laid out on the closest cart.

"They're freshly caught this morning," the vendor said.

"Mm-hmm." I studied the array of slimy creatures before me while dropping a tiny pouch under the table. "Yeah, nah, I'm alright."

"Suit yourself."

Shrugging, I set course for a cluster of barrels further down. While I continue strolling along the pier and placing pouches in strategic locations, the crowd around me thickened. I didn't worry much about it, though. With their eyesight, the elves would be able to keep track of me and the surprise packages I delivered anyway. However, it also meant that the ritual would be starting soon. I threw a quick glance over my shoulder as I neared the pavilion at the far end of the wide walkway.

"Hey! What're you doing here?"

The sudden sound made me jerk my head back towards the pavilion in front of me. A guard scowled at me. *Shit*. While drifting towards the side of the structure, I cast my gaze around for something to use as an excuse. Boats bobbed in the water inside.

"I was told there was a boat for sale." I gave him a light shrug as I reached the wooden wall. "And that I could inspect it before I bought it."

Suspicion swirled in his brown eyes as the guard studied me. "There are no boats for sale here."

"Huh. Must've been someone trying to scam me."

"Yeah, must've."

Just as I was about to turn and begin my retreat, the guard took a few quick steps across the planks. That blooming suspicion had grown stronger when he scrutinized my appearance. I had left most of my visible knives behind in order to not draw as much attention, but I still didn't exactly look like someone who bought boats.

"What've you got in there?" he demanded and nodded at the large black sack full of smaller pouches that I was holding.

Panic shot through me. If he saw what was inside it, our whole plan would be ruined. Still keeping a calm outward appearance, I draped my shoulder against the wall in a casual gesture while expertly tipping the contents of my bag onto the pier. The pouches landed in a small pile in the narrow space between the wall and the water, just outside the pavilion.

"In this?" I asked, shifting the now empty bag to my other hand. "Nothing yet. I was gonna buy some fishing supplies but I haven't found the right ones yet."

Gloved hands snatched at the fabric and peered inside. Once he was convinced that there was nothing in it, he drew back and ran his fingers through his graying hair. He narrowed his eyes at me.

"What kind of fishing supplies?"

"Uhm..." I began.

Man, I should've picked a better lie. I had no idea what one might need in order to fish. And why did this old man need to be so damn suspicious? Couldn't he just let people ruin stuff in peace?

"Well, I..." I tried again.

Excited shouts rang out behind me. I whirled around to see two elves dressed in white make their way onto the pier. The graying guard swore. Shoving the empty bag into my hands, he stalked towards the star elves and the crowd that was pouring onto the docks.

Damn. The plan had been to leave the pier before we set our schemes in motion but it was too late now so I dropped the useless piece of black fabric on the ground and swung around the building until I reached an uneven plank in the outside wall. Old wood groaned as I climbed towards the roof of the pavilion.

"Brave citizens of Sker," the star elf scholar called across the water.

They had gathered about halfway down the pier I was currently stuck on while most of the spectators occupied the same space on the adjacent one. As I rolled over the edge and crawled towards the front of the roof, I briefly wondered if Shade had made it off before that inconvenient cluster of people blocked off the whole walkway.

"I understand that it takes great courage for you to be here today and risk the Staghearts' wrath and I commend you for it," the elf in white continued. "Please form orderly lines and we will proceed with the ritual."

Lying on my stomach, I lifted my head just enough to peek over the edge of the roof while remaining out of sight behind the slightly raised end. Waves slapped against the wood below while nervous excitement hung in the air. The gathered citizens looked both frightened and thrilled at the same time as they shuffled around on the planks further down. Acts of rebellion usually felt like that.

A soft thud sounded behind me. Still pressing myself into the wooden roof, I whipped my head around to find a figure dressed all in black slithering towards me. I rolled my eyes and went back to studying the crowd.

"Weren't you supposed to have left by now?" I asked.

"I could ask you the same," Shade answered. "When I reached the shore, you weren't there."

Keeping my head low, I nodded at the cluster further down. "Yeah, well, the star elves decided to block my escape route. So I figured I'd lay low here until it's done." I turned to peer at him. "But why are you here, if you were already at the shore? And how did you even get here?"

Shade gave me a sly smile in reply. Muttering curses under my breath, I shook my head. Damn assassin.

Atop the city wall, four tall figures rose from behind the battlements and three of them lifted large bows in dark colors that stood out in stark contrast against the pale blue sky beyond. I threw an elbow in the assassin's ribs.

"Showtime."

Flames flickered on the nocked arrows atop the bulwark. Since they were too far away, I couldn't tell who was who, but all three of my elven friends raised their bows and fired their burning arrows towards the pier. The soft whizzing as they flew was drowned out by the star elf's commanding voice. I watched one of them land behind a stack of crates.

Explosions echoed across the waves. Wood and wares flew into the air as the projectiles hit the small pouches Shade and I had been leaving in strategic locations. I grinned. Black powder. It really was a great invention.

Three more arrows sped through the air while people cried out in alarm. A black wooden shaft disappeared under the fish cart I had stopped at on my way over here. Booms rang out. Well-dressed ladies shrieked and flailed their arms around as slimy dead sea creatures sprayed into the air and hit the surrounding pier and spectators with wet slapping sounds.

I tried very hard to keep from chuckling but after one glance at Shade, we both burst out laughing. While fighting off bits of fish that rained down on top of their fine garments, the gathered citizens fled towards the shore. A job well done.

Flicking my gaze towards the top of the city wall again, I saw one of our elven friends shift their aim towards the side of the pavilion. I frowned in surprise. Why would they be shooting here? All the pouches had been left further down the pier. Realization slammed into me like a shovel to the back of the head. *Oh shit.*

Shooting to my feet, I was just about to signal to whoever aimed this way that I was still here but before I had time to make my presence known, they had already fired. Panic set fire to my every nerve. The arrow sped towards its mark. An idea shoved through the alarms blaring in my mind and I reached deep into my soul. If I could just summon some wind, I could blow the flaming arrow off course before it hit.

Everything else seemed to move in slow motion as that burning rage surged from my soul. Black smoke whipped around my body while my dark green eyes turned black as death. I raised my arms. One shot of wind and we'd be safe. With power building inside me, I got ready to slam the torrent forward. *And... now!*

What if I blow up the harbor?

Hesitation froze my body like an ice storm. Nothing happened as I shoved my hands forward in an attempt to create wind. The arrow sped towards its mark with terrifying speed.

"What's going on?" Shade demanded.

At some point he must have climbed to his feet as well because he was standing right next to me, his hand hovering over my arm and the black smoke snaking around it. The darkness snapped back into my soul as I turned to him.

"We should run," I declared.

One of the really nice things about running with other underworlders is that they don't question statements like that. We all know that one second of hesitation can mean the difference between life and death. So when someone says *run*, we run.

Whipping around, Shade and I both sprinted towards the back of the pavilion. Over the clamor from the pier, it was impossible to hear the approaching projectile but my mind swore it could hear it whizzing through the air. The assassin and I reached the edge of the roof. Putting all my strength in it, I pushed off and dove through the air.

A deafening boom spread across the area as the flaming arrow hit the large pile of black powder I had dumped outside the wall of the pavilion when the guard questioned me about the contents of my bag. Heat rolled over my body. Broken planks and chunks of debris flew through the air while the fire whooshed behind us. And then I broke the surface.

Dark water wrapped around me like cold silk as I sped head first into the sea. Twisting around to slow my momentum, I saw the orange light flare across the surface as the flames from the explosion expanded. Holding my breath, I remained under the waves until the bright light had died down. When the world above me was dark again, I kicked towards the land of breathable air.

My soaked clothes weighed me down but it wasn't exactly the first time I had swum fully clothed and armed so I reached the surface without issue. Air filled my starved lungs as I gasped in a deep breath. Falling pieces of wood made plopping sounds as they fell into the water closer to the pier.

"That explosion was a bit bigger than we planned," Shade observed while treading water next to me.

"Yeah, well, that wasn't supposed to happen," I huffed, trying to keep the waves from getting into my mouth.

"What did you do? Dump a whole stack of pouches next to the pavilion?"

That damn assassin was too smart for his own good. I gave him a sidelong glance. "Maybe."

Shade snorted, which turned into a coughing fit as he accidentally swallowed a mouthful of water. I took pleasure in his indignation for a few seconds before jerking my head towards the shore.

"Shall we?"

The coughing Master Assassin nodded and started swimming towards the stony beach. After one last look at the burning wreckage that had once been a pavilion, I followed. There sure weren't any boats for sale now.

Four figures rushed towards us as we neared land. Given the look on Haemir's face, he was probably the one who had fired that last arrow. They stopped at the waterline while Shade and I made our way in.

Water sloshed around my legs as I waded to shore. I performed a quick check to make sure that all my knives were still in their sheaths before I glanced over at Shade. His black clothes were plastered to his skin and his hair matted against his forehead. Muscles shifted under wet fabric as he lifted his arms and ruffled his hair to shake the water out.

"I'm so sorry!" Haemir called as we finally made it onto dry land. "I saw you leave the pouches there and then climb up but I thought it was just to get away. I had no idea that you were still on the roof."

Putting a hand on his arm, I gave it a reassuring squeeze. "It's alright. Promise." I nodded at the chaos unfolding by the docks. "And I'd say it worked like a charm."

The distressed elf turned towards the scene.

People ran in panic from the burning pier while the Sker guards, who had been on their way to strike down everyone who participated in the ritual, instead looked like heroes. Their captain coordinated the effort as the rest of the squad worked together to put out the fire and help people to safety. After this, the guards of Sker, and by extension the Staghearts, were definitely going to get a boost in popularity.

Grinning, I bumped my wet shoulder into Haemir's dry one. Opposite us, Haela matched my grin. A job well done indeed.

Once Haemir had blown out a long breath and nodded in acknowledgement, I turned to Elaran. The grumpy elf had been talking quietly to Shade but now turned to me with a scowl.

He crossed his arms. "Why is it that every time I go somewhere with you, stuff always blows up around us?"

"Bad timing?" I shot him a mock innocent smile.

"I need to start wearing a helmet when you're around," he muttered before turning towards the seaside gate. "Come on, we need to get back before anyone puts two and two together."

Flashing me a mischievous grin, Haela threw an arm around her brother's shoulders and followed Elaran. Shade gave me a shrug and did the same. After squeezing water from my braid, I started out as well. My boots made wet squishy sounds against the rocks as I walked.

"Are you sure you're okay?"

I glanced up to find Marcus peering down at me with concern swirling in his golden eyes. "Yeah, I promise. This ain't the first time I've done something like this." Water drops flew through the air as I tipped my head from side to side. "Well, something similar at least."

"Yeah, Elaran made it sound like stuff like this happens a lot. To you."

A chuckle bubbled from my chest. "He's not wrong." I threw him a sharp look. "But don't tell him I said that."

Rumbling laughter sounded before he transformed his face into a serious mask. "I promise." The severe lines were pushed out by another smile as Marcus turned to study me again. "But seriously, is it always this... messy?"

"Where I am?" I snorted. "Oh you have no idea."

Tipping his head back, Marcus ran his fingers through his hair and let out a long sigh. "I miss my cabin in the woods. Hunting, fishing, hiking through the forest. Sitting by the fireplace." He lifted his broad shoulders in a shrug. "It's a simple life, but I like it."

Strange emotions played over his face. It almost looked like... homesickness. Reaching out, I gave his calloused hand a quick squeeze. He pressed my hand and sent me a grateful smile in reply as we passed through the fortified back gate. My soaked boots left dark footprints in the red sand.

Maybe they were right. Things tended to get kind of messy wherever I was. I wasn't sure whether it was because I was drawn to messy situations or because I was the one who created the trouble. Perhaps it was a bit of both. The distressed cries from the harbor disappeared as we made our way deeper into the red city. I shrugged. Well, at least it was an exciting life.

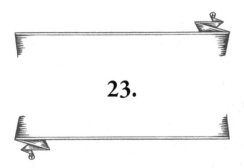

23.

White wax dripped onto the stained wooden table. I pushed the candle a little to the right in an effort to straighten it but only succeeded in making more hot wax run down the side of it. Giving up my futile attempt, I sat back in the rickety chair and crossed my arms.

"Are we sure that's the best play?" I asked.

"Yes." Elaran drew his eyebrows down. "Weren't you paying attention? Lady Beltham is a young widow with a weakness for a handsome face. Seducing her is the fastest way to get her on our side."

I matched his frown. "Young? She's at least ten years older than us."

"She's a lot younger than us," Haela pointed out and motioned at her brother and Elaran. "Like, *a lot*."

"Yeah, but you're not the one seducing her," I muttered.

"No." Shade gave me a curious look. "And neither are you. I am."

Blowing out a sigh, I threw my hands up. "Fine."

Strong winds made the shutters on the windows rattle. The other patrons at The Broken Wing were so busy staring at the bottom of their mugs that they barely looked up at the sound. Pots clanked from the kitchen.

"The explosions yesterday helped." Elaran shot me a pointed look. "But we still need these influential people on our side if we're going to turn the city against Queen Nimlithil."

I smacked my lips and raised my eyebrows in exasperation. "I already said *fine*."

"The three of us have to do the security run for that pompous wine merchant tonight," he continued as if I hadn't commented, and motioned between himself and the twins. "And Shade will be hitting up Lady Beltham." He shifted his gaze to me and Marcus. "I want you to watch his back in case something happens."

A smile tugged at Shade's lips as he turned to Elaran. "Now who's the one giving orders?"

"Shut up. You're always giving orders." The grumpy elf crossed his arms. "Now it's my turn."

Letting out a soft chuckle, the assassin raised his hands in surrender. "Be my guest." He nodded at me. "That one could certainly use some training in taking orders."

"I don't—"

"Guys, focus," Haemir interrupted before I could inform them that I most definitely didn't take orders from either of them.

Marcus glanced between the three of us with uncertainty drifting over his face while Haela laughed and drained her drink on the other side of the table. I blew out a sigh and threw myself back into the chair again. The scraggly thing creaked in alarm.

"Alright," Elaran said once our table had quieted down again. He looked from one twin to the other. "You two, meet me outside in five minutes." Shifting his gaze to Shade, he let out a long exhale. "And you, be careful." When the Master Assassin only replied with a sly smile, the bossy elf stabbed a hand at me and Marcus. "And you two, make sure he *is* being careful. We don't have time to deal with injuries and poisonings and shit like that."

Marcus opened his mouth to reply but then furrowed his brows and closed it again as if he couldn't quite tell if that was a plausible turn of events when seducing a widow. I rolled my eyes at the elf's presumptuous commands but nodded anyway.

"Good." Elaran placed his palms on the table and pushed himself up. "Then let's get to it."

Creaking furniture and scraping wood filled the rundown tavern as we got to our feet and made for the stairs. We all wanted to gear up before heading out so we climbed the stairs in one long line.

Once I had strapped on the rest of my knives, I walked back into the upstairs corridor. The twins and Elaran had already left and the door to Marcus' room was still closed so for a minute, I just paced across the groaning wooden planks in the hallway. Faces of old men long dead stared down at me from the faded paintings. What was taking them so long? I stalked towards Shade's room.

The door had been left open and a shadow moved across the floor inside. After a moment's hesitation, I moved into the doorway. Leaning my shoulder against the chipped doorframe, I took in the scene.

Shade had changed out of his usual clothes and was now busy putting on a slick black suit. Of course. He couldn't very well charm a noble lady while looking like a shady underworlder. Candlelight played over the muscles in his back as he pulled his assassination-friendly shirt over his head and tossed it on the bed. I bit the inside of my cheek.

"You wanna come in?" Shade said. A teasing smile drifted over his lips as the Master Assassin turned to face me. "Or are you just going to stand there staring at me from the doorway?"

"I wasn't staring," I huffed.

The red creeping into my cheeks would suggest otherwise but I hoped he couldn't see it in the flickering candlelight as I took a step across the threshold and leaned back against the wall right inside the door instead.

"You packed a suit for this mission?" I nodded at the fine black pants he wore and the still folded shirt and suit jacket sitting on the table.

"It's about being–"

"Prepared for every eventuality," I finished and barely prevented myself from rolling my eyes again. "Yeah, yeah, I know."

Amusement drifted over his face as he looked at me. I wanted to slap that satisfaction right off his sharp cheekbones but instead settled for a scowl.

"So, you're gonna seduce Lady Beltham, huh?" I said.

"Yeah." Shade tipped his head to the right, his black eyes glittering. "You jealous?"

"Jealous? Me?" I snorted. "I'm pretty sure I'd need a heart for that."

In a few long strides, the Master Assassin had closed the distance between us. When he placed a hand on the wall next to my head and leaned in so close I could almost feel the heat radiating from his body, I became acutely aware of the fact that he still hadn't put on a damn shirt. I had a sudden urge to place a hand on his chest, to push him off or to feel his skin against mine, I wasn't sure.

Shade drew soft fingers along my collarbones. "No heart, huh?"

His touch sent sparkles shooting through my body. I sucked in a shuddering breath as his hand curved around the back of my neck. He leaned in, his muscles shifting against my body, and when his warm lips met mine, I forgot that the rest of the world existed. Everything else became insignificant background noise. All that mattered were his hand on my neck, his body pressed into me, and his lips against mine.

When he finally drew back, I slumped against the wall and kept my eyes closed for another few seconds in order to get my scrambled mind back in order. Drawing a bracing breath, I opened them again. Intense black eyes met me.

He rested his palm against my collarbones again. "How about now?"

Oh that inconvenient thing in my chest had made a whole series of backflips that more than proved its existence, but I shot him a teasing grin and shook my head anyway.

"Nope, still cold and black." I raised my eyebrows. "Yours?"

"Same." A sly smile spread across his lips as he traced his fingers back and forth along my collarbones. "My black-hearted thief."

When I placed a hand on his chest, his heart thrummed beneath his hard muscles. "My cold-hearted assassin."

He let out a dark chuckle. "Let's go seduce that widow."

After flashing me a scheming smile, he drew back and returned to the neatly folded shirt. My skin still tingled from his touch. I shook my head. As he picked up the black shirt, I cast one last look at the lean muscles shifting in the flickering candlelight before I slipped out the door. I needed a clear head in case we ran into trouble, and watching the Master of the Assassins' Guild undress most certainly did not leave me clear-headed.

Shoving inconvenient feelings out of my chest, I stalked down the stairs. We had work to do.

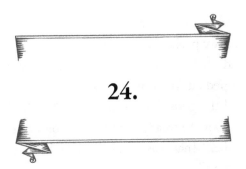

24.

A soft afternoon breeze stirred up dust swirls on the empty road. I watched the red sand twist in lazy spirals before settling again. Next to me, Marcus lounged against the wall. His eyes moved back and forth across the street while his hand rested on the pommel of his heavy sword.

"Are you sure she walks by here?" he asked.

"Yeah." I nodded. "Every time I watched her house, she always took an afternoon walk and then used this road to get back."

Marcus and I were hiding on an empty back porch a few streets from Lady Beltham's home while Shade waited in a side alley, ready to run into her as if he had just happened to be there when the lady passed. There were no shops on this road so the risk of interference was slight. We wanted as controlled an environment as possible for the assassin to work his magic. Putting a foot up on the wall behind me, I crossed my arms. As if he'd need any of that to make women swoon over him.

"Heads up," Marcus whispered. Straightening, he nodded down the street. "She's here."

Both of us shrank back into the shadows cast by the tall buildings as a woman in her mid-thirties strolled by the porch.

Her long blond hair flowed behind her in the soft breeze. Once she had passed, we peeked out behind the wall.

"Oh!" Lady Beltham exclaimed as a man in a well-tailored black suit stepped out right in front of her.

"Oh by all the gods, I'm so sorry," Shade said. He placed a hand on her elbow to steady her while his mouth drew into an apologetic smile. "That was entirely my fault. I wasn't looking where I was going."

The beautiful lady ran her hands over her pink and white dress while shaking her head. "It's quite alright. No harm done."

Shade tilted his head to the right. "Have we met before?"

"Oh." She blinked at him. "No, I don't think so."

"I could've sworn I saw you at the latest party in the Red Fort."

A soundless chuckle made it past my lips. Clever. Telling her that he is important enough to have been at the party in the Red Fort and that he thinks she looks equally important, all in the same sentence.

"I'm afraid I had other matters to attend to that evening."

"I see." The Master Assassin managed to pull off a smile that was both charming and sexy at the same time. He motioned down the road. "May I walk you home?"

Silence fell over the street as Lady Beltham considered. Another soft wind blew strands of blond hair in front of her face. She pushed them back as she ran her eyes up and down the body of the athletic assassin in front of her, no doubt imagining what sort of activities the two of them could spend the afternoon doing. Storm clouds started brewing in my mind and I narrowed my eyes at her.

"Thank you for the offer." She reached up and put a hand on Shade's cheek while a small smile spread across her lips. "But you're not my type."

After giving his cheek a quick pat, she dropped her arm and took a step past the stunned assassin. My mouth fell open. Had she just...? Red crept into Shade's cheeks as he stared at her with both embarrassment and bafflement evident on his face. The lady strode past in a swishing of pink skirts.

"Did he just get...?" Marcus began and turned to me with raised eyebrows.

Fighting the urge to throw my head back and cackle like a villain, I nodded. "Yep, he sure did."

"Shade?" a surprised voice blurted out.

The distinct ringing of swords being drawn echoed between the red stone buildings. I whipped my head towards the sound. *Shit.*

Lady Beltham had backed up the steps to a front door to allow three newcomers to pass. While pressed into the doorway, she flicked her gaze between the two parties. White armor gleamed in the afternoon sun.

"What are you doing here?" Captain Hadraeth demanded.

The sword in his hand was not raised. Yet. But this could turn ugly fast. Motioning at Marcus to keep his sword sheathed for now, I jerked my head towards the road. He gave me a nod and followed me out of the shadows.

Armor clanked as the three star elves shifted their stance to take this new threat into account. Surprise bloomed in Hadraeth's dark violet eyes when his gaze fell on me. I gave him a shrug as Marcus and I took up position on either side of Shade.

The Captain of the Guard narrowed his eyes at us. "Is Elaran here too?"

"No," I said.

He hadn't specified if he meant *here* as in *here in this city* or *here on this street*, so I chose to interpret it as the latter. Suspicion drifted past on his face but he didn't press the matter. Instead, he gripped his sword tighter and lifted it slightly.

"I ask again, what are you doing here?" he said.

I gave him a nonchalant shrug. "We're here on vacation."

His dark eyes flashed with displeasure. "You're here to somehow sabotage Queen Nimlithil's plans."

"Now see, if you already knew that, why did you bother asking?"

He opened his mouth to no doubt growl something rude at me but before he had produced any sound, a look of sudden realization snapped in place on his features. "By the Stars, you're the ones who blew up the harbor yesterday."

"Now you're just being dramatic." I waved a hand in the air. "We didn't blow up *the harbor*. It was just one pier."

"You endangered innocent people!"

"*We* endanger innocents?" I scoffed. "That's a bit rich coming from the guys who use hallucinogenic mist that makes people relive their worst guilt and fear just so that they will go through with your stupid ritual."

The other two star elves cast long glances at their captain but Hadraeth just opened and closed his mouth like a stranded fish. Deciding to press the advantage, I threw my arms out.

"Come on, you have to know that this is wrong."

For a moment, it looked like he was about to say something but then he wiped all trace of emotion from his face and drew himself up. "I have orders, and I intend to follow them." Raising his sword, he pointed it at us. "I'm taking you in."

As the two other star elves raised their swords as well, Shade, Marcus, and I exchanged a look. Without another word, the tall Storm Caster drew his large sword while the Master Assassin produced two long daggers from somewhere in his clothes. I heaved a deep breath.

Steel glinted in the sunlight as I snatch two throwing knives from my shoulders and hurled them at the star elves. Metal dinged against metal as the two white-haired soldiers threw up their swords and batted away the flying projectiles. They bounced off the red stone walls and skidded to a halt further down the street.

Captain Hadraeth was already flying across the dusty ground with his sight set on the assassin. I yanked out my hunting knives as the other two elves barreled straight at me and Marcus respectively. Grinding metal filled the warm afternoon air as blades clashed.

My opponent swung a gently curved sword at my head. Twisting away, I ducked under his arm and swiped my knife across his chest. The sharp point left a rut in the silver-decorated breastplate but did nothing to stop the elf's advance. He whirled around and threw an elbow in my cheek. Man, I hated fighting people in armor.

Red dust crumbled from the wall as I crashed into the building next to me. Blinking black spots from my vision, I almost missed his next attack. With barely a second to spare, I threw up my right-hand blade to block the strike coming for my throat. The knife vibrated in my hand as the star elf slammed his sword into it.

Over his shoulder, I caught a quick glimpse of the other battles. Marcus was holding his own incredibly well. He fought like a block of stone. Swinging his huge sword with powerful strikes while also keeping a tight defense, he appeared to be winning.

Shade, on the other hand, was engaged in a much more evenly matched fight with Captain Hadraeth. Against the captain's long sword, the Master Assassin was at a disadvantage. Since he had been here to seduce Lady Beltham, he'd had to leave his own swords at the tavern. He was using his speed to jab strike after strike at the Captain of the Guard, but just like me, his small weapons had a hard time getting through the well-crafted armor.

Steel ground against steel as the star elf before me pushed his sword further down. My arms shook. With a snap of my wrist, I redirected his blade and forced it to slide down in the empty space next to me. A low growl came from my opponent's throat as I used the second of grace to put some distance between us.

Pulling another throwing knife, I hurled it at him. He yanked up his blade and batted it away almost without breaking a stride. His sword whizzed through the air. I tried to duck away but he was moving too fast so I was forced to parry his sword from an awkward angle. Metallic clattering rang out as my right-hand blade flew from my grip and hit the opposite wall.

The attacking star elf drew his arm in an arc, delivering a lightning fast backhand strike. I threw myself back to avoid being cleaved in two. An armor-reinforced kick landed at the back of my left leg. It buckled and I crashed down on one knee. Red dust swirled into the air in a quick poof as I landed. I rolled forward.

A sword struck the ground in the place I had vacated only a scant second before. Tucking my head in, I rolled right next to my opponent's leg in an attempt to come up behind him. I barely made it to my knees before a heavy boot connected with my back. My breath raced out of my lungs as I slammed hard into the ground while my final hunting knife flew from my grip.

Bracing my palms on the ground, I made sure my legs were on either side of the attacking elf's ankle before I pushed off and twisted around. The surprise force threw him off balance. While the white-haired soldier staggered to the side, I jumped to my feet. This wasn't going to work.

I reached deep into the darkest pits of my soul. Burning rage simmered in there, waiting to be called forth. Right as my opponent charged me again, I gave into the anger and let it surge through my whole body. Dark tendrils whipped out around me.

The star elf in front of me hesitated. Gripping his sword tightly, he held it raised between us but didn't attack. Once I was sure he wouldn't do anything stupid, I leveled black eyes dripping with death and insanity on the Captain of the Guard.

"Hadraeth!" I called across the clamor of steel.

Two battles staggered to a halt as both pairs fighting on the other side turned to face me. Uncertainty flooded Captain Hadraeth's eyes.

"Enough," I growled. "If all three of you don't back off right now, I will pull down these buildings around your heads."

Wind whistled between the red walls as if on cue. The star elf in front of me took a step back towards his captain while the other one flicked an anxious gaze between me and the tall houses. I took a step forward and slowly raised my arms. Black smoke bloomed around me.

"You remember what happened that night in the courtyard." Lightning crackled over my skin. "So you know what I am capable of."

Memories of desperation, of screaming at Shade and Elaran to run, and of a huge chunk of frosted glass toppling from the wall as the storm exploded around me, flashed before my eyes. Dread seeped into my chest, making the black clouds around me shrink slightly. Hoping that no one had noticed, I shoved out the memory. I would most likely not be able to replicate that feat because after all the star elves' mind games, I hadn't been able to get my powers back up to that level again. But Captain Hadraeth didn't need to know that.

"Back off," I ordered. "Right now."

The two other guards cast uncertain glances at their captain while moving closer to him. Hadraeth held my gaze for another few seconds. Black smoke snaked around my limbs as I took another step forward. At last, the star elf captain jerked his chin.

Still keeping their swords out, the three elves backed out of the street in the same direction they had come. I left the darkness in place until I was sure they were gone. Once my eyes were back to their emerald color, I turned to my two friends while massaging my sore cheek.

"You okay?" I asked.

Marcus opened his mouth to reply but was cut short by another voice from further up the street.

"Wow." Lady Beltham peeled herself off the doorway she had apparently been hiding in this whole time and staggered down the steps. "I have never seen anything like this before."

Panic flashed over Marcus' face as he whipped his head between me and the blond lady.

"Relax," I said and waved a hand at him before he could launch into a lecture about the dangers of people knowing about Storm Casters. "The star elves already know I'm Ashaana, remember?"

After a moment's consideration, he gave me a slow nod. While we'd been reconfirming that me using my powers wouldn't actually compromising anyone, Lady Beltham had moved across the alley and stopped in front of Marcus.

"That was incredible." She looked up at him, her eyes glittering. "What a display of sword fighting skills."

"Uhm..." he stammered.

Lady Beltham shifted her gaze to Shade. "You might not be my type, sweetheart." She moved her hungry eyes back to Marcus. "But *you* most certainly are."

A deep red blush spread across his strong jaw. "I... uhm... what?"

"How about joining me for a cup of tea?" Pink skirts swished in the air as she moved next to him and looped an arm through his. "And then you can tell me all about why you and that Ashaana over there hid on that back porch while your friend pretended to run into me. Hmm?"

His face was so red I thought it was about to burst into flames as he cast a panicked glance between me and Shade. While I was busy grinning, the Master Assassin gave Marcus an encouraging nod.

"Yes, why don't you join Lady Beltham for tea?" He shot the Storm Caster a pointed look. "I'm sure you have lots to talk about."

"I... uhm..." Marcus stuttered again.

"Splendid," Lady Beltham said while pulling the flustered man on her arm towards the mouth of the street. "I'm sure we will have a lovely evening together."

"Bet you will," I whispered under my breath before letting out a chuckle.

Twisting his head, Marcus desperately looked back at us for support but when Shade lifted his hands in an apologetic gesture and I just grinned at him, he turned his bewildered stare back to the road in front of him.

"We'd better..." Shade began and nodded towards the roof.

"Yeah."

After retrieving all my missing knives, I followed Shade up the side of the building. We snuck along the rooftops, keeping Marcus and Lady Beltham in sight until they reached the blond lady's house. When she opened the door and motioned for him to step inside, he cast a quick look at the top of the buildings around him. His golden eyes met mine. Grinning, I gave him a thumbs up.

The color on his face had faded to a slight blush, but now it flared back into that alarming shade of red again. His mouth gaping, he stumbled across the threshold and disappeared into the domain of Lady Beltham.

Sun-warmed stones met me as I dropped down on the edge and leaned back against one of the chimneys. After a few seconds, Shade joined me.

For a while, we just sat there next to each other, watching the door to Lady Beltham's house in comfortable silence. Shade's arm brushed against mine as he adjusted his position. I tried to ignore the tingle it sent through my body.

On the street below, people moved about, chatting, arguing, or calling out offers while a rapidly setting sun cast it all in golden hues. Wood rattled as a cart overlaid with small barrels thundered down the dusty road. I drew my knees up to my chest and rested my arms on them.

"What's it like?" I asked.

"What's what like?"

"Being an upperworlder?"

Shade glanced at me from the corner of his eye. "I'm not an upperworlder."

"You're the General of Pernula."

"I'm also the Master of the Assassins' Guild."

My chest shook with a soft chuckle. "Yeah, I don't think you've ever let me forget that." Keeping my elbows on my knees, I tipped my head forward and ran my fingers through my hair. "But you also live in the Upperworld now. What's that like?"

"It's kind of like the Underworld." A teasing smirk spread across his lips. "When I give people orders, they obey."

Bumping his shoulder with mine, I blew out an amused breath. "Bloody dictator."

When I drew back, I didn't move quite as far away as before, so now we sat so close that our upper arms almost touched. I fell silent as shouts rose on the street below. A wind smelling of dry sand and warm stones blew across the rooftops, ruffling our hair.

"I don't think I could do it," I said. "Be an upperworlder, I mean. There are too many rules."

Shade tipped his head from side to side before giving me a sidelong glance. "Yeah, but that's the good thing about being in charge. I get to make the rules."

"I suppose. But there are still so many social rules you need to follow. How to dress, what to say, who to spend time with. Who to love."

Resting the back of his head against the chimney, Shade gave me a sad smile. "Yeah, there is that."

"There is that."

"For now, anyway."

Surprised, I turned to stare at him. "What're you gonna do? Change the whole city?"

"With enough power, there is nothing you can't do."

Letting out a chuckle, I leaned back and rested my head next to his. "Yeah, well, you let me know how that goes."

"Trust me, once I'm done, the whole city will know."

"I bet it will."

Silence settled over the roof again as the Master of the Assassins' Guild and I went back to studying the street below. Somewhere inside the red house opposite us, Marcus was doing gods knew what with Lady Beltham and we would both be staying here until the Storm Caster walked out that door. However late that might be. Because at the end of the day, we always took care of our friends.

25.

"How was the tea?" Haela asked, mischief glittering in her eyes as she looked at the tall Storm Caster who had just descended the stairs.

The three wood elves had been sitting in the almost empty bar area of The Broken Wing when we returned later that night. While Marcus and Shade had gone upstairs to get changed, I had filled in Elaran and the twins on the events of the day before they did the same. Apparently, their protection run had gone much better than our mission.

A furious blush spread across Marcus' cheeks again. "We actually only drank tea. And talked."

"Uh-huh." The teasing twin winked at the embarrassed-looking Storm Caster. "Whatever you say."

"Haela," Haemir chided and swatted his sister on the arm.

Furniture scraped against the floor as both Marcus and Shade pulled out chairs and sat down at the table overflowing with mugs and spilled ale. Elaran crossed his arms.

"I thought I told you to be careful," he said. "In case that wasn't clear, getting into a fight with Captain Hadraeth does not count as being careful."

"What were we supposed to do?" Raising my eyebrows, I shot him an exasperated look. "Just stand there and let him capture us?"

"That's not what I meant," he muttered.

"Then I don't see many other altern–"

Doors banged open. We all shot to our feet right as a horde of men poured through the open doorway. Next to me, Shade magicked a pair of daggers from his sleeves and crouched into an attack position. I was just about to do the same when I noticed the panic flashing over the faces of the rest of my friends. No one else was armed. While I'd been too lazy to climb the stairs, everyone else had gone upstairs to change and drop off their weapons before coming back down.

Shouts rang out as the men barreled forward. I yanked out my hunting knives and shoved them into Elaran's hands. While I ripped out the blades strapped to my thighs and pressed them into Haela's grip, Shade had passed his daggers to Marcus and produced two more knives from his clothes. I shot the stilettos into my palms and slammed them into Haemir's hands just as the first wave of attackers reached us.

A heavy shield sped through the air. I threw myself to the side right before it hit me straight in the face. It whizzed through the room as the owner of the shield whirled it in the other direction. Rolling to my feet, I saw the calamity about to happen.

"Watch out!" I screamed and hurled a throwing knife.

My blade buried itself in the man's arm but the weight of the shield continued forward anyway. A dull thud rang out as it hit Marcus right in the solar plexus. He gasped in a breath before his body convulsed and then collapsed in a heap on the floor.

"Marcus!" I yelled but my scream was drowned out by the chaos around me.

The heavy shield clattered to the floor as the knife in his arm forced the man who had swung it to drop it. While he reached for the blade buried in his forearm, I threw another. He crashed to his knees as the knife penetrated his throat. I only had time to see him toppling over Marcus before flashing steel pulled my attention away.

Ripping out the knife I kept hidden between my breasts, I parried the sword coming for my head and sidestepped the man attached to it. The point of a blade appeared in his throat as Shade rammed his dagger through the back of his neck. I shoved the falling corpse aside and whirled around.

Haela and Haemir were fighting back to back in the middle of the room while Elaran had charged forward alone. Alarms blared through my skull as a man drew back an axe in Elaran's blind spot. I yanked out two throwing knives with my left hand and pitched them both across the room. Elaran's attacker staggered backwards and his swing faltered as the blades buried themselves in his throat. The auburn-haired ranger whirled around just in time to see the axe-wielder topple backwards and collapse on the floor.

A spiked mace flashed in the corner of my eye. My highly developed reflexes were the only thing that saved me as I jerked back just enough for it to miss my chest. Chips of wood flew through the air when the weapon slammed into the wall next to me. I stabbed the knife in my right hand towards the heart of the huge man who had swung it. Bringing down a fist on it, he sent it flying from my grip before it hit.

Returning both hands to the mace, the giant of a man yanked it from the wall. Broken planks clattered to the floor. Throwing panicked glances around the room, I backed away. Shade was fighting three people by the other wall. I sucked in a hiss when he barely managed to evade a sword aimed for his stomach. The mace-carrying man advanced on me. *Shit*.

That simmering rage lay just below the surface. I reached into my soul and pulled at the power that lay waiting there. My eyes started to blacken as I prepared to unleash the storm. Lightning crackled through my body.

If it explodes now, everyone here is going to die.

The darkness snapped back into my soul. *Shit*. Shade ducked out of another coordinated thrust with barely a breath to spare. I snatched two knives from my shoulders and threw them across the room. Steel glinted in the flickering candlelight as they spun over and over again before burying themselves in the chests of two of Shade's unsuspecting attackers.

A deafening roar vibrated off the walls as the man with the spiked mace swung at me. Since I had no weapons to parry with, I ducked under the oncoming death and twisted around while throwing two knives at him. They hit him square in the chest but he kept advancing anyway. Full-blown panic shot up my spine.

"Why won't you die?" I screamed.

Metal spikes sped towards my face. I threw myself backwards and tripped over a chair but managed to stay out of reach.

Splinters sailed through the air as the studded mace buried itself in the wall again. The giant before me braced his hands on the handle to rip it out but this time, it wouldn't budge. He released a howl as the spikes refused to come free. Letting go of the trapped weapon, he whirled on me just as I yanked out another pair of throwing knives.

Sharp thuds rang out as he snatched up a chair to guard against the blades I'd thrown. My knives tumbled through the air when the piece of furniture knocked them off course. I reached up to grab another pair. Dread spidered up my spine. Empty. I'd already used up all my knives.

Continuing to back away, I threw my arms out to find anything to use as a weapon. Ale splashed all over the walls as I threw a half-full mug at the giant's head. He snarled at me and batted away the tankard. Both the chair he had used as a bat and the mug I'd thrown crashed to the floor in a pile of broken wood. Skirting around a table, I snatched up the still burning candle on it and pitched it in his direction.

White wax splattered his face and chest. A howl of raw fury ripped from his throat as he flipped over the table and grabbed its legs.

"Aw, shit," I breathed just before the flat tabletop slammed into my side and sent me flying into the opposite wall.

Pain shot through my whole upper body as I crashed into the wooden planks and slid down the rough surface. Struggling to stay conscious, I blinked repeatedly while scrambling to get up. A boot clamped down on my throat. The weight behind it pushed me back against the floor and prevented air from reaching my lungs.

Shoving out the intense panic exploding in my chest, I dragged my right foot higher. My fingers fumbled. Black spots swam before my eyes from the lack of oxygen. I ripped my boot knife from its fastenings and drew a swift cut through my attacker's heel cord.

The boot disappeared from my throat as he collapsed next to me, screaming in pain. I gasped in a desperate breath. Still coughing and gagging, I forced myself into a sitting position and stabbed my boot knife into the bellowing man's neck. His cries were cut short and replaced by a wet gurgling sound.

I cast a quick glance around the room. Shade and Elaran were fighting off the few remaining attackers by the bar while a terrible ruckus drifted out from the kitchen where I assumed the twins were. On the other side, I just managed to see Marcus struggle to his feet on wobbly legs before something smacked into my cheek.

The dying giant had made one last attempt to take me with him to see the God of Death, but the strike wasn't strong enough to do any real damage. His body, on the other hand... I braced myself for the impact as his corpse toppled onto me.

Too tired to do anything about it, I just let the dead weight pin me to the floor. When his corpse started making it difficult to breathe again, I summoned the last of my strength and shoved him off me. The wooden planks vibrated as his body thudded to the floor.

While I focused on getting air into my lungs, the clamor around me quieted down little by little until only heavy breathing echoed throughout the room. Since no one had come by and shoved a sword through my heart, I assumed we'd won.

"Anyone dead?" I called across the trashed tavern.

"Nope, we're all still alive," Haela replied from somewhere on the other side of the room. "You?"

Slumping back against the floor, I let out a long sigh. "Depends on your definition of dead."

Blood pooled onto the dirty planks next to me, mingling with the red dust and filling the air with a coppery tang. My heart still slammed in my chest. That had been close. Way too close. We had to find out what the hell had happened. Closing my eyes, I listened to my thumping heart. But not right now. Right now, I needed to breathe.

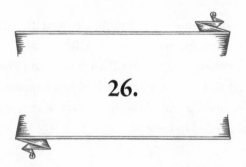

26.

To say that the tavern keeper was angry was the understatement of the decade. He waved a bat around while screaming about compensation and it wasn't until both Shade and I pulled a knife on him that he finally backed off. Fifteen minutes later, all six of us had packed up our things and walked out the door, leaving the grumbling owner of The Broken Wing to sort through his own mess.

"Now what?" Haemir asked as we trudged away from the side gate where we had bought new stabling for our horses.

The makeshift bandage around his upper arm was growing redder by the minute and a couple of nasty bruises were forming along his jaw. In fact, most of us were covered in blood. Ours or someone else's. And I knew for a fact that Haemir and I weren't the only ones who would be sporting wicked bruises tomorrow. Fortunately for us, the streets were mostly empty at this time of night.

"We've gotta find somewhere else to stay." Haela cast a worried glance at her brother. "Somewhere we can dress these wounds."

We all gave her a grim nod in reply. Our first priority had been to get the hell out since we didn't know if whoever had sent those attackers would be coming back to finish the job. But now that our immediate problem had been handled, we had to deal with the next one. We were stranded in a foreign city with no safe house.

"I might have an idea," Marcus said. "Follow me."

Dull pain throbbed all over my upper body after that damn table the mace-wielder had used to smack me into the wall. Nothing appeared to be broken, though. Focusing on the red dirt road ahead, I managed to put one foot in front of the other until Marcus finally came to a halt in front of a moonlit building. I squinted at it. It was very familiar.

"Wait, is this...?" I began.

Marcus climbed the steps two at the time and pounded on the wooden door. "Yeah, it is. And it's our best shot."

Light flickered in the dark windows above. Shade and I exchanged a glance but after one look at the blood seeping through Haemir's bandage and the worried look on his sister's face, I nodded. We had to risk it.

"Have you any idea what time it is?" a miserable-looking man said after cracking open the door and shoving a lit candle through the gap. His eyes widened when the flames danced over our blood-covered clothes. "Oh no, please leave."

He moved to draw the door shut again but Marcus jammed his foot in the doorway before he could.

"Tell Lady Beltham that Marcus needs her help," he said.

The wary servant watched us with narrowed eyes for a moment before finally giving a curt nod and slipping back into the darkened house. I would've paced if walking didn't hurt so much. At last, a blond woman dressed in a nightgown and a dark blue robe pushed open the door.

"Oh by all the gods." Lady Beltham pressed a delicate hand to her mouth. "Marcus, are you alright? What happened?"

"I'm fine." He motioned at the rest of us still standing on the road below. "I'm sorry to involve you in this but we need someplace safe to stay."

"Of course, come inside." She pushed the door open wider and stepped aside before turning back to the servant hovering behind her. "Fetch my doctor."

"Yes, my lady."

While Lady Beltham's servant hurried out the door, she showed us into a spacious sitting room. Large brown couches and armchairs had been arranged in the center of the room while bookshelves made of dark wood covered most of the walls. Side tables in the same material bridged the seating arrangements.

"You can wait here while I get my servants to prepare some rooms for you." She drew back slightly and blinked as if she had just realized something. "Oh, but please don't get blood on the furniture. I will have them draw some baths and find clothes for you to borrow as well. Just... wait here."

"Thank you," Marcus said before she slipped into the hallway again.

I flicked my gaze over our battered group. Haela had looped her arm around her brother's back and was holding him tightly. It didn't appear as though he was about to pass out so I concluded that it was as much for her own sake as it was for his.

"What happened?" Elaran finally said into the dead silence that had settled.

Letting out a long sigh, I shook my head. "I don't know."

"They weren't star elves. They were human."

"Do you think it was the Staghearts?" Marcus broke in.

Shade tipped his head back and raked his fingers through black hair that was matted with blood. "What would they have to gain from it? We're on the same side."

"I don't know." Marcus blew out a breath. "But nothing else makes sense."

Footsteps raced back and forth somewhere upstairs as Lady Beltham no doubt woke her servants and instructed them to help the blood-covered strangers currently waiting in her sitting room. For a moment, that was the only sound piercing the silence. I was so tired that I wanted to lie down right there on the floor, but our hostess had said no blood on the furniture and the fluffy carpets covering the stone floor would definitely be ruined if I did, so I forced myself to keep standing.

"Regardless of who they were, how did they know we were staying there?" I threw out my arms in an exasperated gesture. "No one knew."

"Maybe that Hadraeth dude followed us," Marcus said.

"No one followed us," Shade said. When the muscular Storm Caster opened his mouth to no doubt ask whether he was certain, the black-eyed assassin cut him off. "I'm the Master of the Assassins' Guild. I know when I'm being tailed."

Marcus raised his hands. "Alright. But then how did they find us? And why now?"

We were spared the attempt to figure out questions we didn't know the answer to when Lady Beltham walked into the room again. "Everything is ready upstairs and my doctor will be here soon."

"Thank you." Shade nodded at her before turning back to us. "For now, we'll just lay low. Take a couple of days to rest and heal until we can figure out what we're dealing with."

"Yeah." Elaran motioned at the twins. "Come on, go get that wound stitched up."

He lingered in the doorway while Shade and the twins walked past and disappeared into the hallway. When I made to follow them, his hand shot out and grabbed my arm.

"Hey," the grumpy ranger began and spun me around to face him. "Thanks. For, uhm..." He motioned at all the knives that I had happily given to him and the twins during the fight and that had now been returned to their various holsters across my body. "You know."

A smile tugged at my lips. "Yeah, anytime."

Reaching out, I put a hand over his and gave it a quick squeeze. After a grateful nod in reply, he let go of my arm and stalked out of the room. I followed, a smile still on my lips.

While the rest of us made for the stairs, Marcus approached Lady Beltham. Speaking in a soft voice, he reached out and touched her arm. She gave him a genuine smile in reply. I let out a tired chuckle as I left them behind in the sitting room and climbed the stairs with strained steps. That must've been some cup of tea.

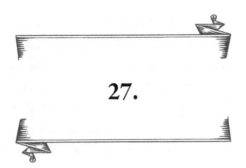

27.

White curtains fluttered in the wind. I paused next to the open door to the balcony and peeked out. Marcus and Lady Beltham were sitting in two wicker chairs surrounded by green plants and white drapes providing shade.

"You could stay here," Lady Beltham said in a quiet voice. "You could just stay here and... be my friend."

"I... uhm..." Marcus stammered.

"Not like that." She released a soft chuckle. "I can have plenty of people for that if I want." Shaking her head, she let out a long exhale. "What I don't have is people who see me."

"What do you mean?"

"Ever since Lord Beltham, my husband, died, everyone either looks at me like this delicate thing to be taken care of or as a prize to win." The blond lady waved a hand at her surroundings. "My husband left me a lot of assets, and that attracts quite a few fortune seekers."

A ray of sunlight fell on Marcus' face, making his golden eyes glitter. "That must be awful."

"I've learned to navigate it." Her lips curved into a wicked smile. "I use them for my own ends too." The expression on her face softened. "But no one has looked at me the way you do in a long time. Not as someone who sees all the wealth behind me, but who sees me for who I really am. So, once you've finished whatever mission you're on, know that you are welcome to stay."

Furniture creaked as Marcus shifted in his chair. I didn't usually have much respect for other people's private conversations but I found myself feeling bad for eavesdropping on this particular one. Darting past the doorway, I left the lady and the Storm Caster alone and continued towards my destination.

Winds carried the smell of dry sand and warm stones to me when I climbed through the ceiling hatch and onto the roof outside. It had been a few days since we'd arrived at Lady Beltham's house, bloody and beaten, and we'd used the time to rest and heal. Everyone was on the mend but we were no closer to figuring out who was targeting us.

Me being, well, me, I didn't do well when confined to the insides of a house, so I had soon found the path to the roof. It was much easier to breathe here. I dropped down on the edge and drew my legs up underneath me. Sun warmed my face.

On the street below, people milled about as if nothing had happened. As if the star elves' white mist didn't keep coming every night and as if large portions of the population didn't end up completing the ritual every day. Though, I suppose, these particular citizens were spared the awful hallucinations since they live too far from the city walls.

"Can I join?"

Turning around, I found a head of dark brown hair sticking up through the hatch. Marcus shot me a wide smile. When I let out a chuckle and nodded, he climbed through and strode over to me. A soft thud sounded as he plopped down next to me on the edge of the roof.

"Lady Beltham asked me to stay," he said without preamble.

I know, was about to roll off my tongue but I caught myself just in time. Instead, I raised my eyebrows and turned to him. "Oh. What did you say?"

"I said no." Leaning back on his hands, he let out a long sigh. "It has nothing to do with this situation with the star elves and she's a very nice woman and this is a very nice house where I would live a very nice life. But it's just..." He trailed off.

"It's just not the kind of life you want," I finished.

He turned to me, surprise and relief mingling in his kind eyes. "Exactly."

With a knowing smile on my lips, I nodded before shifting my gaze back to the street below. In a matter of seconds, people had gone from strolling along the road to pointing and hurrying towards the far mouth of the street. *Oh, not again.* This had been happening several times while I'd been up here and it meant one thing. The star elves were organizing another ritual.

"What kind of life do you want?" Marcus asked, interrupting my internal lament over the fact that we were still forced to lay low and couldn't interfere with the star elves' plans.

"One where I'm free to live life any way I choose."

His face turned pensive as he leaned forward again and braced his hands on the edge of the roof. "What would that look like?"

As soon as I opened my mouth to reply, I realized that I didn't have a clear cut view of what that would look like. All I knew was that *I* wanted to be the one who decided that in the end.

"I don't know yet," I answered honestly. "What about you?"

A pair of seagulls raced by and squawked into the silence while Marcus considered the question. I pushed back a few strands of hair that had blown loose from my braid.

"I want a simple life," he said at last. "I want to hike and fish and laugh with my friends over dinner." The ghost of a smile drifted over his lips as he glanced at me from the corner of his eye. "And a strong woman by my side who could knock some sense into me when needed."

Returning the smile, I gave his hand a short squeeze. "That sounds like a wonderful life."

"Yeah."

The street below had grown empty now that everyone had reached whatever square the star elves had picked for their location this time. Warm winds stirred up clouds of red dust. I watched them swirl for a moment before turning back to the muscled Storm Caster next to me.

"How do you know that you can control your powers?" I asked.

He blinked at the sudden change in topic but recovered quickly. Scratching his jaw, he thought for a second. "It's about trust, I suppose."

"Trust?"

"Yeah. For me, it's not about controlling my powers. It's about trusting them."

Skepticism oozed from my face as I narrowed my eyes at him. "Yeah, well, I'm not exactly a trusting person. And I hate things I can't control."

A laugh rumbled in his chest. "I've noticed."

I swatted his chest with the back of my hand but then winced when I remembered the shield that had struck him there only a few days ago. He shrugged it off with a grin, though.

"But then trust might not be what works for you," he continued. "Everyone handles their powers differently so you just have to find what works for you. But either way, you have to stop thinking about your powers as something external. It's not something separate from you. It is you. You are your powers."

"So that means all the shit my powers have caused is on me and me alone. Like, almost dropping a building on top of my friends." I rolled my eyes. "Brilliant. That makes me feel so much better."

"That's not what I meant."

"I know."

Marcus climbed to his feet with an agility that was surprising for someone of his size. "The doctor should be back now. I have to go see him again for a final checkup."

"Alright." I nodded. "I'll see you later."

For a moment, he just remained standing there. Then, he bent down and placed a quick kiss on my forehead. "Just trust yourself and find what works for you."

Before I could respond, to either the statement or the surprising gesture, he had turned around and made for the hatch. I shook my head. Just trust myself? Years ago, when King Edward had told me he trusted me, I had been surprised because I didn't even know if *I* trusted me. That still held true. After all, I was one hell of a scheming bitch. A grin spread across my mouth. But then again, if that meant my powers had adopted that particular characteristic as well, then we might be able to come to some kind of understanding.

A mass of people shuffled onto the street from the far end. Bracing my palms on the warm stone, I leaned forward to study them. They looked the same as all the others who returned from one of the star elves' rituals. Empty. They might be smiling but their eyes were blank, devoid of all emotion. The spark that was normally present in the eye of the living shone with its absence. It was like looking at a house where all the candles were lit but there was no one home.

Raking my fingers through my hair, I let out a long sigh. We had to stop this. Though we still hadn't figured out who had attacked us, we needed to get back in the game. The city was slipping further into Queen Nimlithil's hands with every passing day and if we didn't do something soon, it would be lost. I jumped to my feet.

These past few days, I'd been plotting ways to stop people from taking part in the rituals and there was one in particular I was in the mood to try. It was an easy one too. Poison. I yanked open the hatch and started climbing back inside. Because what could possibly go wrong with poison?

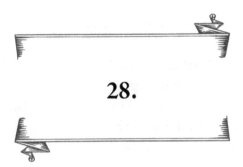

28.

"Something's wrong."

I cast a quick glance at Elaran. "Yeah, I can feel it too."

"What is?" Marcus furrowed his brows and motioned between the Master Assassin standing in the middle of the street and the building with the faded apothecary sign further down. "This is where they sent us, right? So what's wrong?"

"Don't know yet." Shaking my head, I took a step out of the shadows. "But we have to warn him."

My foot had barely made it onto the moonlit road before I screeched to a halt again. Shade had whirled around and darted back towards us. I stifled a chuckle. Of course the bloody Master of the Assassins' Guild could feel when something was off as well.

Slipping onto the darkened back porch, Shade moved grave eyes between us. "Something's wrong."

While turning to Marcus, I tipped my palm towards the assassin as if to say, *I told you so.*

"Yeah alright, something's wrong," the tall Storm Caster huffed. "But what is it that's wrong?"

"When I reached out to my spy network, they said this was the place to buy poison but I don't know..." Shade shook his head. "Something just feels off."

"Then let's go scout it out." Elaran jerked his chin towards the rooftops.

After nods of agreement, the four of us started climbing up the side of the nearest building.

At first, Shade had planned to go alone but Elaran and I had refused to let him leave without backup. Thankfully, the assassin hadn't complained when the two of us and Marcus had tagged along.

Haela had forced her brother to stay behind so that his arm could heal better and had appointed herself his guardian in case trouble somehow found its way to Lady Beltham's house. The exasperated smile on Haemir's face as his other half pushed him into a poofy armchair still lingered on my mind. The sibling love between them was one for the history books.

"I'll take the north side of the bottom floor," Shade said as we skulked across the roof. "Storm, you take the south side. And you two, take the second floor."

"Got it."

We split up. Dark clouds blew across the moon, making the illuminated areas few and far between. But it mattered little to me. The darkness was my home.

I took off at a run and jumped through the air when the building ended. Wind whipped through my clothes. A soft thud sounded as I landed on the other roof and continued my sprint towards the other side of the alleged apothecary's store.

Red dust trickled down the side of the building as I climbed the wall towards the ground again. No candles flickered in the windows as I passed. I whipped my head in every direction to make sure there were no guards outside before dropping the final bit onto the windowsill. Craning my neck, I peered through the shutters.

Dark. And no movement as far as I could see. I stuck a lockpick through the gap and lifted off the latch before gently pulling it open.

The room inside was full of vials and glass beakers but lay otherwise deserted. I snuck forward. Keeping my breathing shallow, I drew up next to the doorway and peered out. Another empty hallway met me. Just to be sure, I waited another few seconds before slinking into the darkness beyond.

Only more deserted rooms awaited me as I passed through the long hall. Maybe we'd been wrong? Perhaps this really was just a sketchy apothecary's store.

A closed door appeared before me at the end of the corridor. I checked for shadows under the door, but since the whole building was dark, it was impossible to tell if there were any. After sending a quick prayer to Nemanan, I pushed down the handle.

The God of Thieves appeared to have heard me because it moved soundlessly. I drew open the door a tiny crack.

A horde of men with raised swords waited in the darkness. My heart leaped into my throat and I narrowly prevented myself from gasping. *Shit.* Okay, this was most definitely an ambush.

While my heart continued slamming into my ribs, I used every smidgen of stealth in my body to push the door shut again without anyone noticing. The handle barely produced a sound as I edged it upwards again. Sending heartfelt thanks to Nemanan, I turned and started back down the corridor.

The floorboards groaned further down. I jerked my head up. A dark shape had stepped into view and now stood staring at me from across the empty hallway. His hand went for the sword at his hip at the same time as he opened his mouth.

Really, Cadentia? While silently cursing the Goddess of Luck, I snatched a throwing knife from my shoulder and hurled it at him.

Before the blade had even struck home, I was darting across the floor. If I didn't make it on time, I was screwed. My throwing knife hit him square in the throat with a sharp thud and cut off his vocal cords before he could raise the alarm. Gurgles spluttered from his mouth.

His knees buckled. I practically threw myself the last couple of strides towards his falling body. If he crashed down on the floor with all his weapons, the whole house would hear it. My heart thumped in my chest.

Just before he toppled forward, I managed to shove my arms under his armpits. His torso slammed into mine. I staggered backwards a step under his dying weight but managed to stay on my feet. Warm blood ran down from his throat and onto my chest. Trying not to huff too loudly, I pulled him with me into the room full of glass vials and beakers.

Once I was through the doorway, I deposited his body next to the wall and sucked in a quiet breath. After yanking my throwing knife from his throat, I wiped it on his pants and stuck it back in its sheath. Without another glance at the dead ambusher, I braced my palms on the window frame and then climbed back into the night.

Shade was waiting for me atop the roof of the shop, so I climbed to my feet and approached him. Silver glittered in his black eyes as the clouds blew clear and bathed us in moonlight.

He opened his mouth but then blinked and snapped it shut again.

Stalking towards me, he grabbed my chin and tilted it up and then to the sides while his gaze flicked over my body.

"You're covered in blood," he stated.

I rolled my eyes and slapped his hand away. "Yes, I'm aware. It's not mine."

"What happened?"

He had released my chin but hadn't stepped back so I was forced to crane my neck to meet his eyes. Spreading my arms, I shot him a nonchalant grin.

"Lady Luck was being a bitch." The smile faded from my lips. "It's most definitely an ambush."

"Yeah, I saw."

Movement at the edge of the roof caught my eye. I turned my head just in time to see Elaran and Marcus climb over the red stones. Shade took a step back as they approached.

"The second floor is clear," Elaran announced.

The assassin and I exchanged a glance. I lifted my shoulders in a light shrug. "We found about fifty men with swords on our floor."

Confusion crept into Marcus' eyes while Elaran grumbled a series of curses.

"What does this mean?" the Storm Caster asked. "First the tavern, and now this."

Only the wind whistling through the buildings filled the silence as none of us had a satisfactory answer to his question. I shifted my weight.

"The only people who knew both things were your spy network," I said. "You think they sold you out?"

Shade crossed his arms. "Sold me out for what? And to who? It doesn't make any sense."

"I agree," Elaran chimed in. "There's no logic in it. We might think they're the only ones who knew but we can't be sure of that." He drew his eyebrows down. "We're missing something."

"Yeah, but right now, all the evidence points to it being my spy network so I won't be using them again until we know for certain that it's not them." The assassin blew out an annoyed breath. "But Elaran is right. We're missing something important. I just don't know what."

Another thick cloud blew across the moon and left our group in murky shadow. I was about to cross my arms but then remembered that I had blood all over my chest so I let them fall down by my sides again.

"What do we do now?" I asked.

"Your plan was solid," Shade said. "Poisoning people who completed the ritual just enough to make them look sick would've help deter others from doing it, but if shit like this," he motioned at the building under us and the ambushers hiding inside, "is going to keep happening, we can't afford to waste time on small things anymore. We need to go straight to the source."

"The mist," I summarized as realization dawned.

"Yeah, we need to get rid of the mist."

Marcus raised his eyebrows. "How are we going to do that?"

The Master Assassin turned to Elaran while a lopsided smile tugged at his lips. "We're going to go see Illeasia again."

Happiness bloomed in Elaran's yellow eyes.

However, when he noticed the smiles on our faces, he drew his eyebrows down again and muttered something under his breath. I swore I could see some color creeping into his cheeks.

While I was busy wiping the grin off my face, Shade clapped Elaran on the shoulder and then jerked his chin. We took off across the rooftops. I stole a glance at the wood elf next to me. Happiness really did suit him.

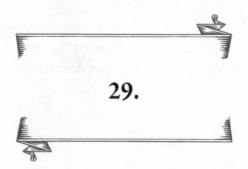

29.

We circled the camp like vultures. The same trick wouldn't work a second time so we had to find another way to Princess Illeasia's tent. I glanced up at the dark blue sky covered in glittering stars. That silver orb glowing bright in the night sky complicated things a bit, though.

Flapping wings and cooing sounds came from behind the white tent I was currently skirting. I drew back and blinked at the pale tarp. Casting a quick glance around me, I made sure no one was about to accidentally stumble into me before I dropped to the sand and lifted the tent wall. White doves ruffled their feathers inside wooden cages in an otherwise empty room.

"Well hello, magic messenger doves that helped me escape the City of Glass," I whispered.

The noise inside the cages increased at the sound of my voice. I dropped the fabric again and shot to my feet as they cooed louder and slapped their wings against the bars.

"Here I was just trying to say thank you and you try to get me caught," I muttered as I darted away. "Damn feather flappers."

Sand sprayed into the air as I screeched to a halt. I glanced back over my shoulder. Magic messenger birds. Of course. A soft chuckle puffed from my lips as I snuck back towards the white tent. Why hadn't I thought of that before?

Once again dropping to the ground by the tent wall, I lifted the smooth fabric and rolled inside. The noise from the birds increased again. I put a finger to my lips and shushed them even though I had no idea if birds could actually be shushed. They completely ignored the command so that was probably a no.

Whipping my head around, I scanned the area. In the corner was a table overlaid with stacks of scrolls and neatly arranged pens. While praying to any god who would listen that the noise from the birds didn't attract attention, I snatched up an empty piece of paper and scrawled a hurried note on it.

Dread filled my chest as I strode back to one of the cages, the note in hand. How was I supposed to get one bird out of there without all of them racing towards freedom? Heaving a deep sigh, I just yanked open the small door and hoped for the best.

No cloud of white feathers erupted around me. Instead, a single dove hopped out and landed on my hand. Huh. I slammed the door shut again before all my luck for the day ran out. The bird on my wrist watched me with curious eyes.

"Don't look at me like that," I huffed. "Lady Luck and I have a complicated relationship."

After unscrewing the tube on the dove's back, I pushed in the rolled-up paper. Footsteps sounded outside. Quickly closing the lid again, I darted towards the back of the tent. The dove cooed in surprise when I put my hands around its body before dropping onto the red sand and rolling under the tent wall. Shooting to my feet on the other side, I quickly whispered instructions to the bird and then released it. White wings flapped into the dark night sky while I sprinted away from camp.

The rest of my companions were already waiting at our rendezvous spot and none of them looked particularly happy so I couldn't stop the satisfied grin on my face as I strolled over to them.

"What are you smirking about?" Elaran grumbled.

"I have just solved all our problems." I tipped my head from side to side. "Well, maybe not *all* our problems. But *this* particular problem."

Shade tilted his head to the right. "Care to enlighten us?"

"I told Illeasia to meet us at the main gate."

"And how exactly did you accomplish that?"

"I sent a magic bird of course." I gave the assassin a short shake of my head as if that should have been obvious.

Marcus flicked confused eyes between the three of us. "Am I missing something here?"

"I'll fill you in," I said before shifting my gaze back to the exasperated-looking elf and assassin. Raising my eyebrows, I spun my hand in the air a couple of times. "Let's go then."

Elaran shook his head while amusement tugged at the corner of Shade's lips, but both of them turned around and jogged back towards the main gate. While Marcus and I trotted after them, I filled him in on the star elves' magical breed of doves.

We didn't have to wait more than a few minutes before a figure in white and silver glided through the darkness. Elaran's eyes lit up as moonlight fell over Princess Illeasia's beautiful features. He strode towards her.

The rest of us shrank back in the shadows while the princess and the ranger embraced each other. A smile drifted over my lips. If someone had told me when I first met Elaran that he would one day be looking at someone with this much love, hope, and vulnerability in his eyes, I would've called them crazy. But the range of emotions playing over his face when he and Illeasia finally released each other from a long kiss and stepped back was one of the most genuine things I had ever seen. A warm sparkling feeling bubbled through my chest.

"Princess," Shade said and nodded at the silver-haired elf.

"General," she replied before shifting her eyes to me. "Do I even want to know how you managed to get a hold of one of our doves?"

I simply grinned back at her.

Letting out a soft laugh, she shook her head. "As happy as I am to see you," she smiled at Elaran, "I don't have long before people will notice that I'm missing."

"I understand," Shade said. "We need your help. The hallucinogenic mist that your mother is sending over the walls every night, we have to stop it."

"Of course." Illeasia scrunched up her eyebrows. "But how?"

Reaching out, Elaran placed a hand on her arm and gave her tired smile. "We have to blow her whole stash."

Princess Illeasia blinked. "Oh. Isn't that a bit drastic?"

"It's the only way to make sure that she can't continue using it as a weapon. We just need to know where she keeps it."

Silence fell over the sands as the princess considered. I leaned back against the city wall and braced a foot on the rough stones behind me. Elaran was just about to open his mouth again when Illeasia finally nodded.

"Okay." A hint of steel crept into her pale violet eyes. "But promise me, *promise* me, that no one gets hurt."

Shade met her gaze head on. "You have my word."

"No one gets hurt," Elaran repeated. "We only want to get rid of the mist."

Once she had seen me and Marcus nod in acknowledgement as well, she let out a long sigh. "The components they use to create the swelling mist are kept in a tent outside camp." She let out a humorless laugh. "My mother doesn't want any of us to get caught in it if there's an accident." Lifting a graceful hand, she pointed towards the far side of the white tents. "At the back of camp, there are lots of supply wagons, carts, and crates. The long white tent at the far end is where you will find it."

"Thank you," the Master Assassin said.

Elaran ran soft fingers down her arm. "I promise, no–"

"Princess Illeasia?" a voice called.

My foot hit the ground with a thud as I straightened from the wall. *Oh shit*. Elaran and I exchanged a panicked glance but before we could do anything about it, Captain Hadraeth strode out of the darkness.

His hand went straight for the pommel of his sword when he saw us. Stopping a short distance away, he cast wary looks between the five of us while his fingers still twitched by his weapon.

"What's going on?" he demanded.

"Nothing," Princess Illeasia said in a hurried voice.

Man, I really needed to teach these people how to lie properly. This was embarrassing.

"They were just leaving," she continued.

Hadraeth narrowed his eyes. "Why were they even here in the first place?" He shifted his gaze to me. "And I thought you said that Elaran wasn't here."

Lifting my shoulders in a light shrug, I shot him a sheepish grin. "Well, when I said *here*, I meant it as in *here on the street*. Not as in *here in the city*."

Displeasure flashed in his dark eyes but before he could say anything else, Illeasia tore herself from Elaran and hurried over to the Captain of the Guard. When she stopped before Hadraeth and placed a hand on his arm, Elaran clenched his jaw hard enough to make the muscles in it shift. I wanted to facepalm. Yep. These people definitely needed a lesson in how to be sneaky.

"Please don't say anything to my mother," the princess said. "It was nothing. They just wanted to talk."

"Princess Illeasia..." he began, a pained expression on his face.

"Please." She looked up at him with a pleading expression on her beautiful face. "You know that I will be in trouble if you tell her."

Captain Hadraeth massaged his forehead while blowing out a deep sigh. "Fine, I won't say anything." When he flicked his gaze to us, his eyes hardened. "But, you four, get out of my sight before I change my mind."

For a moment, I thought Shade and Elaran were going to draw their swords, but when Illeasia sent an apologetic smile in our direction, they backed down. Without another word, the Master Assassin whirled around and set course for the gate. The grumpy archer cast a longing gaze at the princess before following him. Marcus and I weren't far behind.

"Alright, this is what's going to happen now," Shade said in a voice filled with tightly controlled anger while we jogged along the dirt road inside the walls. "All of us are going to go back to Lady Beltham's house. We're going to fill in the twins and then get some sleep. We'll blow the mist tomorrow night so we'll have the day to get supplies and finalize our plans."

"You're giving orders again," Elaran muttered.

"We almost walked into an ambush tonight," the assassin said by way of reply. "That doesn't happen again. We still have a target on our backs from some unknown party and we don't know if Hadraeth will go back on his word." Eyes of steel met each of our gazes. "No one goes out alone. No one. Is that clear?"

"Clear," Marcus replied.

Elaran shook his head in exasperation but then gave the self-proclaimed dictator a nod in affirmation. When I didn't acknowledge his presumptuous commands right away, the Master Assassin leveled hard eyes on me until I smacked my lips in annoyance and gave him a nod as well.

It had just been to get him off my back because I wasn't actually planning on following his orders. After all, doing as I was told wasn't exactly my specialty. He really should've learned that by now. As we turned the corner and jogged onto another silent street, I let my mind sort through my plans. A grin stole onto my lips. Who had time to follow orders when there were plots and schemes to be executed?

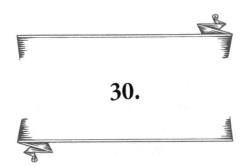

30.

Wings flapped in alarm as I sprinted across the rooftops. The wooden cage bounced across my back in its makeshift straps while the magical doves inside made their discomfort known.

"Oh would you calm down? We're almost there," I muttered at the distressed birds I had stolen from the star elves' camp some half hour ago.

As soon as we had gotten back to Lady Beltham's house, I'd told the others I was heading to bed and then returned to my room. The door had barely clicked shut behind me before I'd climbed out the window and run off to create some more mischief. Those birds were an incredibly fast way of communicating and we would need them in the war to come. So I did what I always do. I stole some of them.

Tiles vibrated under my feet as I landed on the roof of the stable. The guards by the side gate didn't even look back as I shimmied down the side of the building behind them. I approached the front door.

"At least you're punctual," a voice observed.

Twisting my head, I found a lanky man with matted brown hair stepping out of the stable to my right. He stopped outside the doorway before nodding back the way he had come.

"In here," he said.

While unslinging the bird cage from my back, I followed the stable master into the building.

My first stop after leaving Lady Beltham's house had been here. I needed somewhere to keep the doves until we left and I didn't want to bring them to the lady's house, not only because I didn't want to drag her further into trouble but also because I didn't want a certain Master Assassin to know what I had done just yet. And because keeping both our horses and the doves in the same place made sense.

The stable master had laughed quite heartily at my offer and told me that he looked after horses, not birds. That is, until I showed him the bag of pearls I had brought.

"You can put them here," he said and motioned at a table in the back.

Wood scraped against wood as I pushed the cage onto the flat surface. Turning to him, I pulled out the pouch and poured half of the pearls into his hand.

"Half now, and half when you give them back to me, safe and sound," I said, tying off the bag again. Flicking my gaze up, I leveled hard eyes on him. "If you don't treat them well, and if any of them are missing when I return," I shot a stiletto blade into my hand, "losing out on those other pearls will be the least of your worries."

He raised his hands in an appeasing gesture. "Alright, alright, calm down there. If I didn't like animals, I wouldn't be running a stable. Your birds will be fine."

"Good." I retracted the blade again and gave him a nod. "A pleasure doing business."

Hay crunched under my boots as I strode back through the stables. While the brown-haired man rummaged through his supplies at the back of the building, I stopped in front of a stall. A gray mare snorted and poked her head out.

"Hello, Silver," I said.

Silver pushed her muzzle into my waiting palm and let me stroke her soft gray fur. She looked well fed and content so I felt certain that the stable master was taking good care of her and the rest of our horses. The birds would be well cared for too.

"I'll see you soon," I promised and gave Silver a final pat on the neck before striding out the building again.

Warm night winds caressed my face as I climbed back onto the roof and took off towards Lady Beltham's house. Above me, a blanket of stars glittered in the dark blue heavens. I thought about the people sleeping soundly in the quiet houses beneath my feet. How many of them had completed the ritual? How many of them were planning to? Hopefully, blowing up the rest of the mist tomorrow night would be enough to stop this. Otherwise, the city was already doomed.

Pushing off with all my strength, I flew across the last gap between the buildings and rolled to my feet on top of Lady Beltham's roof. Excitement thrummed through my body. Man, I really loved running across rooftops.

A dark figure stepped out of the shadows.

"Didn't I tell you that no one goes out alone?" Shade said in a voice as calm and deadly as poison.

"Yeah, you did." I made as if to skirt around him.

The ringing of steel filled the night as the assassin whipped out his right-hand blade and used it to block my path. "Don't you walk away from me. We have a target on our backs! Do you get that? You could've been killed, sneaking out of here and doing Ghabhalnaz knows what."

"I had stuff to do." Flicking a hand at the blade blocking my way, I took a step forward. "Now get out of my way."

His sword stayed in place.

I leveled an exasperated glare at him and raised my eyebrows. "Really?"

When he still didn't remove his pointy roadblock, I yanked out my hunting knives and slammed them towards his blade. Quick as a viper, he snatched it away and brought it around in an arc while drawing his other sword. Ducking under the swing, I jabbed a knife towards his chest.

Metal dinged as his sword absorbed the impact and redirected the thrust. I danced back before he could press the advantage. He darted forward. Feigning a strike to the right, he shot through the air and brought his blade down on my other side. Throwing up a knife just in time, I managed to evade it and slink away again.

A boot connected with the back of my knee. I crashed to the ground. Rolling with the motion, I twisted around and swiped at his ankles. The assassin jumped back just in time. A challenging smirk spread across his face as he spun his swords in his hands and crouched down before darting towards me again. Zigzagging across the roof, he slammed his blades into mine while backing me further towards the chimney in the middle. My heart thumped in my chest but I succeeded in parrying his thrusts by scant margins.

Shade leaped into the air. *Shit.* I threw up my knives right before his blades crashed into them. Stone greeted me as I dropped to a knee from the sheer force of the blow. Steel ground against steel as the Master Assassin put his full weight behind it and pressed his swords down on my intersecting knives. My arms shook above my head. I tried to use my leg muscles to push myself out of the kneeling position but the assassin's rather impressive force kept me pinned.

Irritation flared through my body. I was *not* going to lose to that arrogant bastard. Reaching inside, I searched for that burning rage deep inside my soul. Flames flickered to life. *What if I blow him off the roof?* I shook my head. Trust yourself. That was what Marcus had said. Letting out a long sigh, I gave in to the darkness.

Black clouds shot around me. The swords above me stopped their advance as Shade stumbled back slightly and blinked at the dark haze now obscuring his vision. *Ha! Take that.* I shot to my feet. He couldn't beat me if he couldn't see me.

That wicked part inside me wanted to truly enjoy seeing him realize that I had won so I started circling him with slow steps. Shade tipped his head to the side as if he was listening for something. He shot towards me.

I let out a startled yelp and stumbled backwards as the assassin came straight for me. Whipping up my knives, I shoved away his swords but the move had taken me by surprise so in my startled backpedaling, I tripped on a loose tile and slammed back first into the chimney behind me. Shade put a hand below my throat and pushed me further into the red stones while yanking up his sword. I snatched up my own blade right as he leaned forward and used the hand on my collarbone to guide the point home.

My hunting knife pressed into his throat while the tip of his sword rested against the base of my throat. I glared at him.

Of course the bloody Master of the Assassins' Guild knew how to fight even without his vision. Letting out an annoyed huff, I pulled the darkness back.

"I told you not to go out alone," he repeated once the black clouds around us were gone. Still keeping the sword to my throat, he shot me a challenging stare. "And I seem to remember telling you that I don't tolerate people going rogue on me and disobeying my orders."

Answering his challenge with a wicked grin, I pushed the knife higher up under his chin. "And I seem to remember telling you that I don't take orders from you."

Even with my blade tilting up his head and exposing his throat, he managed a superior smirk. His black eyes glittered as he glanced down at me. "Whatever you need to tell yourself."

I snorted. "Bastard."

Steel glinted in the moonlight as Shade removed the sword from my throat and stepped back. Amusement played over his handsome face. Shaking my head, I stuck my hunting knives back in their holsters and slid down the side of the chimney. In the distance, thick white mist rolled over the city walls. Just like it did every night.

The Master Assassin returned his blades to his back before sitting down next to me. "It's been a while since we did that."

"Yep."

"It was fun."

Casting him a sidelong glance, I let out a chuckle. "Yeah, it was." My knives made scraping sounds against the stone as I adjusted my position and went back to staring at the empty roof in front of us. "How did you learn to fight in the dark?"

"My old master locked me in a pitch-black room and sent his best assassins in there to beat me up until I learned how to fight back without my vision."

I snorted. "Right." When he didn't laugh as well, I whipped my head towards him. "Wait, really?"

He nodded.

Letting out a low whistle, I raised my eyebrows. "Wow. That's kinda awful."

"Yeah." A smirk tugged at his lips. "But without that training, I wouldn't have won our fight just now."

I gave his arm a shove. "You didn't win. It was a tie."

"Uh-huh. Keep telling yourself that."

When he straightened from my shove, he leaned further in and only stopped once his upper arm was brushing against mine. Resting my head against the chimney, I tried to ignore the sparks shooting across my skin at the near touch.

For a while, we just sat there on the roof and watched the night in silence. The dark sky sprinkled with silver dust seemed endless above us as I watched it stretch all the way to the hulking city walls in the distance. Moonlight bathed the red city in pale light. Still resting the back of my head against the stones, I let out a deep sigh.

"Are you ever afraid?"

As soon as the words had left my mouth, I wanted to kick myself. Had I really just asked the Master of the Assassins' Guild if he was afraid? Idiot. Of course he was never afraid. A soft wind blew across the roof while I braced myself for his laughter. But Shade only turned to me with curious eyes.

"Why do you ask?"

I shook my head. "Never mind." When his intense black eyes just continued staring at me, I raked a hand through my hair. "I don't know, it's just..." I turned to face him head on. "Do you ever think that all this power makes us evil?"

Shade tilted his head to the right while continuing to watch me with that strange look in his eyes. "Power isn't good or evil. It just is. It's what we do with it that defines who we are."

Picking up a few pebbles that had crumbled from the chimney, I pitched them across the roof. They clattered against the stone before rolling over the edge and falling down towards the street.

"Alright, point taken. But I can summon black clouds and lightning and apparently also drop a building on people if I'm pissed enough. And you're both the Master of the Assassins' Guild and the General of Pernula. You can have anyone killed with a wave of your hand. That's a lot of power." I blew out another deep sigh. "Aren't you ever afraid you'll make the wrong decision?"

"No," Shade said with so much certainty that I turned towards him in surprise. His steady gaze was locked on me. "The only bad decisions are the ones you don't make."

Silence settled over the roof as his words sank in. There was a lot of truth to them. Making a decision, even if it turned out to be the wrong one, was always better than not making one at all. As I had learned firsthand many years ago, hesitation only got people killed.

I furrowed my brows at the assassin next to me. "How the hell did you get both brains and good looks?"

Satisfaction swirled in his eyes while his lips drew into a smirk. "Did you just call me handsome?"

"Shut up." I gave his arm another shove. "I said nothing of the sort."

His rippling laughter echoed across the rooftop. Damn assassin.

After watching the glittering stars for another few minutes, we exchanged a glance and climbed to our feet. White mist continued rolling over the city walls in the distance. I had enjoyed our fight and our talk afterwards more than I wanted to admit but unfortunately, we did need sleep. Tomorrow, we had another full day and night ahead. After all, we had shit to blow up. A wicked grin tugged at my lips. Again.

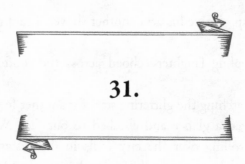

31.

"We'll create the distraction."

Haemir sent his sister an impatient glower. "I've already told you, I'm fine. There's no need to keep me away from the thick of it."

"I'm not keeping you away from anything," Haela protested. "I just really like creating distractions."

"You also like blowing stuff up."

"Oh shush." She swung an arm over her brother's shoulders and fired off a beaming grin in our direction. "We'll take care of the distraction."

Scattered chuckles echoed from the rest of our group while Haemir grumbled under his breath.

Night had fallen across the red sands and the supply area was mostly empty but we didn't want to take any chances so we had opted for a distraction on the other side of camp as well. Dark clouds blew across the heavens at high speed. Tilting my head up, I watched them whirl past. I had a feeling that a storm was brewing just beyond the horizon so we'd have to act fast.

"Good," Elaran said and tilted his head up to watch the sky as well. "But hurry. We need to light the fire before the rain comes."

"Aye aye, captain." Haela raised her hand in a mock salute before pulling her brother with her towards the other side of camp. "Distraction is my middle name!"

Another bout of laughter drifted through the air as we watched them trot away. After shaking our heads at their retreating backs, the remaining four of us started in the opposite direction.

Only a few guards patrolled the supply area when we arrived and their white and silver armor made them easy to see against the dark background. We stopped just out of range to study their patterns of movement. Once Elaran was satisfied, he turned to me and Shade while drawing his eyebrows down.

"Don't kill anyone."

"Why are you looking at us?" I put a hand to my chest in mock affront. "As if we would ever do something so gruesome?"

Exchanging a glance, the Master Assassin and I both let out a snort. Elaran crossed his arms and muttered something about underworlders while Marcus released a soft chuckle. After one final shake of his head, the grumpy elf jerked his chin.

"Let's go."

Since I was the only vertically challenged person in our quartet, I had been deemed bait. While the others, who could actually reach around a star elf's neck without having to stand on a crate, were in charge of knocking them out, I was in charge of making sure they weren't looking at my taller companions.

I blew a sharp whistle. The star elf in front of me whipped his head towards the sound right as Marcus snuck up behind him and looped a muscled arm around his neck. The guard swatted at the thick limb cutting off his oxygen before passing out. The tall Storm Caster and I repeated the procedure on another unfortunate soul while the assassin and the ranger held their own on the other side of the supply stash.

"All clear?" Shade asked.

Letting out a huff, I pulled the unconscious star elf the last bit and laid him next to the others behind a stack of crates before nodding. "Yeah."

"Then let's go blow it up."

All four of us darted towards the long white tent at the far end. The shiny fabric snapped in the strong winds and I could smell the rain in the air. We had to hurry.

Rows upon rows of barrels and smaller containers met us when we threw open the tent flap and stepped inside. I stared at the labels specifying things I'd never heard of. This was what they used to create the mist.

"Take a corner each," Shade said.

Yanking out the bag of black powder I was carrying, I wove my way through the maze of chemicals. Once I reached the corner, I pulled open the stopper and began my trek back while pouring gunpowder in a long line across the ground. My three friends met me in the middle where we poured a large stack on top of a barrel.

"Get outside," Elaran said. "We have to do this before the guards wake up and–"

Fabric rustled as the tent flap was thrown open. I whipped around to find a star elf in full armor staring at us.

"I knew it!" Captain Hadraeth drew his sword. "As soon as the alarm sounded on the other side of camp, I knew you were using it to sneak in on the other side." He flicked his gaze around the tent. Once his eyes fell on the black powder, they widened slightly in surprise. Gripping his sword tighter, he raised it in our direction. "I can't let you do this."

Next to me, Elaran and Marcus drew their swords as well. While I pulled the hunting knives from my back, I realized that Shade had gone missing.

"You have a lot of honor and integrity," Elaran said. "You know using this mist is wrong."

The Captain of the Guard shifted his gaze between the three armed intruders advancing on him, but stood his ground. "It doesn't matter what I think. I have my orders."

I had to bite my tongue to keep from saying, *sounds like someone else I know.* But Elaran appeared blissfully ignorant of the similarities as he pointed his blade at the star elf captain.

"Don't make us hurt you."

Holding the blade steady, Hadraeth raised his chin with a defiant look on his face. "Come try it."

A black sleeve shot around his throat from behind and yanked back. The sword clattered to the ground next to him as the captain tried desperately to break Shade's grip on his windpipe. After a few seconds, he went limp.

The Master Assassin nodded at Marcus. "Help me lift him over to the others. We need to get this done. Right now."

While the two of them hauled Hadraeth's unconscious body to the other side of the area and laid him next to the rest of his guards, I threw open the tent flap and fastened it to the wall. Strong winds ripped it loose several times but I finally managed to get it to stick. Thick dark clouds blew across the sky as I sprinted back to where my friends had gathered.

"Are you sure you can do this?" I asked. "With winds this strong, I mean."

Elaran replied with an offended glare while unslinging his huge black bow. After nocking an arrow, he lit it on one of the torches burning at the edge of camp and drew back. "Watch."

The muscles in his back and arms tensed. He took a breath, and then he released the arrow. A flickering speck of fire shot across the red sand as the arrow flew towards its mark.

Deafening booms reverberated through the air as the burning projectile hit the stack of black powder and set off a chain reaction inside the tent. White fabric flew into the night as the whole tent lifted from the ground before being ripped apart by the explosions.

Even though we were far away from the danger zone, I threw a hand over my face and ducked as falling debris rained down across the area before us. Flames of yellow, green, and violet licked the wood as the fire devoured the chemicals that had been stored inside.

Shade slapped Elaran's chest with the back of his hand. "Nice shot."

The auburn-haired archer grinned in reply. I shook my head. *Elves.*

While the fire destroyed any chance Queen Nimlithil had at drugging the city, the three of us jogged back towards our rendezvous point. We only made it to the edge of the city wall before heavy drops started falling from the sky. When we joined up with the twins, the rain was falling in earnest.

It mattered little, though. Deluge or not, the explosion had already served its purpose and wiped out all of the star elves' chemicals. Satisfaction burned through me as we slipped into the city. The mist was gone.

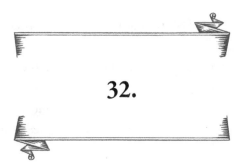

32.

Angry voices called obscenities at the walls of the Red Fort. The crowd that had gathered outside the royal palace stirred and shifted in outrage but the large gates remained closed.

"Murderer!" a woman shouted and jabbed a fist in the air.

"Traitor!" someone else joined in.

Shade and I exchanged a glance. We had been on our way to the Red Fort to tell Malor that the mist would no longer be a problem, when we'd run into the furious mob. Stepping around a puddle from last night's storm, we slunk through the mass of bodies.

"How could she do this?" an older woman demanded. "Kill her own people just because they want to be happy?"

The younger woman next to her crossed her arms. "I heard she got the new General of Pernula to do it. Shade. Apparently, he's an assassin."

"Partnering with a foreign assassin and blowing up her own people." The old woman shook her head. "And she thought we wouldn't find out."

Said assassin frowned and took me by the arm, pulling me away from the crowd. Once we were out of earshot from the furious citizens screaming about bloody murder, he drew us into a private alley closed off by a dead end on the other side and let go of my arm.

"What the hell is going on?" he hissed. "No one died in the explosion."

"I don't know." I shook my head. "But it sounds like someone's spread the word that Kristen Stagheart hired you to blow people up."

Shade raked his fingers through his hair. "This is bad. If the queen blames us for this then–"

Steel rang and armor clanked just outside the alley mouth. Shade had his swords in his hands in the blink of an eye while I yanked the hunting knives from the small of my back. A horde of men rushed into the alley, blocking off the way out. They wore the symbol of the Red Fort on their chests. The assassin and I lifted our weapons.

"Don't," a man with graying hair said from the middle. Crossbows were pointed at us from the whole row of guards. "Queen Kristen only wants to talk."

As things were now, the situation was still salvageable but if we started killing her guards, we would definitely make an enemy of the redheaded queen. After exchanging a brief glance to confirm that we were thinking the same thing, Shade and I nodded at each other.

Relaxing our grip on our weapons, we stuck them back in their holsters.

"Alright," Shade said. "Then let's talk."

The guard with the graying hair snapped his fingers, and two younger members approached us with handcuffs. I gave them an internal eye roll. *Seriously?* Amusement played at the corner of Shade's mouth as he watched the exasperated expression on my face but we both held out our arms, palms up, without complaint. Cold steel wrapped around my wrists. I had no doubt that both Shade and I would be finished picking the locks on those manacles before we'd even exited the alley.

Placing a hesitant hand on my arm, the young guard urged me forward. The squad of soldiers led us in through the same side door we had left by last time and along the red stone corridors towards the same hexagonal meeting room.

Firelight flickered over Kristen Stagheart's furious face as she stood before the rows of crowded bookshelves and messy desks. Her brother and Malor were nowhere to be seen.

"I want you out!" she hissed.

"You're the one who just brought us here," I observed.

When her face flashed red with anger and lightning practically leapt from her eyes, I knew that had been the wrong thing to say. Shade shot me an exasperated look.

"I want you out of my city!" the Queen of Sker screamed. "A plebian mob is outside my gates calling for my head." She stabbed a finger at us. "And it is your fault!"

"We didn't kill anyone," Shade said in a calm voice. "It's the star elves spreading lies. All we did was blow up their supply stash so they can't create any more mist." He shrugged. "Once people find that out, they will be grateful."

Kristen sucked in a breath and drew back. A malicious glint crept into her eyes as she looked at us, the shrieking madness of the previous minutes completely blown away and replaced by eerie calm. Sudden dread drew its icy fingers down my spine. We had just blundered head first into some kind of trap we hadn't even seen.

"So it is true," the queen whispered. "I didn't want to believe it but your own words betrayed you."

"What are you talking about?" Shade demanded.

"You are here to steal my country." Murderous clarity sparkled in her blue eyes. "Fighting off the star elves' invasion was never about helping me save Sker. It was about stealing it from right under my nose. While the star elves were making me look bad, you would look like the perfect hero, swooping in to save them from both the invaders and their own wicked queen."

Shade furrowed his brows. "That's absurd."

"No, it makes perfect sense. Why else would the General of Pernula come here personally instead of sending one of his men?"

The Master Assassin opened his mouth again but was cut off when Kristen sprang across the room. Strong hands clamped down around our arms while the Queen of Sker drew a bejeweled dagger and placed it against Shade's throat.

"No one is going to steal my country," she growled in his face. "Not you and not the star elves."

Her hand trembled with rage but Shade looked more disinterested than worried as he glanced down at the blade. I cleared my throat.

"Yeah, I can see that you're angry," I said. "But killing the General of Pernula while your city is already under siege from another foreign power... You might wanna think about that move for a second."

Kristen Stagheart clenched and unclenched her hand several times before finally yanking the dagger from Shade's throat.

"Get them out of here," she snapped at her guards before turning her murderous glare on us. "If you're still in the city after nightfall, you're dead."

I frowned at her. "I feel like we've had this conversation before."

"Get them out!" she screamed.

While suppressing a chuckle, I let the guards drag me into the empty red corridor again. Our feet thumped against the cool stones but other than that, the walk back out into the sunlight was a silent one. I could feel Shade itching to say something, though.

Once the guards had deposited us outside and shut the side gate in our faces, the Master Assassin turned to me with bafflement written all over his face.

"How the hell has no one slit your throat yet?"

I blinked at him. "A valid question. But is there anything in particular that brought it on?"

"You. Firing off snarky remarks in the faces of furious queens." Shade shook his head. "How no one has killed you yet is a bloody miracle."

A chuckle slipped from my lips while I tipped my head from side to side. "Well, to be fair, it hasn't been for a lack of trying on their part."

Shade let out an amused breath. "True. Come on."

The warm fall sun did its best to soak up the puddles that had smeared out the red sand while Shade and I skirted around the angry mob still shouting profanities at the Red Fort. We nimbly stepped out of the way as a pair of muscular men rolled a cart forward. Rotting vegetables sent a waft of truly gag-worthy air in our faces as it passed.

"Both blaming the explosion on me and making Kristen think I'm here to steal her country." Shade shook his head. "Nimlithil is a lot smarter than I gave her credit for. Malor was right. It's as if she has been studying the political situation around our cities for years."

"Yeah. Her spy network is a lot deeper than I thought." I turned towards him as a sudden explanation snapped in place. "It must be the other Storm Casters. The ones she convinced to give up their powers. Back in Starhaven, they talked about them leaving after finding their purpose. This must be it."

Shade considered for a moment before giving me a slow nod. "That makes sense."

The smell of wet stones drifted in the air as a strong wind blew through the red streets while the assassin and I continued our trek back towards Lady Beltham's house. More neutral voices replaced the angry shouting the further away from the royal palace we got. One question had been lingering in my mind ever since we left the furious queen in the meeting room so when we turned onto the final street, I glanced up at the General of Pernula.

"Tell me the truth, were you planning on taking over the city?"

A sly smile spread across Shade's lips. I snorted and shook my head as we climbed the short steps to Lady Beltham's house. Damn assassin.

33.

The market square was packed with people. Apprehension, excitement, and irritation all mixed in the noon air as the crowd stirred restlessly while waiting for their king and queen to arrive. I snuck along the roof.

"You think this is in response to yesterday?" Marcus asked and nodded at the square below just as I reached our scheming group.

Shade's face was an unreadable mask. "Has to be."

We had filled in everyone else on the meeting with Queen Kristen, along with the threat and the accusations she'd been spewing. The first decision had been an easy one. Despite the hotheaded queen's promise to kill us if we stayed, no one had voted to leave. I guess I wasn't the only one who didn't specialize in doing as I was told. As far as the queen's accusations went, Shade had neither confirmed nor denied anything, but I think we all had a feeling that there was some truth to her words.

The assassin shifted his black eyes to me. "Find anything?"

"No." I shook my head. "But something is definitely up."

"Alright, we'll take a side each then." He nodded at the twins. "You two, take this side." Twisting slightly, he motioned at me and Marcus. "And you two take the south side. Elaran, you cover the north. I'll take the east."

I narrowed my eyes at him. "I thought you said no one goes alone."

"If the rumors are true that the star elves had another stash and really are planning on dosing the Staghearts with mist during this speech, then we have to stop it. We need to cover every side."

"Fine." Crossing my arms, I glared at the bossy assassin and the grumpy elf. "But be careful."

"You're one to talk," Elaran muttered.

"If things go sideways," Shade interrupted before I could retort, "we meet back at the Beltham house. Now go."

Elaran and Shade clasped forearms while I pulled Marcus towards the edge of the roof. After lifting a hand to her brow in a mock salute, Haela unslung her bow.

The tall Storm Caster still hadn't gotten quite used to jumping between buildings but he did his best as we made our way towards the south side of the market square. Tension still hung heavy in the air below.

"How much do you trust that star elf princess?" Marcus asked as we landed on the next roof.

Twisting my head towards him, I frowned. "Why do you ask?"

"Do you think she lied to us about this mist? That she's really on her mother's side and had us blow up something else while the real stash was left untouched?"

Our feet thumped on the red tiles as we continued towards the next gap.

"No, I think Illeasia loves Elaran more than she loves her mother." I blew out a resigned sigh. "But that doesn't mean Queen Nimlithil didn't lie to her daughter."

"Hmm."

We sped up as we reached the final house on the west side before the buildings made a sharp turn to the left. Veering towards it, we pushed off the edge and leaped through the air. Excitement sparkled like fireworks in my chest as the wind whipped through my clothes and hair. Marcus looked like he was trying very hard not to think about the death waiting for us far below if we missed. Intense relief washed over his face when our feet at last found purchase again. I let out a whooping laugh and jabbed an elbow at him.

"Lighten up! This is fun!"

An only half disgruntled smile tugged at his lips. "Careful now. I'm going to repeat that to you when I introduce you to all my favorite pastimes in the mountains."

I shot him a challenging grin. "Bring it on."

Once we had gotten about halfway across the south side of the buildings boxing in the huge market square, we slowed down to a trot before finally coming to a halt. Apart from the increasingly restless crowd below, everything was quiet. If the star elves were planning something, they weren't here yet. I paced back and forth for a few minutes before giving up the futile attempt to spot any attackers.

"Alright, let's split up."

Marcus whipped his head towards me. "What? No."

"Not *split up* split up. Just..." I flapped my arm towards the other half of the roof. "We spread out a little so we can see better." Shaking my head, I ran my hands over the stilettos hidden in my sleeves. "I just... I have a bad feeling about this. Something's gonna go down."

"Okay." He nodded but then jabbed a finger at me. "But stay within earshot."

"Yeah."

That uncomfortable prickling sensation still stabbed into the back of my neck as I drifted a little further back towards the west side. I didn't know what, but something bad was about to happen.

The carts and stalls that usually crowded the huge red square had been removed to make room for the enormous mass of bodies packed on the dusty ground. Only two things remained standing: the gigantic bronze statue of the warrior astride his horse and the large podium in the middle of the square. At least the hazy overcast sky kept the temperature down.

Startled cries rang out from the other side of the market place. I whipped my head up. A large procession was making its way towards the center stage. Guards in full armor marched with determined steps while creating a clear path behind them. Inside their well-rehearsed formation, figures strode. Flaming red hair billowed in the wind. The King and Queen of Sker had arrived.

Moving closer to the edge, I kept my gaze sweeping across the gathered spectators in search of anything white and silver. My heart thumped in my chest. If anything was going to go down, it would happen soon.

Kristen Stagheart held her chin high and gazed out at the crowd as she strode onto the podium while her brother mostly stared at her instead of his subjects. Throwing back her fur-lined cape, the redheaded queen held out her arms. The crowd quieted.

"Our beloved citizens," she called in a strong voice that carried across the whole square. "We have come before you to address the lies our enemies have been spreading and to assure you that our proud nation will never be broken."

A ripple went through the audience. I shifted my weight on the red tiles but kept scanning the scene. No star elves yet. Casting a quick look at Marcus, I got confirmation that all was clear on his side as well.

"You have been told that I hired the General of Pernula, the man also known as the Master of the Assassins' Guild, who cheated his way to power in our neighboring country." Kristen Stagheart slashed an arm through the air. "That is a lie. Just like the pale wolves at our gates, he is only here for one thing: to steal our country!"

Gasps echoed from the people below. A group of finely dressed woman put their heads together and whispered behind their hands while two burly men gestured expressively at the podium.

The Queen of Sker threw out her arms, making her dark-green cloak billow around her. "No one will steal our country. Not Queen Nimlithil and not General Shade. Our nation is a proud one and our people are warriors! We answer to no one."

Cheers of support and agreement rose from several parts of the audience. Kristen raised her voice even further and stabbed a hand in front of her.

"To show Pernula that we do not let the murder of our people go unpunished, I issued a proclamation yesterday. As of now, if General Shade and his coconspirators are found in our city, they will be captured and executed." She slashed an arm through the air again. "Let everyone know that Sker will never bow to Pernula or to–"

Her head snapped back. The fur-lined cloak seemed to flutter in slow motion as the queen fell backwards. Red hair flowed around her face while the previously so determined blue eyes stared blankly up at the heavens. A heavy thud sounded. Metal dinged against wood as a heavy gold crown with crimson jewels rolled across the stage before wobbling to a halt by the edge.

And then the screaming started. I stared in utter disbelief at the large dagger protruding from Kristen Stagheart's forehead while blood flowed into an ever-growing pool around her head. The Queen of Sker was dead.

"No!" A heart-shattering howl ripped from Kristian Stagheart's throat as he collapsed next to his sister's corpse. "Kristen! Kristen!"

He shook her violently while the guards around him tried to pull him away. The ring of soldiers had their weapons drawn and whipped their heads in every direction in search of the queen's assassin. Panicked shrieks rang out from the crowd as the people closest to the stage tried to get away but their stampede was halted by the tightly packed rows around them.

"There!" someone shouted.

"Look! There he is!"

Several people were pointing at the east side of the square. Still paralyzed by shock, I hadn't moved at all in the minute since the Queen of Sker had been assassinated, but now I finally managed to snap out of the stupor and jerk my head in the direction they were indicating.

A man with black hair and dressed in tightfitting black clothes was scrambling up the side of the building on the east side of the square. Two swords gleamed across his back.

"It's General Shade!" someone called.

"He killed her!"

"The assassin Shade murdered our queen!"

"Oh gods save us!"

The figure dressed in black had made it onto the roof and ran south along the edge before turning east again and darting away from the square. Shooting to my feet, I sprinted towards him.

Marcus, his mouth hanging open, was staring between the disappearing assassin and the dead queen but whirled towards me as I approached. The tiles vibrated underneath me as I thundered forward.

"Come on," I yelled. "We've gotta follow–"

"Look! His accomplices! They're all over the roof."

"Get them!"

A crossbow bolt whizzed through the air. I ducked just in time. It sped past in the space my neck had just vacated before disappearing on the other side of the roof. *Shit*. Both Marcus and I threw ourselves flat against the tiles as the next volley shot towards us. Sharp thuds rang out as the thick arrows connected with the adjacent building.

"We have to..." I trailed off as a clamor rose from the east side of the roof.

Rolling across the tiles, I peeked over the edge. A horde of men were making their way up the wall towards us.

"Oh for Nemanan's sake!" I pounded a fist on the red stones before jumping to my feet. "They're coming. We've gotta go."

Marcus was already on his feet when I reached his side so we both took off towards the west side of the square. Angry shouting followed us. The pursuing men had made it onto the roof and were sprinting to catch up with us. After casting a hurried glance behind me, I willed my legs to run faster.

"This way!" I yanked at my friend's sleeve. "We have to lose them."

Taking a sharp turn, we switched direction and jumped the gap between the houses on our left. I rolled to my feet easily on the other side but Marcus staggered and tripped into a chimney after the long leap. I screeched to a halt and darted back towards him. The men had seen our direction change and had jumped onto the building further down. Once Marcus had found his footing again, we raced towards the next roof.

"Summon a wind," I panted between heavy breaths. "Blow them off the building or something."

He whipped his head towards me. "No one can know I'm Ashaana, remember? So unless you want me to kill them all, I can't use my powers."

That was exactly what my plan had been. However, the expression on his face told me that killing all those men was highly unacceptable to Marcus so I kept my mouth shut. Morals. What an inconvenience.

"*You* have to do it," he said as we leaped onto the next red stone building. "Summon a wind and push them back along the roof."

"I can't summon wind!" I snapped.

"Yes, you can. Don't try to control it. You are the storm. You don't need to control it."

Don't control it. Right. Twisting around, I got ready to push my hands forward in a shove. *What if I blow us off the roof too?*

A frustrated scream tore from my throat as I whirled back around and continued running. I couldn't make these kinds of decisions when I didn't even have time to think. My heart thumped in my chest. I cast a panicked glance behind me. All that indecision had done was slow me down so that our pursuers had gained even more on us.

"At the end of this roof, don't jump," I said. "Climb down the wall and bust through the first window you get to."

"They'll see that."

"No, they won't." Skidding to a halt, I whipped around. "Just do it!"

The thudding feet behind me informed me that Marcus had done as he was told and continued towards the edge of the roof. As the men hunting us closed in, I jammed my hands into my belt pouches and yanked out two items. A vial and a glass orb. My mouth drew into a malicious grin as I lobbed the vial towards them.

Glass shattered, followed by a loud whoosh as if something huge had caught fire. The men yelped in surprise as black smoke bloomed around them. I threw the orb and ran.

A deafening explosion racked the red tiles as the exploding orb landed in the middle of the artificial darkness that the blackout powder had created. I slid over the edge of the roof and scrambled towards the closest window.

Ever since the attack at The Broken Wing, I had started keeping as much of my tools and gear as possible on me at all times. I was always armed with knives, of course, but knowing that I was a Storm Caster had made me lax when it came to bringing things like exploding orbs and blackout powder. After all, if I could create something similar myself, why should I bother with the extra weight? However, after the attack and my hit-and-miss attempts at actually using my powers, I'd decided to play it safe. Good thing.

Wood rattled as I jumped into the room and slammed the shutters closed. Marcus was doubled over in the middle of a small bedroom. Hands on his knees, he sucked in desperate breaths. I drew a couple of deep ones myself in an effort to slow my racing heart.

"That wasn't you, was it?" Marcus asked and pointed a finger at the ceiling.

"Nope." I let out a soft chuckle. "That was the chemical genius of Apothecary Haber. He's an interesting man. You should meet him sometime."

The tall Storm Caster flopped onto the messy bed and stretched his muscled body while resting his arms above his head. "I think I'll pass." Lifting his head, he peered at me with curious eyes. "Why aren't you more rattled? Every time something like this happens, you just take it in stride."

Sitting down on the edge of the bed, I shrugged. "Things like this are pretty normal to me."

"You have a very strange view of what's normal."

I chuckled. "Yeah, I know."

The mattress creaked in distress as I lay down next to him. Adjusting his position, he moved his arm around my shoulders so that my head rested on his muscled bicep. I let out a long sigh. A few minutes' rest and then we'd sneak back out and deal with some more normal stuff. Like, the assassination of a foreign monarch. Yep. Completely normal indeed.

34.

Fluffy carpets were mercilessly trampled beneath my boots as I paced back and forth across Lady Beltham's sitting room. He wasn't back yet. Though Haela was sprawled on a brown couch in a comfortable position, she drummed her fingers on the dark wooden table next to her in a manner that betrayed her worry. I shifted my gaze to the doorway. Elaran was glaring at the door as if it was its fault that the black-haired assassin hadn't walked through it yet.

The handle was pushed down. Relief surged through my whole body when a man in tightfitting black clothes strode across the threshold. Marcus shot to his feet as Shade entered the sitting room.

"Did you do it?" he demanded.

Oppressive silence hung like a thick blanket over the tastefully decorated room. The Master Assassin cast him a sidelong glance.

"No."

"The assassin looked exactly like you. He was coming from the side *you* were supposed to be watching." Marcus took a step towards him and threw out his muscled arms. "And we all know that what the queen said was true. You *did* come here to take over the city."

He was making some great points but I still had a very hard time believing that Shade was the one who had killed Queen Kristen. If he had done it, he would've told us. I think.

Lifting his eyebrows, Shade threw him a disinterested stare. "Are you done?"

"No." Marcus closed the distance between them. "You're the bloody Master of the Assassins' Guild, for Werz's sake! Are you seriously telling me that all of this doesn't add up to you being the one who killed her?"

Elaran stepped between them and jerked his chin at Marcus. "Back off. If he said he didn't do it, he didn't do it."

Throwing his arms out, the muscled Storm Caster looked to the rest of us for support. When he received none, he blew out a breath and ran his fingers through his hair before retreating a couple of steps. Elaran remained standing in front of Shade with his chin raised until the assassin placed a hand on his shoulder. The Master Assassin's black eyes were filled with unspoken words as he held Elaran's gaze and gave him a nod.

"A group of star elves showed up," he said once Elaran had nodded back and taken a step to the side. "I went after them. That's why I wasn't at the east side when everything went down. They baited me and I fell for it."

"Sounds like a perfect setup," Haemir said from the couch.

"Yeah. Making them look like me, leveraging my assassin ties, luring me away so I wouldn't be able to stop it." He blew out a forceful breath. "From what I heard on my way over here, they even did it right when Kristen was screaming about how awful I am."

"Yeah, it was perfectly timed," I said.

Shade slammed a fist down on the back of a brown armchair, sending a poof of dust swirling in the air. "We played right into their hands! How the hell does Queen Nimlithil know so much about the strained relationship between Pernula and Sker?"

Only a strong wind rattling the shutters answered the assassin's question. Glancing down, I tried to smoothen out the rut I had created in the fluffy white carpet with all my pacing. It just served to flatten it further.

"Sorry." Marcus heaved a deep sigh and shifted his gaze to Shade. "For accusing you and snapping at you and all that." Raking fingers through his dark brown hair, he shook his head. "It's just, all this..." He spun a hand in the air. "...craziness. It's getting to me."

The Master Assassin gave him a nod in acknowledgement before a slight smirk ghosted across his lips. "And for the record, if I did decide to assassinate a foreign monarch, I wouldn't be so sloppy as to get seen doing it."

I chuckled. Now *that*, I believed. Soft laughter spread across the room as the rest of my friends no doubt thought the same thing.

After swinging her legs off the comfortable cushions, Haela sat up straight. "Alright, we walked right into their trap. Now what?"

"Now the whole bloody city is looking for us," Elaran muttered and drew his eyebrows down. "We need to lay low for a while."

"I agree." Shade nodded at the grumpy elf. "The whole city is on high alert and we still have that unidentified party painting targets on our backs. We need to take a few days to figure out what we're doing before we step into another trap."

I lifted my shoulders in a shrug. "We might have to just get Malor and get out. And leave Sker to its fate. We can't help them if they don't want our help."

"We're not there yet." The assassin swept his gaze across the room. "Kristian Stagheart is a pushover. If we can just get him to see that this was the star elves' doing, we can get him to do whatever we want."

A wicked grin grazed my lips as I gave Shade a quick rise and fall of my eyebrows. "So you can take over Sker?"

"Shut up." He shook his head at me before turning back to the rest of the room. "Alright, complete lockdown. No one in or out until we figure out how to handle this."

"Aw, seriously?" Haela placed a hand on her forehead in a dramatic gesture. "However shall I pass the time locked indoors for days on end? I am a free spirit. I need the great outdoors."

Haemir arched an eyebrow at her. "How about spending it working on your nonexistent patience?"

Reaching behind her, Haela picked up a decorated pillow and hurled it at her brother. "Party-pooper."

After nimbly catching the flying décor, Haemir strode across the room and pulled up his sister from the couch. "Come on, let's head to the library at the back."

"Aha! I knew I could count on you." A grin spread across her mouth. "The library is the perfect room to practice martial arts."

Surprised laughter rippled through the room and we all shook our heads at Haela as Haemir pulled her towards the stairs. I made one last attempt at returning the carpet to its original state before giving up and following the twins. With a slight smile still on his face, Shade raised his voice.

"Alright, you can all occupy yourselves in whatever manner you see fit, but remember: complete lockdown. Don't do anything stupid."

The stairs creaked as I stalked up them. While the twins continued towards the library to read or practice martial arts, the rest of us headed towards our rooms. White curtains fluttered in the open window when I pulled open the door. The wind carried air smelling of dry sand and warm stones to my lungs.

Complete lockdown. Sure. I braced my palms on the edge of the wooden shutters and climbed out the window. First, I just had some things to take care of.

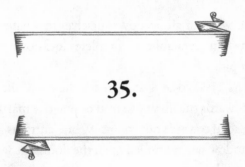

35.

Our footsteps echoed between the walls of smooth red stone as we made our way deeper into the Red Fort. I swept my gaze restlessly over the empty corridor. Next to me, my friends did the same.

"If this is a trap..." Shade warned.

"Then it's not of my making," Malor cut off before the assassin could finish. "If it was, why would I be sneaking you into this meeting fully armed?"

After considering in silence for a moment, Shade gave him a nod. "You expect a trap too?"

"Kristian is not the sneaky scheming kind, so ordinarily, no. But after the death of his sister, it's impossible to tell." Sadness crept into Malor's reddish-brown eyes. "Kristen was his whole world. He's beside himself with grief. After her death, he spent the whole week crying and now I fear that he has lost himself in despair and depression. A few days ago, he withdrew into himself and spent all his time just staring blankly out the window. He's shut everyone out." Malor heaved a tired sigh. "Even me. I haven't seen him in days."

A twinge of pity for the King of Sker went through me as memories of that awful time in Starhaven when I thought Elaran was dead flashed unbidden through my mind. The death of a loved one could certainly be enough to break anyone.

"This morning, I was finally able to convince him to send for you so that you can handle the real threat, the star elves, together." Caution was written all over his face as Malor turned to the six of us. "But yes, there is a slight chance that this is a trap. I still haven't been able to see him so I'm not sure what state he's in. Stay alert."

We nodded at him just as we reached a nondescript wooden door. My heart pattered in my chest. If it was indeed a setup, we were about to find out. I felt the comforting weight of all the blades strapped to my body as I willed my pulse to slow. Malor put a hand on the handle. *Here we go.*

The vast throne room filled with large red pillars appeared before us. After surveying the area in silence for a few seconds, Malor lowered his hand and gave us the nod to proceed. Guards were positioned along the walls and by the main entrance but there didn't appear to be an excessive amount of them present. If it had been a trap, there should've been a lot more of them.

Burning candles cast flickering shadows over the red hall as we strode through the forest of stone columns and approached the raised dais at the back. The twin thrones made of the same red stone as the rest of the city remained on top of the platform even though only one of them was occupied.

Kristian Stagheart was slumped on the sturdy seat of power, his elbow propped up on his knees and his head in his hands. Muted red curls fell down over his eyes and the gleaming crown he wore seemed heavier than usual.

"Everyone is saying that you killed my darling sister," he whispered, the vaulted ceiling above carrying the sound to us as we stopped below the dais. "Everyone except Malor."

"Malor is correct," Shade said. "The star elves murdered Queen Kristen and they are framing us in order to turn Pernula and Sker against each other."

A deep sigh escaped from the grieving king as he finally dropped his hands and straightened. The red curls fell away from his face. I drew in a sharp breath. *Shit.*

Blue eyes devoid of all emotion stared down at us. They were the eyes of a person who had been robbed of the ability to feel pain. The eyes of someone who had completed the ritual.

"I was almost convinced by your lies," King Kristian said in a hollow voice. "But they made me see."

Doors slammed shut behind us. I yanked out my hunting knives as the soldiers stationed in the room pulled their swords and advanced on us.

"They want a world free of pain," Kristian Stagheart droned on. "And you, *assassin*, all you do is inflict pain. How could it be anyone but you who murdered my beloved sister?"

Shade had drawn his twin swords from behind his shoulders, while the elves unslung their bows and Marcus whipped out his own blade. With eyes shifting between the approaching guards, the six of us formed a circle with our backs to each other.

"How could you, Kristian?" Malor said. He remained standing next to our defensive formation with his arms crossed and a disapproving look on his face. "How could you disrespect Kristen's memory by bowing to the star elves in this way? I am ashamed of you." Raising his voice, he waved a hand at the guards. "Stand down. The king's mind has been compromised by our enemies."

All around us, feet shuffled against stone as the soldiers hesitated. Uncertain eyes flicked between the senior advisor and the King of Sker. While the guards came to a halt, their weapons still raised, Kristian Stagheart rose from his red throne. The fur-lined cloak around his shoulders rustled as he straightened, strode towards the edge of the dais, and swept a bland gaze around the room.

"Malor is a traitor to the crown," he said matter-of-factly. "Anyone here who refuses to follow my orders will be branded a traitor and hanged alongside him."

A ripple went through the high-ceilinged hall. Flames danced over faces that appeared torn between the respect they had for the senior advisor and the loyalty they had to the crown. Weapons were raised tentatively again.

King Kristian moved his empty stare to us. "The rest of you are lucky. Queen Nimlithil is on her way. She said she has a use for you." He waved a lazy hand. "Take them all."

Metal clanked as the Sker soldiers loosed a battle cry and charge towards us. In a heartbeat, Elaran and the twins took a step back and formed a smaller circle while Shade, Marcus, and I positioned ourselves in front of each elf. I raised my knives.

Since we had expected this to be a trap, we had already formed a plan for how to get out alive. The elves and their ranged weapons were responsible for taking down the attackers while the rest of us protected our archers.

Air vibrated next to my cheek as Haela's arrow sped past my face and buried itself in a charging guard.

The only one who didn't know the plan was Malor. I whipped my head around in search of him but the red-eyed advisor was suddenly nowhere to be found. A surprised frown flashed across my face before movement in the corner of my eye pulled my attention back.

Steel clanked as I threw my knife up to absorb the impact of the sword. The guard who had swung it grunted and shoved my blade to the side in an attempt to hit his true target. Haela. The black-haired twin didn't even flinch at the movement while firing arrows at the other guards barreling for us. She trusted me to keep her safe. And I would. By Nemanan, I would.

Right as my knife slashed through the air after being pushed off course, I flicked up my other blade and jabbed it forward. Wet sliding sounds rose as I pushed the hunting knife through the gap between my opponent's breastplate and helmet. He drew a sharp breath. Yanking the blade back out, I kicked his body backwards. It crumpled to the ground in a clanking of metal.

"Side door," Shade hissed from my left.

Neither of us wasted any breath responding and instead just started moving towards the side door we had arrived through while keeping our formation intact. Bows twanged behind me.

The charging guards had recovered from the shock of finding themselves picked off one by one by the skilled elven archers inside our defensive circle and had drawn back to regroup. King Kristian was standing behind a wall of soldiers and watched the scene with expressionless eyes. We moved towards our exit as quickly as possible while the guards on the floor strategized.

Another shout bounced off the red walls as the soldiers scattered and darted for the large pillars around us. Elaran and the twins loosed arrows over our shoulders. Wood snapped as the projectiles struck the columns that our attackers now used very effectively as cover.

"Watch out!" I called as a guard jumped out from the shadows to my right.

Marcus jerked back but then swung his longsword towards the surprise threat right in time to save Haemir from getting skewered. The heavy weapon whooshed through the air and buried itself in the guard's side, nearly cleaving him in half. Marcus yanked his sword free as we continued moving towards the side door. Arrows whizzed through the air.

"Call for backup!" someone shouted from behind a pillar right before Elaran hit him straight in the eye.

While the body clattered to the floor in a thudding of armor and dead limbs, the command was repeated across the room as the rest of the guards pulled back again. They kept their weapons raised and followed us from a distance as we made our way towards the exit but no one was in a hurry to attack again. The elves kept their drawn arrows shifting between them in order to discourage anyone who might be brave and stupid enough to try another charge.

My heart thumped in my chest. We just needed to get through the door before their backup arrived. And then get out of the palace without anyone noticing. Before the elves ran out of arrows. Shit. This was not going to be easy.

Wood crashed into stone as Shade kicked open the side door. Marcus and I moved in front of the others as they entered the doorway while Elaran remained standing just behind our shoulders with his bow raised. Once everyone was through, the tall Storm Caster and I backed across the threshold as well. I slammed the door shut and whirled around.

"Back gate," Shade whispered and nodded down the empty corridor.

Still keeping our weapons raised, we followed him down the red stone passageways in silence. Only the soft echo of our feet betrayed our movements as we hurried towards our freedom. Shade and I exchanged a glance. He shrugged in response to my wordless question: *where the hell is Malor?*

Elaran threw up a hand. We skidded to a halt right before a bend in the corridor. The auburn-haired archer snuck forward and peeked around the edge. Drawing back, he jerked his hand across his throat a couple of times. *Damn.* Guards were blocking the way down there. We started retracing our steps towards the last intersection we'd passed.

Feet slapped against stone further down. Alarm flashed over our faces before we all broke into a sprint. *Shit.* The guards in the throne room had finally gotten their backup and they were now closing in from behind as well.

Wall-mounted candles cast their flickering light over yet another red corridor as we veered left and charged down the empty hall. Marcus threw an arm to the right. We disappeared down another passageway right as shouts rose from the one we had just vacated.

"Have you seen them?"

"No, sir, they haven't passed us."

"They can't have gotten far. Let's go!"

Hunting footsteps and clanking armor echoed off every surface as we took turn after turn in the hopes of finding another way out of the Red Fort while our pursuers were snapping at our heels. My heart slammed against my ribcage. We were never going to make it.

A woman in a feather mask of black and gold appeared before us as we rounded yet another corner. Marcus crashed into me from behind as I skidded to a halt in order to avoid running her over. Tripping forwards, I swung my arms around to keep my balance until the muscled Storm Caster put large hands on my arms and steadied me.

"This way," the woman said in a quiet voice.

Her sheer dress flowed around her as she turned and started down the hall. A cloud of perfume wafted towards us. I squinted at the lace underwear visible inside the see-through garment. An escort.

The six of us exchanged quick glances before following her down the corridor. Clamor rose around us as the guards closed in. We picked up speed.

"Why?" I asked as I hurried behind her.

She didn't even bother turning around when she replied, "I'm from the Pink Lily. It's the least I could do after you rescued Milla."

Huh. I opened my mouth to ask her how she had found us but a ruckus from not too far behind shut me up. Casting a panicked glance over my shoulder, I continued running behind the escort in silence.

Dread spidered up my spine when the corridor ended in a closed door but our savior pulled out a key and unlocked it before slipping inside. We followed her. The door led to a narrow staircase that was only lit by a few torches along the walls. Flames danced across the red stones as we made our way down. The air was getting cooler with each step until it evened out in a level coldness when we reached a long corridor at the bottom of the stairs.

"Where are you taking us?" Shade whispered.

His voiced bounced off the walls in the tight space, making them unnaturally loud in the otherwise dead quiet hallway.

"There is a secret exit that leads to the beach," the escort replied. "We use it when we're visiting clients in the Red Fort who require more discretion than our usual customers."

A thick stone door appeared before us. The blond escort put a slender shoulder against the red stones and pushed. It scraped against the floor as it moved inwards. Once she had created a small gap, she slipped through. My friends followed her while I brought up the rear and slunk through after them.

The door banged shut behind me. I whipped around but the closed door had caused oppressive darkness to smother the room so I couldn't make out my surroundings. A strong hand wrapped my wrist in an iron grip and twisted my arm behind my back. I sucked in a breath to scream but the warning died on my lips when a gloved hand slammed across my mouth and something cold pressed into my throat.

Flames flickered to life around us. Fire cast dancing shadows over a circular room made entirely of stone and over the metal bars that dotted the unforgiving walls. Soldiers were positioned along the whole room. My eyes widened. White and silver glimmered in the darkened room as light fell across the face of Queen Nimlithil.

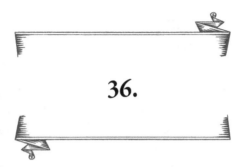

36.

The Queen of Tkeister stood in the middle of the room with a look of superiority on her beautiful face. Her silver dress cascaded onto the dusty red floor while the sparkling headdress she wore glittered in the firelight. White bows were drawn and pointed at us from every direction. Queen Nimlithil motioned at the door where Haemir and I stood with swords to our throats.

"Think very carefully about your next move," she said.

The two of us had been the last to enter the room which had apparently earned us the role as hostages. Gods damn it. I yanked against the hand trapping my arm behind my back but it only served to have the star elf soldier tighten his grip on my wrist and mouth.

With weapons raised, the rest of our friends whirled around to see the precarious position Haemir and I were currently in. Lightning flashed in Shade's black eyes but it was Haela who spoke up.

"If you hurt him, hurt them, I will slaughter you all," she growled at the room full of star elves.

"You are not in a position to make threats," Queen Nimlithil said matter-of-factly. "Now, surrender your weapons and get on your knees before me or they will both die."

A brief nod from his queen made the guard behind me force my head up and expose my throat further to the blade his companion held against it. Tense silence filled the room. Then, steel clattered against stone as Shade and Marcus dropped their swords while Elaran and Haela lowered their bows. I watched my friends disarm while a sinking feeling spread through my stomach.

Once all weapons had been discarded, a pair of star elves removed them from reach while the ring of archers tightened around them. The grip on my wrist disappeared. Yanking my arm free, I spun around to face the guard who had kept me hostage.

Dark violet eyes I knew very well met me. I drew in a sharp hiss between my teeth while my fingers twitched by my sides. Captain Hadraeth stared me down.

"Disarm," he commanded.

For one rebellious second, I considered shoving a stiletto blade through his windpipe just to see the surprise in his eyes but the arrows pointed at my friends crushed that impulse. Rage brewed inside me as I yanked out knife after knife and handed them to the star elf next to me. Once I was done, the Captain of the Guard shoved me into the ring of archers while the soldier to my left did the same to Haemir.

"You did well, my child," Queen Nimlithil said to the escort standing forgotten by the wall.

"Thank you," she replied and nodded at the elven queen before slipping towards the door.

I bared my teeth at the treacherous escort. "Why?"

She had removed her feather mask and when she turned to face me, I immediately understood the reason. Eyes devoid of all emotion met me.

"We have suffered so much," she said in her quiet voice. "Queen Nimlithil showed us that we don't have to suffer anymore. No one at the Pink Lily has to suffer anymore."

Before I could figure out what to say, she had disappeared out the door again. I shook my head. How were we supposed to win against someone who could promise people an existence free of pain and strife? Of course people would fall for that. And when they finally realized that they were only given a half-life in return, it would already be too late.

"Kneel," Queen Nimlithil ordered.

The storm boiled in my soul, begging me to let it out. White arrows hovered only an arm's length from my friends with a silent promise of death at the first sight of trouble. I pushed down the darkness into the deep pits of my soul. No one would die because of me. Shoving my pride aside, I got down on my knees in front of the silver-haired queen.

"You only have one choice," Nimlithil said as she swept pale violet eyes across the six kneeling prisoners before her. "Complete the ritual. Then, you will go back to your respective nations and convince your people to do the same." Her gaze locked on me. "And you will also give up your powers to Aldeor the White."

"Not gonna happen," I growled, biting off each word.

Queen Nimlithil looked like a mother trying to convince her unruly children that eating vegetables was good for them, when she peered down her slender nose at us. "You will do the ritual. Everyone does it." Something wistful, and incredibly dangerous, drifted over her face as she smiled. "Eventually."

Panic washed over me like ice water at the sight of her lethal smile.

Next to me, Shade narrowed his eyes at her. "You said no one could be forced to do the ritual. That it had to be done by their own free will."

"Correct." She shifted her gaze to the assassin kneeling next to me. "But some people require a little extra motivation to agree to it."

"What does that mean?" Elaran demanded.

Fanatical determination blazed in the queen's eyes. "It means that you *will* do the ritual." She waved an elegant hand in a lazy gesture. "If I hurt your friends enough, you will agree to do the ritual voluntarily."

My breath hitched as dread wrapped its cold hands around my heart and squeezed. The lunatic queen was going to torture our friends until we broke and did what she wanted. And she did it all in the name of freeing the world from pain. Only a dangerous zealot could believe that those kinds of means justified an end like that.

In the shocked silence that descended on the dungeon, only the hissing torches broke the stillness. Masks of horror mirroring my own met me as I looked at the rest of my companions. I knew without a doubt that I would let the crazy star elf queen do whatever she wanted to me before I let her hurt any of my friends. And I had a feeling they were all thinking the same thing.

"You have until nightfall to decide," Queen Nimlithil said. "If you have not agreed to do the ritual by then, we will proceed to the next step."

A hand grabbed my shirt and yanked me to my feet as the queen made for the door. She waved a hand at me and Shade as she passed.

"Make sure these two are locked up thoroughly. They possess some skills that can prove an inconvenience."

While I stared daggers at the exiting queen, the star elves hauled us all towards the cells at the back of the room. Arrows were still pointed at us from every direction.

Captain Hadraeth oversaw the work as his men chained us to the walls. For the twins, Elaran, and Marcus, they were apparently satisfied using the manacles and chains bolted to the walls throughout the cell. The assassin and I, however, had another treatment coming.

Flat iron bars with two bulges at the end had been fastened in the stone. Hinges squeaked as the elven guard to my right opened the outer bar and held it open while his partner shoved me against the wall and forced my arms up over my head. Cold metal pressed against my wrists as he slammed the bar shut and locked it on the side. I yanked against the contraption trapping my hands far from each other above my head and away from all my lockpicks.

Across the room, Shade was in similar restraints. Only, the iron bar locking his hands above his head was positioned much further down on the wall so he had been forced to his knees in order to fit his wrists into the waiting bulges in the metal. Cold fury burned behind the assassin's eyes.

"Let's go," Captain Hadraeth said to his men.

I glared at him as they all filed out of the cell before locking it behind them. The Captain of the Guard kept his face neutral. Once the final lock had clicked shut, he barked orders about guard shifts and then stalked back out the door.

Silence fell across the dungeons of the Red Fort as the star elves left by the stone door, taking the torches with them. In the thick darkness, I could no longer make out the faces of my friends. I swallowed against the panic rising in my throat. How were we supposed to get out of this mess?

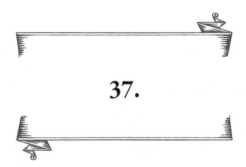

37.

Two thuds echoed outside the stone door. Straining my eyes, I tried to see through the oppressive darkness. A metallic click sounded. I held my breath.

With nothing to measure the time by, it was impossible to know for certain how long it had been since Queen Nimlithil and Captain Hadraeth had left us in this dungeon. We had tried to find a way out of it but with our group's only two underworlders trapped with our hands far from our lockpicks, we were all still chained to the walls. No one had wanted to talk about the ultimatum the Queen of Tkeister had given us, so after a while heart-pounding silence had fallen over the room as we fought against the manacles and the bleak future awaiting us.

Stone scraped against stone as the door was pushed open. Torchlight flickered through the gap. It couldn't be nightfall yet. It couldn't. I yanked against my restraints in another futile attempt to get free. We were supposed to have more time. I wasn't ready to watch my friends get hurt or to give up my powers and my ability to feel. Not yet. By Nemanan, I needed more time.

White and silver gleamed as flames bounced off the red walls. I stared at the elf striding across the stones.

"Illeasia?" Elaran breathed from further down the cell.

"*Shh*, we have to be quiet," Princess Illeasia said as she stuck a key in the cell door to unlock it. Metal clinked faintly as she stepped across the threshold while flipping through the keys on the sturdy iron ring. "And we don't have much time, so go get your weapons as soon as you're free."

Thankfully, I was one of the first people she set free because I had quite the arsenal to strap back on. I gave her a grateful smile and squeezed her hand when she removed the iron bar from my wrists. She smiled back before continuing to Haemir. There would be time for proper thanks later.

I gave my body a good stretch before sticking all the blades back in their holsters. By the time I was finished, everyone else was free and armed too. Illeasia put a slender finger to her lips and waved us forward.

Keeping our weapons at the ready, we filed out of the dungeon. Two star elves lay slumped against the walls outside. I arched an eyebrow at Illeasia but she just shook her head and urged us forward. We slunk through the corridor on silent feet. After climbing the stairs at the end, we paused and glanced back at the princess who brought up the rear. There could be an army waiting for us on the other side. However, when Illeasia nodded at us to proceed, Shade pushed down the handle and slipped through.

Two more star elves lay slumped on the floor outside the doorway but apart from that, the hallway was empty. Once our group had gathered in the red corridor that we knew was finally on ground level again, we exchanged a few quick glances.

"Now what?" Marcus said. "How do we find our way out from here?"

"I'm not sure where all the Sker guards are but–"

Steel rang as a sword was drawn from its scabbard around the corner. I gripped my hunting knives tighter right before Captain Hadraeth appeared in front of us. His dark violet eyes flashed.

"You killed my men," he growled and nodded at the two figures lying on the floor.

"No," Princess Illeasia interrupted before any of us could respond. She elbowed her way through our tightly packed group and planted herself between us and the furious captain. "They're not dead, only passed out. I'm the one who drugged them."

Hadraeth lowered his sword slightly, uncertainty blowing across his face. "Princess Illeasia?"

Taking a step forward, Shade advanced on the Guard Captain and raised his right-hand sword. "Step aside."

"No." He shook his head and raised his own blade again. "I can't let you leave."

Bows creaked as the three wood elves nocked and drew back. A predatory grin flashed over Shade's mouth.

"Then give me one good reason why we shouldn't kill you right here."

Princess Illeasia whirled around and backed towards Hadraeth with her arms thrown out. "Because I care about him."

Panic flared across Elaran's face as the princess was now right in the path of the arrows so he swiftly lowered his bow and motioned for the twins to do the same. The Master Assassin cocked his head to the right.

"This is my price for saving you." Illeasia lifted her chin. "You owe me. You will not hurt him."

Confusion, hope, and pain drifted over Hadraeth's face at her words. After a second of hesitation, he reached out and pulled her backwards. A hiss escaped Elaran's throat but died down again when he realized it had only been to get the princess out of the way of a potential fight. With Illeasia safely behind him again, Captain Hadraeth took a step forward and squared his shoulders.

"You'd better kill me then." Raising both his sword and his chin, the captain stared us down. "Because I still can't let you leave."

"What are you doing?" Princess Illeasia protested behind him. "My mother is going to torture them until they do what she wants. You *know* this is wrong."

Desperation crept into his voice. "It doesn't matter what I think! I'm the Captain of the Queen's Guard. I can't keep doing this. I can't keep looking the other way. Without my loyalty, without my honor, I am nothing. She's my queen, I have to follow her orders."

Oh he sounded *a lot* like someone else I knew but I decided it best not to point that out. Especially when that someone was currently glaring at the captain while his fingers twitched by his huge black bow.

"Men." Princess Illeasia heaved and threw her arms in the air while shaking her head. "Stop being ridiculous." She moved eyes of steel between Hadraeth and us. "And let me remind you that if this turns into a fight where someone dies, I'm the one who will get hurt the most."

I could almost feel the heartbreak radiating off Hadraeth as he closed his eyes against the onslaught of hopeless choices. Tipping his head back, he heaved a deep sigh while raking a hand through his dark silver hair. When he opened his eyes again, all the fight in them was gone.

The tip of his sword dinged against the stones as he lowered it and stepped aside. "You have a five-minute head start, then I'm sounding the alarm."

Shade studied him through narrowed eyes before giving the defeated captain a slow nod and sticking his swords back in the sheaths. The rest of us did the same. Boots thudded against the floor as the six of us made our way past Hadraeth and continued into the corridor. Holding his gaze, I gave the captain a nod as I passed. He just looked back at me with tired eyes.

"Thank you," Princess Illeasia whispered and squeezed his arm before she followed us down the hall.

Casting a glance over my shoulder, I watched him slump back against the wall and lean his head against the red stones while staring blankly up at the ceiling. Whatever my general thoughts about the star elves might be, I found that I did have a certain respect for the Captain of the Guard. Even if he only helped us because of his own selfish reasons concerning Princess Illeasia. Or perhaps because of that. After all, I was a selfish bastard too.

Armor clanked and feet slapped from down the hall. I jerked my head up. *Shit.* Weapons were about to fly when the Princess of Tkeister instead shoved us in the opposite direction.

"I'll distract them." She flicked a hand over our heads. "I think there's a way out somewhere in that direction. Go!"

"Thank you," I whispered while the words were repeated by the rest of my friends as well.

Elaran drew her into a kiss but she pulled away after only a second as the clamor from the approaching guards grew louder. She traced soft fingers down his cheek.

"I will see you soon," she whispered, pain lacing her words, before she pushed him towards the other side and flicked pleading eyes to us. "Keep him safe."

"Always," Shade promised as he grabbed a hold of Elaran's shirt and hauled him away from the woman he loved.

We darted through the red stone corridor as shouts rose behind us. There had to be a way out here somewhere but without having scouted the passageways beforehand, we were running blind. My heart slammed against my ribs. It would only be a matter of time before we ran head first into a wall of soldiers.

Candles flickered in distress as our bodies created strong drafts while racing through the Red Fort. Everywhere, shouts and clamor hunted us. The noise bounced off the stone walls, making it seem like our enemies were closing in from every direction. We sprinted through one corridor only to have it blocked by guards and having to retreat again while hoping they hadn't spotted us. Veering into yet another passageway, I sent a desperate prayer to Nemanan that we would find our way out of this maze of red stone.

A door banged open and a callused hand shot out. Grabbing a hold of my shirt, it yanked me inside a room. I let out a yelp as I stumbled across the threshold.

"In here," a voice hissed.

While the rest of my friends barreled in through the door after me, I whirled around to face the person attached to the hand that had grabbed me. Malor peered down at me with those reddish-brown eyes. I blinked at him as he strode to the door and slammed it shut after everyone had darted through it.

"I would've come for you sooner but finding you was a lot more difficult than anticipated because you were running around like headless chickens," the senior advisor grumbled, and crossed his arms. "Now, listen up because I have a way out for us."

Shade took a threatening step forward. "You vanished into thin air as soon as King Kristian ordered his men to take us. How do we know you weren't the one who set us up?"

Malor shot forward and in a heartbeat, he had the Master Assassin pressed up against the wall. With one hand twisting his arm up and behind his back and the other clamped around the back of his neck, Malor kept Shade in an iron grip while pushing the assassin's cheek into the red stones.

I would've smirked at seeing someone outmaneuver the arrogant Master of the Assassins' Guild in such a way if I wasn't so worried that we had stepped into yet another ambush. The hunting knife was in my hand and pressed against Malor's throat before I had even taken a breath. On the other side, Elaran's blade lent weight to mine.

"Because if I wanted to hurt you, boy," Malor said in response to Shade's previous question, "we wouldn't be having this conversation."

Malor didn't even acknowledge the blades as Elaran and I pushed them higher up under his chin. With his cheek still pressed into the wall, the assassin pressed his jaws together while lightning danced in his eyes.

The muscled senior advisor looked him up and down. "Distrusting, strong, and scheming." His gaze finally traveled to the gleaming blades at his throat. "And capable of inspiring loyalty this strong in your friends. You would make a great leader."

In a few swift moves, Malor released the fuming Master Assassin and stepped back. Elaran and I kept our blades raised while Shade dusted himself off before turning to face the man who had outmaneuvered him as easily as one would a child.

Steel crept into the assassin's eyes as he leveled them on the black-haired advisor. "I am already a leader."

Malor let out a chuckle. "Arrogant, too. We can work with that." Raising his hands to show that he had no interest in further fights, he met each of our gazes. "Yes, I disappeared before. You see, Nimlithil and I have a... very complicated history. I couldn't let her or any of the other star elves see me." Amusement twinkled in his strange eyes. "But you seem to have managed just fine on your own."

"We also had some help," Elaran said with pain from the hurried goodbye still lingering on his handsome face.

"I see." Malor shifted his gaze to me. "Well, I'll accept your offer to help me escape now."

I wanted to say something snarky in reply but I also wanted Morgora to train me, and for that I needed to get Malor out, so I kept my mouth shut and simply nodded at him instead. Once Shade and Elaran had come to the conclusion that the red-eyed senior advisor had indeed not been a part of the trap, they nodded as well.

"You said you had a way out?" Marcus said while pushing past the twins who exchanged a glance before shrugging their agreement that Malor wasn't a threat.

"I do." The muscular advisor moved towards the door. "Follow me."

As the six of us joined him and snuck through the secret passageways of the Red Fort, I studied our guide. He was able to disappear from the throne room without anyone noticing and locate us in a maze of tunnels. His body moved with the grace of a warrior, and wisdom as well as cunning swirled in his reddish-brown eyes. Furthermore, he had successfully outmaneuvered the Master of the Assassins' Guild who was the most dangerous and skilled fighter I knew. Power and confidence radiated from his whole being as he led us towards the secret exit.

Who was he? Who was he *really*? And what was his connection to Morgora? I watched the muscles in his back shift as he pulled open an iron gate at the far side of the fort. Sunlight bathed the courtyard outside in soft light. Maybe one day I would find out. But for now, we had a hostile city on high alert to break out of. I heaved a deep sigh. One problem at a time.

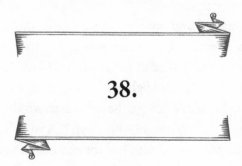

38.

Metal clanged behind me. I whipped around, ready for a fight, but only found a merchant pushing a cart filled with pots and pans along the dusty road of packed dirt. Letting the stiletto blades slide back into my sleeves again, I pulled my cloak tighter around my shoulders.

We had made a quick stop at Lady Beltham's house, both to pick up our things and to thank her for letting us stay, but the blond lady hadn't been there so we had just grabbed our packs and left again. It was probably for the best. I had a feeling that she would've tried to convince Marcus to stay again, and we didn't exactly have time for that.

Casting a quick glance over my shoulder, I met Elaran's eyes from further down the road. He gave me a nod. Wind caressed my cheek as I turned back around and continued slinking down the street.

The guards were looking for a large group trying to flee the city. In order to avoid attracting attention, we had decided to split up. We all followed the same route but we kept a slight distance between us so that we looked like seven separate people traveling by ourselves. Shade led the procession, followed by me and Elaran. Since he was our main objective, Malor stayed firmly in the middle, with the twins behind him and Marcus bringing up the rear with his heavy longsword and Storm Caster powers.

I glared up at the building on my left. The Pink Lily. Everyone inside had performed the ritual and would sell us out to the star elves in a heartbeat. As one of them already had. That's what I got for actually daring to trust someone.

A yelp echoed from up the street. My eyes scanned the crowd until I spotted Shade's back through the throng. He had stopped dead in the middle of the road while ladies clutched their skirts and hurried away in the other direction. All my instincts were screaming at me to rush over to him but I forced myself to keep a casual pace. If nothing was wrong, I couldn't break formation yet.

The startled crowd was rapidly clearing the street. Blood pounded in my ears. *Please let it be nothing, please let it be nothing.* When Shade drew his sword in slow movements, I threw caution to the wind and darted forward. The assassin's blades hit the street with two sharp thuds. I picked up speed. Skidding to a halt next to him, I tried to process the scene before me.

Lady Beltham was standing in the middle of the road. Tears streamed down her beautiful face and she was clutching her pale blue dress as if the glittering fabric was the only thing keeping her tethered to this world. A brown-haired man was standing directly behind her. Two swords pressed into her throat while the man kept her pushed up against him. I had never seen him before but based on the fury burning like blue flames in Shade's eyes, I had a feeling that he knew who this person was.

"You too," he said and jerked his chin at me from behind his human shield. "Weapons on the ground."

I glanced between the weeping lady and the smoldering assassin next to me. Shade gave me a brief nod. While I started stripping off my knives, Elaran screeched to a halt next to me. His feet sent a cloud of red dust swirling into the air.

"Any more of you coming?" the unidentified man barked after having ordered Elaran to disarm as well.

"No," the auburn-haired archer said.

In my mind, I winced at the too fast and too forceful reply. At least he hadn't looked at me and Shade while he did it, so there was that.

Elaran glanced at the two of us. I almost facepalmed in exasperation but managed to restrain myself. Man, I really needed to teach him how to lie convincingly.

However, the man holding Lady Beltham captive was too preoccupied with watching Shade's every move, so he missed the telltale signs of Elaran's lies. Though, if I knew anything about that strategizing ranger, there was at least some truth to his statement. He had probably sent Malor on ahead.

"Why?" Shade said in a calm voice dripping with poison.

The man behind the trembling lady just smirked at him. After another second of deadly silence, the Master Assassin flicked his gaze between me and Elaran.

"Rooftops," was all he said.

Casting a quick glance at the buildings around us, I tried to figure out what he meant. Ever since the citizens of Sker had left the area, yelping and clutching their skirts, the street had been deserted. Shutters had been drawn closed on the surrounding houses, and dark red curtains had been pulled across the windows of the Pink Lily further back. I squinted at the empty rooftops again.

A haughty snickering slipped from the brown-haired man's lips. He waved a hand in the air. All around us, figures rose from the red tiles above until the edge of every roof was lined with men and women. Every pair of hands had a crossbow bolt trained on us.

Lady Beltham whimpered in her captor's grip. *Shit*. At least it explained why Shade hadn't attacked yet. Schemes flew through my head as I picked up and discarded plan after plan in an attempt to find a way out of this that didn't involve the three of us turning into hedgehogs.

"Well, if it isn't the new General of Pernula and his scheming little friends."

My blood turned to ice in my veins. Moving very carefully, I turned to stare at the source of the voice. A muscular man with dark-brown hair and a curved sword at his hip appeared from a building on our left and strode towards us with confident steps.

Marcellus bared his teeth at us. "The thieves who stole my country."

Letting out a humorless laugh, Shade shifted his gaze between the former General of Pernula and the man holding swords to Lady Beltham's throat. "So that's why my spy network sold me out."

"*Your* spy network?" Marcellus clapped a hand on the sword-wielding man's shoulder and shot him a wide smile. "They were *my* spy network for far longer than they've been yours."

I stared at him with wide eyes. By Nemanan, I had not seen that coming. At all. But in hindsight, it all made sense. The attack at The Broken Wing, the ambush at the poisoner, it *had* been because Shade's spies in Sker had betrayed him. How the star elves knew so much about the political climate here. It had all been because of Marcellus.

"Oh by all the gods," I blurted out as another sudden realization snapped in place. "*You* framed *us* for an explosion and spread a rumor that people had died in it."

Wicked satisfaction gleamed in Marcellus' eyes. "I hate when that happens. Don't you?" The arrogant former General of Pernula, who *we* had framed for an explosion when we stole his country, rested a hand on the pommel of his sword. "I could barely believe it when Captain Hadraeth came back to camp and informed Queen Nimlithil that you, of all people, were here in Sker. The gods must truly be on my side. To think that I could get both my target and my revenge in one fell swoop."

A strong wind cut through the stone buildings and ripped at my cloak. Sun glinted in the red dust that filled the air. Despite the warm rays, I pulled my cloak tighter around me because I suddenly found myself chilled to the bone.

"You're working for Queen Nimlithil?" Elaran ground out between gritted teeth.

"Yes. Since you stole *my* country, I had to seek out other opportunities. When that ambitious queen got here, I offered her my services." A malicious smile stretched his lips. "For a price."

Shade locked hard eyes on him. "You're getting Sker."

"It is a rather brilliant plan, isn't it? Killing Kristen, who was the real power behind the throne, which then sent her frail brother spiraling into pain and grief, which in turn made it easy to convince him to do the ritual. A weak puppet king who would then hand over power to me." Satisfaction gleamed in his eyes. "And all I had to do was kill one person."

Another gust rattled the shutters up and down the street. I cast a quick glance at the crossbow-wielding ambushers around us. Even if Marcus and the twins somehow skirted around them and attacked from behind, there were still way too many of them to take out.

"Now what?" Shade spread his arms. "You're going to kill us all and get your revenge?"

"No, little assassin," Marcellus crooned. "Now, I'm going to take you back to the Red Fort and break you. I'm going to use every means at my disposal. Torture, hallucinogenic mist, the star elves' pain ritual. Until I shatter you all into tiny little pieces and turn you into the thing you fear most." His brilliant white teeth glinted in the sun. "I will make you an enemy and a traitor to your people."

For a moment, only Lady Beltham's soft crying broke the dead silence that had descended on the red street. Then, Marcellus jerked his head towards the buildings on the right.

"And you," he snapped. "Whoever you are lurking there in the shadows, why don't you come out and show your face before I get it in my head to put a crossbow bolt through one of your friends just for the spite of it."

A tall and muscular man strode out of the shadows with his spine straight and his chin held high. Sunlight fell across his dark-brown hair and strong jaw.

Marcus leveled hard eyes on the man in front of him. "Hello, Father."

39.

The air was sucked right out of my lungs. I whipped my head between Marcus and Marcellus while the two tall and muscular men stared each other down. Marcellus was Marcus' father?

"You are no son of mine," Marcellus snarled. "You took your mother's side."

"You killed her!" Marcus screamed.

"She *betrayed* me." He slashed a hand through the air. "I was on track to becoming the General of Pernula. If she'd run away with a smuggler, *a smuggler*, all my work would've been for nothing."

"You killed her," Marcus repeated.

Marcellus sneered at his son. "And you tried to blow me up."

"How about I give that another shot?"

"Ah, ah, ah." Marcellus held up a finger in the air.

Next to him, the brown-haired man pushed the swords further into Lady Beltham's throat. Wood creaked above us as the men and women on the rooftops stirred.

"Remember," the former General of Pernula continued, "I know what it looks like when you access your powers. And if you do, he will kill the lady here and they," he flicked a hand between the sword-wielder and the crossbows above, "will kill your three friends over there."

Deeper into the city, stamping feet and clanking armor echoed. The soldiers of Sker were on their way. If we didn't get out soon, we'd have to fight the whole military might of this city as well as the ambushers currently surrounding us. Blood pounded in my ears and my head spun from all the revelations. I had to find a way out of this.

While Marcus was staring down his father, Shade and I exchanged a quick glance. *Fight?* I mouthed at him. The assassin shifted his gaze to Elaran, who gave an almost imperceptible nod. Turning back to me, Shade replicated the gesture. The tall Storm Caster next to us was too preoccupied with decades of unresolved feelings to respond to any attempts at making eye contact. He looked to still be deciding whether he was going to carry out his threat and blow his father to kingdom come regardless of the consequences. Based on the searing hatred rolling off his body, it appeared to be a strong possibility. Marcellus watched his son with a malicious smile on his lips.

I had no idea if the twins and Malor were coming or if they were already at the stable waiting for us, but if we were going to fight, we had to do it now. Shade flicked his gaze between us and then to his hand. Down by his thigh, he held out five fingers. Then, he ticked one off. Four seconds.

My heart slammed in my chest. Three seconds. There was no way we'd be able to fight our way out of this without anyone getting hurt. Two seconds. I couldn't let my friends get hurt. Sweeping my gaze over the ground, I calculated how long it would take to reach my discarded blades. My fingers twitched by my sides. One second.

Pebbles trickled down the street. Whipping our heads around, we all found a small girl with short black hair walking towards us. She watched the armed people around her with curious dark eyes.

"Milla?" I breathed.

"Are they hurting you?" Milla asked, staring straight at me with eyes that shone with emotion.

At least one person from the Pink Lily hadn't done the ritual, then. Frowning at her, I was still trying to wrap my mind around the fact that the girl I had rescued from the Trader earlier had just strolled right into a warzone when she stopped between me and Marcellus. Her shoulder-length black hair swung in the breeze as she looked between us.

"Why is she crying?" she said as her dark eyes stopped on Lady Beltham.

"I don't know who you are, girl," Marcellus said, "but this is no place for children. Run back to where you came from and leave this to the grownups."

Tipping her head to the side, she studied the former General for a few moments before turning back to me. "Is he like the Trader?"

Clanking armor and trampling feet grew louder in the distance. I shifted my weight. The soldiers would be here soon and we couldn't fight if there was a child standing in the middle. If we did, she was bound to get hurt. I had to get her to leave.

"Yes, Milla." I swept a hand over Marcellus, the sword-wielder, and all the people with crossbows. "All these people are like the Trader. They will hurt you if you stay, so please, go back to the Pink Lily. You just go back, lock the door, and pull the curtains. And then you stay there until everything is quiet again. Can you do that?" Flicking desperate eyes down the street, I added emphasis to the word. "*Please.*"

"I don't like people like that," she replied.

"I know. So just go home, okay?"

The strange child studied me with those dark eyes of hers before turning her back on me. We all watched in shock as she took another step towards Marcellus.

"I don't like people who hurt other people," she said in a voice that sounded both terrifyingly empty and full of rage at the same time.

Lady Beltham whimpered next to Marcellus. The man with the swords to her throat drew them tighter, making the scared lady cry even more. Milla had stopped a few strides from them.

Marcellus flicked a hand dismissively. "Girl, you'd better–"

I slammed into the wall. Winds strong enough to toss a man around like a leaf threw everyone against the red stones. My discarded knives smattered as they came to an abrupt halt on the wall around me. Men screamed. Shrieks echoed across every surface when they were blasted off the rooftops all around us and the noise mingled with the person at the center who howled like a banshee. Black clouds whipped like snakes around her. Milla.

Crumpling to the ground as the wind died down, I stared at the strange girl with wide eyes. She raised her hands and another raw scream tore from her lips, sending dark smoke and more blasts shooting towards the roof. Bodies toppled and heavy thuds sounded as they met the street below. I sucked in a sharp breath. Milla was Ashaana.

At least that explained the trashed room when she was taken from the Pink Lily and the Trader's strange comments. I shook my head. Who'd seen that coming?

While the child Storm Caster kept all our enemies busy, I armed myself again and darted over to the black heap on the ground that was Shade. The Master Assassin rubbed a hand over the back of his head while struggling to his feet. Elaran was heading towards us as well while Marcus had helped Lady Beltham to her feet. With steady hands on her shoulders, he cast a hurried glance at the chaos around him before locking eyes with the still trembling lady.

"Thank you. I'm sorry." He let go of her shoulders. "Run."

For a moment, she remained rooted in place, sadness filling her eyes as she drew a soft hand down his cheek. Then, she whirled around and disappeared around the corner in a fluttering of pale blue skirts without so much as a goodbye to the rest of us. Though, given the death and violence she had just witnessed, I didn't blame her.

As soon as the blond lady was out of harm's way, Marcus launched himself across the street. Strength was draining rapidly from the small Ashaana and he had to throw himself the last bit to catch her before she collapsed from exhaustion, the black clouds snapping back into her body. He gently placed the unconscious Milla on the ground before whipping towards his father.

By the wall, Marcellus was climbing to his feet while drawing his sword. A growl ripped from Marcus' throat as he broke into a run and charged right at him. Metal dinged and grunts echoed off the red stones as the tall Storm Caster swung his heavy sword right into his father's blade.

"I should've killed you long ago!" Marcus screamed while bashing his weapon into his father's defense.

Marcellus deflected the strokes but the two were evenly matched in both strength and skill. And more importantly, they both fought using the same technique. Like blocks of stone with powerful blows and tight defense. That, in combination with Marcellus still trying to recover from being slammed head first into a wall, proved his downfall.

While still blinking to clear his head, Marcellus stumbled back after a heavy strike and twisted his sword in the wrong direction. Steel clattered against stone as the blade flew from his grip. Marcus swung his sword with deadly accuracy straight towards his throat.

Silence descended on the street. Panting from exhaustion and anger, Marcus held the blade still right above his father's exposed throat. Marcellus spread his arms.

"At least you inherited your fighting skills from me." The former General of Pernula lifted his chin. "Do it."

With hands shaking, Marcus pushed the edge deeper into his skin. Blood ran down from the shallow wound.

"Come on then!" Marcellus yelled. "Do it!"

Marcus let out a long scream. And then dropped the blade. It vibrated on the ground while the golden-eyed Ashaana stepped back and shook his head.

A triumphant smirk spread across Marcellus' lips. "I knew it. You're weak. Just like your mother. You can't even kill me, kill the man who you have wanted dead since the day you watched me murder your mother. Pathetic. Weak pathetic coward." He spat on the dusty ground. "You are no son of mine."

Anger and tears of shame for a promise to his mother that he couldn't fulfill blew over his face but Marcus made no move to follow as his father retreated down the street. The clamor from the approaching soldiers was reaching deafening levels.

"I want you dead!" the distraught Storm Caster called.

"But you will never get your wish." Marcellus shot his son a malicious smile. "Because just like your pathetically weak mother, you are not a murderer."

A sharp thud sounded. Marcellus' eyes widened as he stared back at us for a second before his knees buckled.

"No." Closing the distance between us, I yanked out the throwing knife buried in his throat. "But I am."

The former General of Pernula toppled to the ground. Fresh blood mingled with the red dust as the man who had murdered his wife for a political advantage bled out a nobody on a foreign street.

Marcus stared at his dead father for a moment before turning to me. Relief filled his eyes as he gave me a grateful nod. I nodded back. Marcellus had been right. Marcus was not a murderer. And there was no need for him to go down that path because once you let the darkness in, it never comes out. My heart and soul were already black so what was one more dead body? Better I bear it than he.

Shouting rose as the advancing soldiers rounded the corner further down the street. *Shit.* I stuck the blade back in its holster and darted to my friends.

"Shall we?"

They nodded in reply.

"I sent the twins and Malor to the stables," Elaran said. "But they said they'd be waiting for us to catch up."

Marcus motioned towards the other side of the road. "I'll get Milla."

While he ran over to the unconscious Storm Caster lying on the ground, Shade flicked eyes of steel between me and Elaran.

"And, you two, let's get something straight. If you see me very clearly walk right into a trap, you *do not* follow me into it!" He blew out a forceful breath. "You get the hell out. Is that clear?"

"As if I'd leave you trapped alone in an ambush." I furrowed my brows at him as if that was the stupidest thing I'd ever heard. Which it was. "Not gonna happen."

Elaran drew his eyebrows down and looked from me to Shade before jerking his chin in my direction. "What she said."

We were spared Shade's exasperated cursing because Marcus had finally scooped up Milla. Soldiers screamed and charged towards us.

"Let's go!" he called and took off, Milla bouncing in his arms.

Not hesitating a second, we sprinted after him. Boots smattered against the packed dirt as the guards of Sker pursued us.

This was going to be a close call. We had to make it all the way to the stables, get on the horses that the twins and Malor had hopefully already saddled for us, and then gallop through the gate before that mass of armed men caught up with us. I cast a hurried glance over my shoulder. The soldiers were practically snapping at our heels. This was going to be a *very* close call.

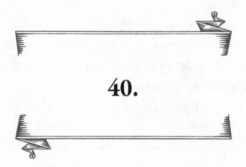

40.

Steel clashed beside me. I skidded to a halt and whirled around to face the racing soldiers who were attacking us from behind. Shade met the swiping blade with his own before shoving his left-hand sword through the attacker's gut. A bowstring twanged next to me as Elaran loosened an arrow into the wall of charging men.

"Milla," Marcus yelled desperately somewhere behind me because he couldn't fight with an unconscious child in his arms.

"Go!" I screamed over my shoulder. "We'll be right behind you."

Shade and I both knew that was a lie as we darted towards our archer and formed a protective barrier in front of him, but I hoped that Marcus' strong protective instincts made him leave with Milla. There was no time to turn around to find out because the first wave had reached us.

A sword slashed through the air. I ducked under the oncoming blade and rammed a hunting knife into the soldier's armpit. He cried out in pain right before I yanked it out and swiped my other blade across his throat. Arrows whizzed past over my head as Elaran fired into the charging mass.

Shoving the dying soldier backwards, I barely managed to evade the next attacker who stabbed at my chest. I threw down a fist on his outstretched hand but he kept his grip on the blade. Black stars danced across my eyes as he slammed his other elbow into my cheekbone. Twisting down and around, I succeeded in getting inside his guard before his sword could strike home. Still blinking dark spots from my vision, I feigned a swipe at his throat while burying my other blade in his heart. A soft grunt escaped his lips before he tipped backwards.

Shade was fighting two opponents a few strides in front of Elaran. The assassin's blades were a flurry of silver in the warm fall air as he took his opponents down with swift strikes. A black shaft sped through the air over my shoulder as the auburn-haired archer behind me brought down another charging soldier.

Battle cries rang out before me as the second wave surged towards us. Shade returned to his position next to me while Elaran picked them off from afar. Dread clenched my heart. These first ranks of scouts were thinning out and the bulk of the soldiers would soon be upon us. We would not survive that.

Steel vibrated through the air as three attackers bore down on us. The Master Assassin next to me threw his blades up and stopped the swords meant for my head while I danced in front of him and rammed my hunting knives into two of the attackers' windpipes. Wet sliding sounds echoed as I yanked them out while Shade shoved away the remaining sword above my head and whirled towards a fourth approaching attacker.

Spinning around I landed a kick at the back of my opponent's knee. He crashed to the ground but rolled with the motion and came up behind me. Returning the favor, he planted a boot in my lower back. I stumbled forward. Whipping around, I prepared for the coming strike. A dark arrow pushed through the back of his head and protruded from his eye on the other side. I sent a quick nod of thanks to Elaran before I had to deflect another blow.

While stabbing a knife in the kidney of Shade's attacker from behind, I slashed through the air and caught another soldier in the throat. Blood splattered all over my face. And for a moment, everything was still around us. The scouts were dead. All that remained now was the main bulk of the soldiers. And they were barreling straight for us. This would never work.

"Get back!" I screamed at my two friends while sticking the hunting knives back in their holsters and stalking forward.

If I could blast them with winds, I could blow them back and create distance between us long enough for us to escape to the stables. My heart slammed against my ribs. I raised my arms.

Self-doubt was screaming in my mind. *But you can't create wind! If you try this and it fails, you will have lost any chance to escape! It won't work!*

It has to work. Closing my eyes, I drew a deep breath. *Trust yourself. Find what works for you. You are the storm.* Dark clouds shot out around me as my eyes turned black as death. I raised my arms slowly, feeding the rage inside my soul. Sparks leapt through the deep pits and caught fire with a whoosh. Black smoke billowed around me.

The soldiers were getting closer with each second. Panic tried to claw its way up my throat but I shoved it down and smothered it with the raging wildfire inside me. Thunderclaps echoed off the red stone buildings in deafening booms and lightning flashed in the darkness around me. I sucked in a deep breath. *Now.*

If you do this, it might blow back on your friends! It could drop a building on them! The uncertainty inside me was banging furiously on the walls I was slamming up around my mind. *It could hurt them! Are you sure you're willing to make that decision?*

Calm certainty spread through my soul like a steady river. I smiled at the mist and thunder around me. *The only bad decisions are the ones you don't make.* The terrible power coursing through me didn't need to be feared. It needed to bow to my will because the darkness was mine and I was its master.

I slammed my arms forward. Hurricane winds shot out before me and swept the black smoke and lightning with it as it sped down the red street. Screams of terror rang out when the force picked up the charging soldiers and flung them backwards. Armor and weapons clanged as the guards slammed into one another. Rank after rank flew through the air. By the time I whirled back around to my friends, the wide street was clear for several blocks. Power thrummed through my body.

"By Nature's grace," Elaran blurted out.

"Let's go!" I snatched at both of their shirts as I ran past and set course for the stable down by the side gate.

After one more second of stunned silence, the elf and the assassin took off after me.

Exhilaration sparkled inside me. I had done it. I had created wind. While the darkness pulled back into the deep pits of my soul, I grinned triumphantly at the large red wall rising in the distance. I had done it.

Then, the tiredness set in. Exhaustion washed over my body like a tidal wave and I had to shake my head to keep from drowning in its dark embrace. If I used my powers one more time right now, even just a little, I would pass out. Forcing oxygen in and out of my lungs, I sprinted down the dusty road next to my friends while trying to keep the unconsciousness away.

"So, you finally stopped being afraid of your powers, huh?" Shade threw me a lopsided smile as we ran. "Marcus is a good teacher."

"Yeah," I pressed out between breaths. "Yeah, I guess he is."

It was actually Shade's words about indecision that had helped push me the final bit across the barrier of doubt, but I decided not to tell him that. We had already established that there could never be anything between us so what would that accomplish? And besides, I would die before admitting to that arrogant bastard that he had been right about something.

"There they are!" Haemir's voice cut through the fog building in my mind.

The stable by the side gate rose before us. And more importantly, the seven already saddled and ready horses that stood outside on the stone yard.

"Mount up, they'll be here any minute!" Elaran bellowed back at them.

Malor was already seated on a large black horse, as was Marcus, who had placed the unconscious Milla in front of him on the saddle. The twins let go of the reins they'd been holding as we skidded to a halt before them. Hay and dust sprayed through the air.

After wiping a sleeve over my face to clear off some of the blood, I slipped through the waiting animals until I reached Silver. My gray mare snorted as I shoved a foot in the stirrup and hauled myself up. Surprised cooing and flapping came from a wooden box that had been tied to the back of my saddle.

Leaning against the doorway, the stable master smiled and nodded at me. I yanked a full pouch from my belt. Pearls rustled against each other as I threw the brown leather pouch towards him. Lifting a hand to my brow, I grinned back at him before spurring my horse on.

"Keep the change!" I called as I charged after my six companions.

The guards at the side gate yelped and ducked out of the way as seven large horses barreled out through the open doorway. Behind us, the clamor was increasing in strength. We would soon have the soldiers of Sker on our heels again.

Red dust swirled around stampeding hooves as we galloped across the sands. Sun beat down on us from above while winds whipped through my cloak and hair. Despite the exhaustion and the pursuing guards, I had the strangest urge to laugh.

"Woohoo!" I called into the clear blue sky before a mad laugh tore from my throat.

Haela responded with a victorious whoop of her own. Scattered laughs of relief spread through our whole group as we tried to process the fact that we had actually survived all of that.

The merriment was short-lived, however, as rows upon rows of Sker soldiers poured through the side gate and spread out across the red sands. Crossbow bolts whizzed past in the air. I threw myself against Silver's neck.

"Marcus!" I called as more bolts sped past us. "I've already used all my powers. You have to use yours and blow them back."

"This many? And from this distance?" He ducked as another shaft hurtled past. "It'll take all I have."

"Do it! As soon as we're away from them, we're in the clear."

Horses neighed as Marcus pulled on the reins and turned his mount in a sharp circle while the rest of us slowed down as well. He gently leaned Milla against the horse's neck before straightening. A crossbow bolt sped right past his cheek. Marcus raised his arms.

Black smoke bloomed around him and he slammed his arms forward. The cloud of dust he stirred up with winds far greater than mine was large enough to obscure all our visions as it plowed towards the unsuspecting soldiers. Screams rose.

When the red dust had finally settled, the guards of Sker lay sprawled along the edge of the gigantic stone walls. A calm stillness settled over the area. While the soldiers who had been blown away by unnatural winds for the second time today struggled to their knees, we urged our horses on again. These people would not be following us.

Tiredness swept over Marcus and his eyelids drooped slightly, but he kept a firm grip on the reins and Milla as we charged across the sand and towards our freedom.

After we had put some distance between us and the large red walls of Sker, we slowed our horses to a trot. We still had to make it all the way back to Pernula and that would take days, so we couldn't push them too hard.

The pale sun blazing down from the bright blue heavens deepened to a golden color as we continued our trek towards Pernula. I had to see Malor safely behind the city walls before I could leave for the White Mountains again. And my other friends too, for that matter. After that, Marcus and I would be continuing on to the hidden Ashaana camp along with Milla. Leaving a Storm Caster child in a city filled with star elves, and in a home that was already loyal to the silver-haired elves, had not been an option. She would be much better off with her people in the mountains.

I glanced at the sleeping girl and the muscled man holding her. She would be alright.

Thundering hooves echoed across the gold-painted landscape. Panic flashed over all our faces as we turned in our saddles to stare at the horizon behind us. White and silver glimmered in the low sun.

"They're here." Malor watched the approaching riders with a resigned look in his reddish-brown eyes. "The star elves are here."

I cast a hurried glance in the other direction. It shouldn't be far now. If we could just make it...

"Come on," Shade barked and spurred his horse on.

We pushed our mounts into a gallop again and raced towards the other horizon while the wave of silver and white chased us from behind. Brittle bushes crunched under stomping hooves as we sped through the dry grasslands. Every time I threw a look over my shoulder, the star elves had gained a little more on us.

When our horses were panting and staggering forward with dangerous exhaustion, Elaran reined his in and slowed until the two of them came to a halt on the grass.

"If we keep pushing them, they will die," he said. "And then we'll never make it anyway."

The rest of our group had come to a halt as well. Haela had already dismounted and was patting her tired horse on the neck while nodding at Elaran.

"I agree," she said.

Haemir swung his leg over his own horse and dropped to the ground. "So, what do we do?"

I gazed at the empty horizon behind me. Gods damn it. We were so close. I didn't want to accept that my plan had failed but

Elaran was right. If we forced our horses to run any longer, they would die, and that wouldn't save us either.

"We make a stand." Shade led his black and white horse towards a cluster of bushes nearby and left him there. "Here."

Marcus did the same. "I guess here is as good a place as any."

When everyone had placed their horses in the somewhat protecting vegetation, we strode across the grass. I heaved a deep sigh and pulled out my hunting knives.

On both sides of me, my friends spread out until we formed a long line. Steel sang as Shade and Marcus drew their swords. Elaran and the twins rested their bows on the ground while the wall of silver closed in on us. One Storm Caster was still lying unconscious by the horses while the other two had already used up all our powers. We would never win this. Sker had already fallen. And soon, we would too.

Glancing towards the end of the line, I found Malor glaring at the oncoming attackers. Uncertainty flickered in his eyes while difficult choices seemed to dance across his strong features. If he did in fact have any special powers, I hoped he intended to use them.

The noise from the army of charging horses drowned out everything else as they closed the distance with terrifying speed. I swallowed. Gripping the hilts of my knives tighter, I sucked in a deep breath to steady myself. Shade and I exchanged a glance filled with desperation. We both knew that this might be our last moments together. After this, we would be dead. Either physically or emotionally. I tightened the grip on my knives even more. We could almost see each individual star elf now.

Shade raised his twin swords. "Get ready."

Next to me, Elaran and the twins nocked and drew back their large bows. Marcus and I exchanged a look before raising our weapons as well. Battle was upon us.

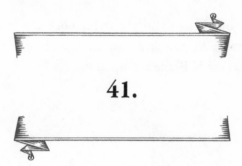

41.

Arrows whizzed over our heads. Startled yelps rang out from our line as we ducked when another cloud of sharp arrows sped past above us. I whirled around just in time to see a huge black cloud swallow the surrounding area. Relief so strong I almost wept surged through me. They were here.

The dark smoke shot through us and hurtled towards the ranks of charging star elves, knocking them backwards as the blasts of wind finally struck. My friends stared in open-mouthed shock at the mass of people behind us.

Black-clad assassins fired arrow after arrow into the elves attacking us while still seated atop their panting horses. To their right, elves and humans raised their arms and slammed them together in synchronized claps that sent strong winds flying forward in wide formations. I sank to my knees on the dry grass and braced an exhausted hand on the ground while letting out a long sigh of profound relief. The Assassins' Guild and the Storm Casters had come.

Cries of alarm came from the attacking star elves as they were pushed back by forces of nature and arrows fired with deadly accuracy alike. Horses neighed and elves shouted as they scrambled to defend themselves. Until finally, the sweetest sound in all the world echoed across the plains. A horn blaring retreat.

Their gleaming armor cast glittering light across the brown and green grasslands as they whirled around and raced back towards the distant horizon and the already fallen city that lay there.

"Marcus!" Cileya jumped down from her horse and jogged over to the flabbergasted Storm Caster a few strides away from me while I struggled to my feet again.

"How are you here?" Marcus shook his head. "And why did you...? Don't take this the wrong way but you just showed the star elves that there's a whole host of Ashaana still out here."

The mountain elf flicked her red and gold hair back over her shoulder before crossing her arms and drawing up before him. "If we can't use our powers to help our friends, then we don't deserve to have them."

Marcus blinked at her and then pulled her into a hug. She stiffened in surprise but then hugged him back. From across her shoulder, Marcus met my gaze while still addressing Cileya. "You sound a lot like someone else I know." A genuine smile spread across his lips as he drew back and placed both hands on her shoulders. "Thank you."

Blond hair flowed in the breeze as Faelar wove through the crowd that was quickly gathering around us. Brotherly love radiated off the both of them as he and Elaran greeted each other.

"Master," a man called as he pulled his horse to a halt on my left and leaped down. "Are you unharmed?"

A small smile spread across my tired face as I watched Shade and Man-bun clasp forearms. So, he had come anyway, even though I had sent the message to Slim. After all, I still didn't know what Man-bun's actual name was.

"Yes," the Master of the Assassins' Guild replied and then demanded, at the same time as Marcus and Elaran did, "How?"

Man-bun, Cileya, and Faelar all turned to me. A sneaky grin flashed over my lips.

"So, yeah, I might have gone back to Queen Nimlithil's camp and stolen a small cage of magical messenger doves. I'm a thief, remember?" I waved vaguely at Silver and the other horses behind the bushes where said cage of stolen birds was located. "And then when shit hit the fan and we went into lockdown, I might have snuck back out again to send a message to Pernula and the White Mountains to tell them that we might end up needing an escort back." Shrugging, I grinned again. "Just as a precaution."

Genuine laughter, of joy, of exasperation, and of gratitude filled the afternoon air. Haela swung by me and clapped a hand on my shoulder.

"I knew I could count on you and your scheming brain to get us out of trouble." She sent me a beaming smile. "And I knew coming on this trip with you was a good idea. I haven't had this much fun in ages!"

Haemir shook his head at his sister but gave me a grateful nod before pulling Haela towards the horses again. On the other side, Elaran was bringing Faelar up to speed on the situation while Marcus did the same with Cileya and the other handful of Storm Casters who had joined her. Sweeping my gaze across them, I found Malor standing a little to the side. I jerked back slightly when I realized that he was staring straight at me. Wheels turned behind his reddish-brown eyes as if he was seeing far larger things than the thief covered in blood and dust before him.

"You okay?"

Twisting back around, I found Shade standing in front of me. "Yeah."

He placed soft fingers on my jaw and tilted my head to either side as if to really make sure that the blood on my neck wasn't mine. My skin tingled from his touch after he let go. I smothered those ridiculous feelings and instead shot him a satisfied grin.

"Aren't you glad I *disobeyed* your orders and snuck out to steal those birds now?"

His pleasant laugh filled the warm air between us. Gold from the low sun glittered in his black eyes as he reached out again. For a moment, his hand hovered in the air but then determination pushed out the uncertainty on his face and he placed the hand on the back of my neck.

Lightning shot through my body as he pulled me towards him and pressed his lips against mine. His toned body shifted against mine as he drew me close. I raked my fingers over his muscled back before knitting them through his hair. Space and time slipped my mind as we lost ourselves in a kiss full of relief and desperation.

All too soon, he drew back. His breath was hot against my skin as he let out a low chuckle and drew soft fingers from the back of my neck towards my collarbones. A shiver went through me.

"My little thief," he whispered against my neck before pulling back.

The rest of the world came trickling back into my consciousness and I suddenly became acutely aware of the fact that there were other people here. Other people who were staring at us. A flush crept over my cheeks. From atop her brown horse, Haela was grinning widely at me.

A satisfied smirk tugged at Shade's lips before he broke eye contact and sauntered over to his black and white horse. I shook my head while trying to force the blush away. Damn assassin.

The rest of the journey back to Pernula was fortunately entirely uneventful. Both regarding attacking enemies or... other activities. Before long, the enormous stone walls of Pernula rose before us.

While Silver and the other horses gulped down well-deserved water at the stables inside the gates, the rest of our party gathered on the gray stones. Haela had swung an arm over her brother's shoulder while the rest of us leaned against whatever support we could find. Though, for some of us, the journey wasn't over yet.

"I think I'll stay here in Pernula," Malor announced into the growing silence. He shifted his gaze to Shade. "I would like to be your advisor. If you're interested?"

The General of Pernula locked eyes with the former Senior Advisor of Sker. "Yes, I would be very interested in that."

"Good." He nodded. "Then there might be a chance yet."

I was too tired to frown at the strange comment so I just skipped right past it and waved a hand at Marcus and the other Storm Casters. "We'll spend a night here so both we and our horses can rest, but then we're heading off again."

"Be careful," Haemir said.

"Always am."

My friends chuckled at the blatant lie. After pulling me into a hug and telling me to be careful again, Haemir wandered off to say goodbye to Faelar who would be leaving with me as well.

Haela flashed me a grin and winked at me before following her brother.

"Don't get into any fun mischief without me," she called over her shoulder.

I chuckled in reply. Across from me, Elaran stood glowering at me with his arms crossed. Raising my eyebrows, I opened my mouth but he got there before me.

"Don't burn anything down," he muttered. "And don't get yourself killed."

A sly smile spread across my lips. "You know I can't promise that."

Shaking his head, the grumpy elf stalked over to Faelar while still muttering under his breath about troublesome underworlders. While I directed the Storm Casters towards the tavern we'd be staying at, Shade and Malor remained standing by the horse pen, staring at the people milling about.

Spices on a warm summer day still filled the air even though we were far into fall. I drew a deep breath of fragrant air as the elves and the Storm Casters finally cleared the area. Marcus threw me a quick smile before leading Milla away by the hand.

"We will meet again, the Oncoming Storm." Unspoken promises about great things swirled behind Malor's strange red eyes.

I frowned at him. "Yeah, okay, if you say so."

"I do." A wry smile tugged at his lips. "Oh, and tell that old bat that I know it was her."

"I have no idea what you're talking about."

"Yes, you do." Malor spun on his heel and stalked up the street while still muttering curses about Morgora under his breath.

For a moment, only snorting horses pacing across stones filled the silence as Shade and I faced each other. Shifting my weight, I nudged a stray piece of hay with the toe of my boot before looking back up at him. I didn't like goodbyes, so instead I let a smirk spread across my lips.

"So, how does it feel to lose?"

The Master Assassin narrowed his eyes at me. "I don't lose."

"You did now."

"*We* lost."

"Speak for yourself. I got what I wanted." With that smirk still playing over my lips, I gave him a nonchalant shrug. "You went there to make sure that Sker didn't fall to the star elves." Tipping my head from side to side, I let out a chuckle. "Or to take it over. Either way, that didn't happen. I went there to rescue him." I pointed at the muscled advisor waiting further up the street. "I did that and now Morgora will teach me."

A soft chuckle escaped his lips as Shade shook his head at me. "Uh-huh."

Silence descended over the stone courtyard again as neither of us wanted to say the words we knew were coming next. The ordinary people chatting around us seemed very far away.

"So," Shade finally began, breaking the silence, "you're leaving again."

"Yeah." I nodded at the obsidian spires of the palace reaching for the heavens behind Shade. "And you're going back to your strategically important daughter. Sorry, *daughters*."

"And you to your powerful Storm Caster."

There wasn't, and never had been, anything romantic going on between me and Marcus. How could Shade not have seen that? However, what good would come of pointing that out? So in the end, I just shrugged.

"Whatever it takes to win."

Shade reached out, and for a moment it looked like he was going to lean in further, but then he just drew soft fingers along my jaw. "Whatever it takes."

And with one final smile, he was gone. I stared at his retreating back until the crowd had swallowed up both him and Malor.

Whatever feelings I might have for that infuriating assassin, and whatever feelings he might have for me, there couldn't be anything between us. Not right now, anyway. Because that's what you do when you care about someone. When you *really* care about someone. You don't force them into something that you know will kill their dreams and trap them there until they suffocate. Instead, you let them go so that they can follow them.

His deepest desire was to become the sole ruler of Pernula and I would never want to stand in the way of that. Just as he would never want to stand in the way of me learning to master my powers. But afterwards, who knew...

Shaking my head, I pushed my inconvenient feelings aside and strode towards the tavern now filled with Storm Casters. Who had time for a normal relationship when we had a world to conquer?

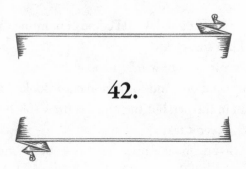

42.

Brisk winds rattled the bare branches around me and sent a gust filled with the smell of damp soil and murky leaves to my lungs. A soft smile spread across my lips as I watched the Storm Casters of the White Mountains welcome their friends back. Faelar gave me a nod before slipping away with Cileya.

"I have to know," Marcus said to me once the satisfied crowd had dispersed. "Did I ever stand a chance?"

I blinked at him in surprise as we made our way through camp. "At what?"

"At, well, you and... me?"

"Oh." Understanding dawned on me with all the elegance of a brick to the face. "*Ohh.*"

Man, maybe that damn assassin was more perceptive than I gave him credit for.

Amusement twinkled in Marcus' golden eyes. "Wow. My subtle attempts at flirting with you went right over your head, didn't they?"

A sheepish grin spread across my face. "Sorry."

Fallen leaves crunched under our boots as we neared the longhouse. Morgora was seated in the chair outside, her steel gray eyes watching the proceedings like a hawk. The muscled

Storm Caster next to me placed a hand on my arm and pulled me to a halt before we moved into earshot.

"So, was there ever a chance?"

I gave him an apologetic smile.

He let out a soft chuckle. "I figured as much."

"I'm sorry. I guess I'm just not a settle down and retreat into a cabin in the woods kind of girl."

"I know." A genuine smile blew across his face. "I've known that since the first time I met you. You're not a dim candle flickering in the wind. You're a wildfire. If you were put in a cabin, you'd burn it down." Marcus placed a hand under my chin and tilted it up towards him. Strength gleamed in his golden eyes. "Don't be a candle. Be a wildfire."

After placing a quick kiss on the top of my head, he strode away. I watched him go before turning towards Morgora who had finally risen from her chair. A cool wind whipped through my hair as I made my way over to her.

"Well?" the old woman demanded.

"Malor is safe in Pernula and currently enjoying his new position as advisor to the General of Pernula."

"How do I know you're telling the truth?"

I blew out a sigh. "Aside from my general trustworthiness?" When Morgora just continued glaring at me, I rolled my eyes. "Before I left him in Pernula, Malor said, and I quote: *tell that old bat that I know it was her.*"

"Ha!" The powerful old woman barked a laugh. "That's Malor alright. Ridiculous old fart." She jerked her chin. "Come on, then. You held up your end of the bargain. I will hold up mine."

Birds flapped in the trees above us as I followed Morgora into the woods. The naked branches shivered in the wind as another cold mountain breeze disturbed their slumber. Except for the birds and the odd squirrel scurrying past, our walk was a silent one. I turned to Morgora in surprise as the lake Marcus had taken me to appeared through the trees.

"Now," Morgora said as she stopped at the waterline. "Show me what you can do."

Reaching into my soul, I fed the burning rage inside. Black clouds shot out around me as I raised my arms. Twigs snapped along the edge and waves pushed the water further out as I sent wind and dark smoke flying across the lake. No more hesitation. No more doubt.

A satisfied chuckle rumbled in Morgora's chest. "You've finally stopped being afraid of your powers. Good." She turned to me, a grin pulling at her wrinkled face. "*Now*, the real work begins."

I raised my arms again. Black smoke billowed around me and lightning danced across the dark blue water. Drawing a deep breath, I gathered more force. Thunder boomed around me as the darkness surged from my blackened soul. Next to me, Morgora cackled, urging me on.

War was coming. Sker had fallen and Pernula was now the only unoccupied country left on the continent. It wouldn't be long before Queen Nimlithil led her armies to Pernula's gates as well. My friends were going to need me and I would do anything to make sure they survived the battle to come. I would even let Morgora bully me for months on end, if that was what it took, because I swore to myself that the next time I saw my friends, I would have mastered my powers. Black clouds spread through the woods as I fed the raging fury inside my soul without a shred of fear or doubt.

When the war finally came, I would be ready. Power crackled around me. I slammed my arms forward and unleashed the terrible storm inside me. Exhilaration coursed through my body at the sheer force that flattened the landscape before the lake. I did not fear the darkness. The darkness feared me.

Acknowledgements

Fear and doubt can be crippling. Sometimes, I wonder how many extraordinary things the world has missed out on just because that horrible hesitation prevented people from doing their thing. Please don't listen to that nagging voice telling you that you will fail. That you'll never make it. That you're not good enough. If you have a wildfire soul, don't hide from the world by pretending to be a candle. Trust yourself. Burning fiercely. And make your insecurities scurry back to whatever hole they crawled out of because you don't bow to them. They bow to you.

As always, I would like to say a huge thank you to my family and loved ones. Mom, Dad, Mark, thank you for the enthusiasm, love, and encouragement. I truly don't know what I would do without you. Lasse, Ann, Karolina, Axel, Martina, thank you for continuing to take such an interest in my books. It really means a lot.

Another group of people I would like to once again express my gratitude to is my wonderful team of beta readers: Deshaun Hershel, Jennifer Nicholls, Luna Lucia Lawson, and Orsika Petér. Thank you for the time and effort you put into reading the book and providing helpful feedback. Your suggestions and encouragement truly makes the book better.

To my amazing copy editor and proofreader Julia Gibbs, thank you for all the hard work you always put into making my books shine. Your language expertise and attention to detail is fantastic and makes me feel confident that I'm publishing the very best version of my books.

Dane Low is another person I'm very fortunate to have found. He is the extraordinary designer from ebooklaunch.com who made the stunning cover for this book. Dane, thank you for the effort you put into making yet another gorgeous cover for me. You knock it out of the park every time.

I am also very fortunate to have friends both close by and from all around the world. My friends, thank you for everything you've shared with me. Thank you for the laughs, the tears, the deep discussions, and the unforgettable memories. My life is a lot richer with you in it.

Before I go back to writing the next book, I would like to once again say thank you to you, the reader. Thank you for being so invested in the world of the Oncoming Storm that you continued the series. If you have any questions or comments about the book, I would love to hear from you. You can find all the different ways of contacting me on my website, www.marionblackwood.com. There you can also sign up for my newsletter to receive updates about coming novels. Lastly, if you liked this book and want to help me out so that I can continue writing books, please consider leaving a review. It really does help tremendously. I hope you enjoyed the adventure!

Printed in the USA
CPSIA information can be obtained
at www.ICGtesting.com
LVHW041318090923
757485LV00011B/25